UNDER THE INFLUENCE

LAYNE DEEMER

For Liz
because TikTok
because "shotties in the cave"
because you are you and I am so glad

MY MOUTH ROUNDS as I take in the scene before me. We've been out here many times over the past few weeks, but it wasn't ours then. Now, as we park in *our* driveway and admire *our* house, *our* yard, *our* land, I'm in awe. "It's perfect," I whisper.

The house is a modest but beautiful old log cabin. Built over fifty years ago, it's brimming with rustic charm and historic character. It was renovated from top to bottom a few years ago, but the restoration was done without losing any of the original beauty that made it unique.

"Marcus, we actually live here now," I say with a smile so wide it almost hurts.

"What are we waiting for? Come on!" My husband takes my hand and tugs me toward the front door. We sprint to the wraparound porch, and when we reach the door, I hold out my hand, stopping him from going any farther.

"Listen. Do you hear that?"

He tilts his head to the side and a wisp of brown hair

falls in front of his eye. Running a hand through the strands, he quirks his mouth. "Baby, I don't hear a thing."

I grin. "Exactly. No blaring horns, no barking dogs, no gunshots." I grimace.

"April, that was one time and it was just some kid with a cap gun."

I shrug. "Still counts. But we won't have any of that out here. It's so peaceful and exactly what I need."

"Can't argue with you there." He rests a hand on my shoulder, giving it a squeeze.

A light clicking sound gets our attention, and we turn to find our bulldog, Clyde, lumbering up the steps onto the porch. He wanders a few paces and then collapses into a heap on top of a square of sunlight. Within seconds, he's snoring softly.

"There's the Clyde stamp of approval." I giggle.

Marcus laughs. "I don't think his list of demands is very long."

A car door slams, and the sound of my mother's incessant complaining breaks through the quiet. And just like that, our peaceful moment is over.

I steal a glance behind me and find her tromping toward us with a severe look in her eyes. Marcus takes my hand, weaving our fingers together.

"Do you have any idea how long it took your father to drive *all* the way out here?"

I pinch the bridge of my nose. "Mom, you act like we live a million miles away, but it's just—"

"Thirty minutes! It may as well be in another country. And you," she glares at Marcus, "how could you agree to this? You know how she is. She's going to lock herself up in this house and we'll never see her!"

"That's enough, Gracey." Nana's melodic voice is like a salve as she sidles up next to my mother. "Now I know you loved having your daughter close, but that tiny apartment wasn't right for her. Was it, sweet pea?" She asks, turning to me and resting a warm hand on my cheek. I lean into her touch and close my eyes.

When I open them, I blink up at my mom. "It wasn't good for me there, Mama. There were too many noises and too many people. I could never relax."

"I just worry." She sighs. "It's like you're running away and instead of facing your fears, you're embracing them."

She's not wrong, though I'll never say that out loud. I've been dealing with anxiety for most of my life, but the older I get, the more afraid I am. At this point, it would take less time for me to list the things I'm not scared of. Dr. Lesser says I have agoraphobia, but with her help, I have it under control.

Still, situations can exacerbate my condition, and with our apartment located right in the heart of the city, my fears were paralyzing. Even though we were close to everything and everyone, I never felt safe. But out here, away from the world, I finally have a sense of security. We're tucked away with nothing but forest surrounding us. Any sounds we hear are from nature and it's hard to feel threatened by that.

Out here, I can lean in to who I am. I know my limits.

"What are you all doing standing outside?" Emma's booming voice zings through the air and demands every-one's attention. In third grade, she overheard Sam Kells making fun of my pointy ears and calling me "April the Elf." She leaned in and whispered something in his ear that made his face turn red and his body shake. No one knew what she said, and to this day, I still don't, but he never bothered me again after that. She's been my best friend ever since. Next to my nana and Marcus, she's one of the most impor-tant people in my life. She commands every situation she enters, and this one is no different. Breezing past all of us, she grips the knob on the front door and pushes it open. "Well, come on now. Everybody in. April's gonna give us the grand tour!" She winks at me, and I mouth a silent, "Thank you." Emma has witnessed the tension between my mom and me more times than I can count. She knew what she was walking into, and just like that day in third grade, she saved me.

"All of this has been totally redone," I say, extending my arms and twirling in a circle. We're in the living room, but a few walls have been knocked down, making the floor plan nice and open. The kitchen, dining room, and living room blend together while still maintaining distinctively separate spaces. Original wood beams line the ceiling and a grand stone fireplace takes up most of the sidewall in the living room.

"Oh, honey, this is lovely," Nana delights. The corners of her eyes crinkle. "I'm so proud of you." She beams.

My mom crosses her arms and surveys the space with a questioning look. "I still can't believe you can afford all of this just by talking about makeup on the Internet." She scoffs.

"Mom, you know that's only part of what I do. Sure, it's mostly beauty related, but I'm considered a lifestyle influencer. And what can I say? I got lucky starting out on YouTube when I did. There weren't a ton of us at the time and for whatever reason, people wanted to watch me." I wrap my arms around myself, hugging my middle the way I wish my mother would.

"Well, I, for one, think it's fantastic," my dad quips. "Now how about we let April continue her tour, huh?" He gives my mom a hard smile.

"Fine," she says, looping her arm with his. "It's definitely beautiful. No argument there."

Oh, there's an argument for sure. With her, there always

is, but for the moment, she's backing down and I plan to enjoy it while it lasts.

Which ends up being about five minutes.

Marcus and I lead the group to the hallway, and my mom claps her hands wildly. "Look at all of these bedrooms! Please tell me you'll be filling some with grandbabies?"

I smack my palm to my forehead. "Mom, we've been over this. If we have kids—and that's a big if, by the way—it won't be any time soon."

She frowns. "But—"

"That's enough, Grace," Nana scolds. Her voice takes on an almost menacing tone and her eyes narrow into slits. I hardly recognize her. My mom seems to, though. This must be the same voice Nana used on my mom when she was a little girl. She seems to shrink hearing it now. "April and Marcus are twenty-five. They're practically still children themselves. They've only been married a few years and they just bought a house. Let them enjoy life, for Pete's sake."

My mother clears her throat and has the good sense to keep her thoughts to herself. I don't know what I'd do without Nana. She's the perfect buffer between my mom and me. My dad does what he can, and sometimes, like earlier in the living room, he's successful, but most of the time, she turns her venom on him, too.

I motion to the room on the left. "This will be my studio. I plan to film most of my videos in here and we're going to put a desk over there by the window so I can edit in here as well." I'm so excited to finally have a dedicated room to work. In our apartment, I made a makeshift set up in the living room, but I had to tear it down every night so we could use the sofa. It was far from ideal.

Emma strolls over to the only door in the hallway that's

closed. There's a lock on the outside and she probes it with her finger. "Well, this looks ominous." She smirks.

"Yeah, that's because it kind of is." I scrunch up my nose.

Emma's eyes bulge. "Do tell."

"Hold up," Marcus interjects. "It's only a basement and the last owner put the lock on it so his little kid wouldn't go wandering down there. And April," he says, turning toward me, "I already told you. I've got plans to make it more homey."

"Well, what is it if it isn't *homey*," my mom chides.

Marcus cocks his head, giving me a *you need to fix this* look. "It's just the only room that hasn't been remodeled and there's an old sump hole down there that makes it kind of creepy. But aside from the washer and dryer, I don't really have a reason to go down there," I backpedal.

My mom looks as though she'd like to say something, but my dad clears his throat. "What are your plans for the other room?" He asks, gesturing to the open door across from my office.

Marcus strides across the hall and stands in the middle of the empty room. "This one's for me."

"For you?" Emma's brow lifts. "What do *you* need a room for? Wait, wait, let me guess. You're gonna get an actual job and use this space for the nights when you bring your work home with you, right?" There's a challenging edge to her voice. As hard as I try, I can't make these two do more than tolerate each other. Most of the time, they ignore each other, but sometimes, like right now, Emma can't help herself.

"Cute." Marcus grunts, crossing his arms over his chest. "Actually, I'm moving my gaming set up in here. There's a door so April doesn't have to hear me and the guys." He grins, proud of himself.

"Aha," Emma sings. "So it's not an office. It's a game room. I should've known." She rolls her eyes, and Marcus looks like he might say something he'll regret.

I clear my throat and move quickly toward the back bedroom. "You guys are not gonna believe this last room." I push the door open and dance inside. "Just look at all of these windows!"

"A wall of windows in a bedroom. Just what everyone wants. What are you, an exhibitionist, now," my mom deadpans.

I grit my teeth and turn to face her, but just as I open my mouth, my words are cut off by the sound of beeping outside. "Saved by the moving van," Marcus mutters under his breath.

We all gather outside to watch Marcus's best friend, Zach, attempt to back the large U-Haul into the driveway. Marcus tries to direct him, but from where I'm standing, it looks as if Zach is doing the opposite of what he's being told. "Um, he's not going to crush my rose bushes, is he?"

"Nah, he'll be fine." Marcus waves off my worry.

After a close call with the mailbox and several expletives later, Zach finally puts the van in park and hops out. He strolls confidently over to Marcus, where they greet each other with their secret handshake that I swear lasts at least two minutes. "What's up, my guy?" Zach claps him on the shoulder and then turns his head to find me. "There she is!" He smiles wide, and it erases all of my irritation from his lack of driving skills.

"Hey, Zach," I say, giving him an easy smile.

Zach has been in Marcus's life since before we met. He's the brother Marcus never had but always wanted. Looking around right now, it's not hard to see how unbalanced things are. Both of my parents, my nana, and my best friend are here, but for Marcus, it begins and ends with Zach.

Marcus doesn't like to talk about it, but he had a really rough time as a kid. His mom was severely depressed and his dad was severely absent. But even when his dad was around, he wasn't really there. He showed no interest in Marcus other than to tell him to shut up and he had no tolerance for his wife. Marcus's mom spent a large portion of his childhood in and out of hospitals, but it never seemed to help. In fact, he told me it almost made things worse. She'd be okay for a few days when she got home, but pretty soon, she'd start to slip back into her old ways, flip-flopping between mania and indifference. As Marcus got older, he noticed his mom would sleep whenever his dad was around. At first, he thought it was a coping mechanism, but when he was eighteen, he caught his dad stirring a white powder into his mom's glass of juice. He'd been drugging her to make her "easier to deal with." He told Marcus that he was helping her because she couldn't be sad if she was asleep. Marcus came to me that night, snuck into my room through the window, and roused me from sleep. I could tell he'd been crying, and when I asked him what happened, I wasn't prepared for what he would say. "He told me we were a waste of time, April. My own father. Then he packed up his shit—what little he still had at the house—and left, but not before he let me know he was never coming back. What kind of dad does that?" His face crumpled and he collapsed into my arms. As sad as I was for Marcus, I had hoped that things would improve with his dad finally out of the picture. I couldn't have been more wrong.

Two weeks after his father walked out, Marcus came home from school to find his mom hanging from a rafter in the garage. He called 911, and then he called me. I'll never forget the look on his face when I got there. He was devastated in a way I'd never seen before, and it's a look I hope I never see again.

"Sweet pea," Nana calls. "Show me those roses of yours, would you?"

We walk across the expanse of grass to the modest patch along the top edge of the driveway. The previous owner clearly had a green thumb and an eye for landscaping. All of the plants, shrubs, and flowers look as though they materialized naturally. Even the roses have been planted in such a way it's hard to imagine them not being there.

Nana hobbles along beside me. At nearly seventy-one, she's still pretty spry, although I've noticed her knees have been giving her some trouble lately. I've been trying not to focus on it. Each new ache and pain only serves to remind me that she's getting older, which inevitably makes me think about death, and I refuse to go there. If I do, I'll wallow. I can't imagine life without her in it.

"So, what do you think? They're nice, huh? Not as nice as yours, of course." I beam at her.

"They're gorgeous, especially the red ones. Say, did I ever tell you why I started growing roses?"

I think on it a moment. "You mentioned once that your grandma grew them so I just assumed that's why you did."

"She did, you're right about that, but it was actually your grandfather who convinced me to grow them."

"Really?" My grandfather died when I was twelve. I have a few memories of him, but time has blurred them. When I think about him now, I remember his crooked smile and the way his eyes would dance whenever my nana walked into the room.

"He was quite the romantic," she says, a wistful smile blooming on her face. "Every Friday for years, he would bring me a dozen long-stemmed red roses just like these." She pinches a petal between knobby fingers. "I started growing them after he died."

"That's beautiful." I swipe at a lone tear trickling down my cheek.

She clears the emotion from her throat. "Now, you'll need to take good care of these. I'll come over when it's time to prune them and show you how to do it."

I take her hand in mine, giving it a light squeeze. "I look forward to it."

Two Years Later

I HAVE no idea where I am or how I got here. All I know is I'm standing in a field, completely surrounded by a towering maze of corn. In rural Pennsylvania, fields like this are a dime a dozen. I could be anywhere.

There's a chill in the air—the kind that comes when the day is just beginning. Morning dew glistens along the stalks, catching bits of the rising sun's light. It's hard to appreciate the beauty when you're not in control of a situation. Everything feels ominous.

My toes curl into the moist dirt. *Where are my shoes?* I close my eyes and think back on the last thing I remember. I was climbing into bed. It was late again, but that's nothing new. I glance down at myself, and sure enough—I'm wearing my paper-thin striped pajama pants and charcoal gray tank top. They're no match for the cold. I wrap my arms around myself, but it does little to warm me.

I inhale deeply, catching a faint whiff of citrus. It's out of place here in a cornfield, but it doesn't stop me from whipping my head around in search of an orange grove. Nothing but eight-foot stalks surround me.

"Marcus?" I call out my husband's name, but it catches

in the wind like a boomerang and swirls back toward me. The echo of my own voice pounds into me from every angle.

The wheat-colored corn tassels dance as the wind picks up. The orange scent is gone and in its place is the sweet, almost honey-like smell of the field. The stalks bend, forming an archway in front of me. I move forward—or maybe backward. It's impossible to tell. I have no idea how deep into this field I am, but aside from the smacking of leaves on the corn, there's no other sound. No cars on a distant road. No crows cawing overhead.

The silk peeks out of the husks and tickles my arms as I trudge through the field. I should be feeling more than just confused right now. I should feel concern that I'm lost, anxiety that I'm alone, fear that I have no memory of getting here. But all I feel is a mild curiosity.

The daylight begins to dim, and I cast my eyes to the sky. A sea of rich, black clouds rolls overhead, and it's unlike anything I've ever seen before. It's as if the day is turning to night at a rapid pace—without the gradual ease I'm used to. The wind whips my long hair in front of my face, and I grab at the strands, shoving them behind my ears.

I'm somewhere between a walk and a jog when I hear the faint sound of a train. The low rumble begins to gain momentum. I must be getting close to it. It's so loud now, I half expect it to appear right in front of me. At that moment, something does appear, but it's not a train.

Oh, shit. Those dark clouds have clashed and swirled to form a giant funnel that's just about to touchdown. And then it does. A tornado, the likes of which I've only seen in movies, begins its torment, assaulting everything in its path. Trees are uprooted and tossed into the air. The corn is ransacked and obliterated.

I should move, but instead, I stand statue-still, hypnotized by the wonder of nature in front of me. The ground rumbles and quakes with fury as the spiral seems to set its sights on me. It moves toward me with deliberate precision, and I start to run—or at least, that's what I'm attempting to do. My legs move like they're underwater. Fear begins to settle in, winding its way around my neck like a noose. No. I can't die here. Not when no one knows where I am.

I do that thing that everyone does when they're being chased; I look over my shoulder instead of keeping my gaze fixed in front of me. The tornado is gaining on me, licking at my heels. My toe catches on a vine, and I'm propelled forward. My fingers claw at the dirt, and my head bounces off the ground with a *thud*.

"Baby, wake up. You're having one of those dreams again."

"Marcus?" My voice sounds distant and not entirely like my own.

A firm hand presses down on my head, pushing it into the ground. Only it doesn't feel like the hard earth or gritty dirt. It feels like a soft pillow. "Damn, April. You're straight up moaning. That shit is creepy."

I blink a few times and then spring up, ramrod straight. Four familiar gray walls surround me. I'm in my bedroom, not a cornfield. I hold my hands in front of my face and pull the skin back behind each nail, inspecting them for dirt. They're still squeaky clean from my shower last night.

Well, this is new. I'm used to waking up in a blind panic after one of my tornado dreams, but I've never felt compelled to double-check and make sure it was only a dream.

"Earth to April?" Marcus singsongs from somewhere to my right.

I tilt my head down and roll it side to side, letting it loll back and forth like a pendulum. On a deep sigh, I angle my chin toward Marcus and catch a glimpse of his taut chest as he stretches a T-shirt over his head. He grins when he finds me staring at him. "Baby, you better get up. You have a Zoom call with Dr. Lesser at eleven. And then you've got that video to edit for the lipstick company with the weird-ass name—Petal Pushers or whatever the hell they're called." He chuckles, but his voice is gravelly like the static on an untuned radio. I'm pretty certain he's smoking again. And he's been smelling awfully minty lately—a sure sign of a cover-up.

"Petal Pout." I chuckle but stop fast, gripping the sides of my head. That dream really messed with me. I've been plagued by recurring tornado dreams for as long as I can remember. And for as often as I see them in my sleep, you'd think I'd been traumatized by one in real life, but the truth is, I've only ever seen them on TV. It's not a huge stretch for me, though. Spending too much time worrying about natural disasters is kind of my specialty.

I'm not sure I put a ton of stock into dream analysis, but I'd be lying if I said I never researched the phenomenon. As it turns out, dreaming of swirling black clouds on repeat is a sign of anxiety. And that word could practically be my middle name. Anxiety governs every move I make, every relationship in my life, every thought I have.

I groan, closing my eyes, and begin massaging my temples.

"Shit. It was a bad one, huh?" I feel his eyes on me.

I nod, and even that hurts.

He slides onto the bed and wraps his large arms around me, cocooning me in warmth. His hand rubs slow circles on my back, and he kisses the top of my head. This is a side of Marcus that most people in my life rarely see, or if they do, they never acknowledge it. He's been written off as a mooch who lives in his game room, but the truth is, I'd be lost without him.

Marcus may be twenty-seven on paper, but in his head, he's perpetually seventeen years old. It isn't really his fault. Honestly, it may be mine. My job makes it possible for him not to have one. Well, that's not entirely fair. He may not have a typical nine-to-five gig, but he still has responsibilities. He took over handling my emails and scheduling sponsorships once my channel grew too large for me to keep up. He helps keep me organized, and without him, I'd be even more of a disaster than I already am. But his job is flexible and doesn't take much more than about two to three hours of his day to complete. The rest of his time is devoted to the true love of his life. The one I jokingly like to say I play second fiddle to—his PS5.

He's a giant kid in a giant body, but he also has a giant heart—and right now, it's on full display. "Shh, it's all right now, baby. You know we don't see too many of those around here, right?"

I heave out a breath. "I know, but still, it *could* happen. I mean, last year, twelve tornadoes touched down in Pennsylvania."

He leans back and places his hands on either side of my face. He's wearing his trademark lopsided grin, the one that made me agree to dance with him at our junior Christmas formal. It was just supposed to be one song, but it turned into another and another. We've been each other's only dance ever since. That was ten years ago. Wow. Ten years. I hardly ever let myself think about time. Growing older terrifies me.

Marcus's laugh pulls me out of my thoughts. "Where do you go in there?" He taps my forehead. Before I can answer, the mattress dips, and we're suddenly joined by sixty pounds of love. Clyde pushes his way between us, tripping over my legs in the process. Marcus and I shake our heads, laughing at our oafish dog.

"Uh-oh, is somebody hungry?" Clyde drags his tongue from my chin to my forehead, eliciting a gag from me. His breath is unreal. "Ugh." I swipe at my face in an ill attempt to remove the drool. "Okay, I'll get you breakfast as soon as I get dressed." He chuffs in agreement and stumbles off the bed.

I stand and stretch my arms overhead. Marcus had started to lift himself off the bed, but he pauses mid-movement to watch me. His eyes shoot to my feet and make a slow travel up the length of my body. His finger joins his eyes and moves up my thigh, stopping just above the waistband of my pajama pants. He hooks his finger around the elastic and lightly tugs. "Still upset from that dream? Bet I could make you forget all about it."

I bark out a laugh. This is another one of the ways Marcus never grew up. He still has the libido of a teenage boy. Most of the time, I appreciate his sexual impulses, but not after the dream I just had, and let's be honest, never first thing in the morning, either. I don't know who these people are in movies and TV shows, but I need a toothbrush before I'll even consider fooling around, and I'd also much prefer to have some coffee in my system, too.

When I don't react, he scoffs and removes his finger. "Pssh, you don't have an impulsive bone in your body, April."

"You're just figuring that out now?" I tease.

"Whatever. Come find me when you need a distraction." His eyebrow arches.

I toss a pillow at the back of his head as he leaves the room. It ricochets off his white baseball cap, and he responds with a shake of his ass. He's ridiculous, and I love him for it. Marcus hasn't changed in all the years I've known him. My best friend, Emma, likes to talk about the importance of growth. She once said, "April, I don't know how you stay married to a guy who still behaves like a teenager when he's pushing thirty." But that's the thing, what she finds frustrating, I find comforting. I like it best when things don't change. I can only handle so much *new* all at once before I feel like I can't breathe. And after all that Marcus has been through, he deserves to be happy and have the carefree life he was denied when he was a child.

I wait a few seconds until I hear the telltale click of his game room door as it latches. He knows I can't do my job with him yelling, "Shotties in the cave," in the background, and while the door isn't completely soundproof, it helps.

Once I'm sure he has his headphones in place, I call out, "Alexa? Play 'Walking on Sunshine.'" Within seconds, the familiar drumbeat starts, and my feet instantly respond. I sway back and forth, and when the trumpet joins in, I'm full-on dancing. I sing into my hairbrush as I spin and twirl around my room.

This song has been my morning anthem for a while now. My nana used to play it on rainy days to help encourage me to get out of bed. I'd roll my eyes and groan, but I secretly loved it. I'm not a kid anymore, but it still has the same effect. It's just hard to feel down when I hear this song. If I thought Marcus wasn't aware of my routine, I'd be deluding myself. We just never talk about it, like it's some unspoken rule. He knows I need my alone time before I work. I imagine it's a bit like a prizefighter psyching themselves up for a match or a soldier preparing for battle. Okay, maybe those are a bit dramatic as far as examples go, but still. The idea remains the same. I'm preparing myself for the day ahead, and I'm not about to give up this tradition.

When the song ends, I traipse over to my closet and

fling the double doors open. It's a disaster. Everything is in complete disarray. Cardigans are heaped in piles on top of sweatshirts, while most of my hangers are free of clothing aside from one rogue flannel shirt that's hanging on by an arm. Marcus tried organizing it once. He arranged all of my clothes in color order and while I could appreciate the pleasing visual, what I could not appreciate was my total inability to find anything. He was stunned and said, "But baby, it's simple. You want your orange cardigan, you look in the orange section." Only that's not how my brain works. I remembered that I put my orange cardigan underneath my black hoodie in the back left-hand corner of my closet, so when I tried to picture that cardigan, I knew exactly where to find it. Marcus's reorganizing messed with my system. To him — and everyone else — it looks like chaos, but not to me. To me, his color-coded situation made absolutely no sense.

Fall is beginning to set in, and there's a slight chill in the air, so I decide on an oversized brown cardigan that I find tucked away under a pile of jeans. It took me less than three seconds to locate it because my system works. I smile smugly as I skip over to my dresser. I need a black tank top, and I'm sure I stashed one in the back of my underwear drawer. I root through the balled-up pairs, and sure enough, my fingers curl around a strap. I slide the tank top over my head, followed by a pair of black leggings that I also managed to find rolled up in the same drawer.

With my cardigan in place, I'm just about to step into the hallway when I catch a whiff of fresh cinnamon and apples. I breathe in deep, and my stomach answers with a weighty growl. But there's something else. Something that makes me stop and close my eyes. Nana. The pain of loss hits me immediately. We moved into this house two years ago and lost her three months later.

This smell is so familiar. It reminds me of her apple crisp. She made it every fall right around this time. I inherited her recipe cards and I'm sure it's written down on one. They're stashed somewhere in the basement. I haven't been able to bring myself to look for them.

The day she died, my mom remembered Nana saying she was going out to the garage to try and find her box of recipes. My breath hitches as I recall my mother's words. "She told me, 'April should have my recipes. They're in those boxes collecting dust. I'm gonna go grab them for her.'" And that was the last thing she ever said. Nana meandered out to the garage, and an hour later, my mom went to check on her. She found her lying on the ground. The boxes had cushioned her fall and lay crushed around her head, but it didn't matter. They told us it was a massive pulmonary embolism. It killed her before she ever hit the floor. Even after almost two years, I'm still in shock that she's gone.

"Marcus?"

I hear the whirl of wheels on his gaming chair as it spins toward the door. When it opens, my husband pokes his head out and slides his headset down. "What is it, baby? I was just about to start."

I know the answer to the question before I even ask it, but my curiosity wins out. "Are you *baking* something?"

He throws his head back and laughs. "You," he wheezes. "You think I"—he points to himself—"am baking? Me?" He roars like this is the funniest thing he's ever heard, and sure, he rarely cooks, neither of us do. We're pretty big fans of takeout and delivery. And he's certainly never baked anything since I've known him, but are these theatrics really necessary? His laughter ends in a coughing fit. Yep, he's definitely smoking again.

I roll my eyes and wait for him to get himself under

control. He holds out a hand and releases a long, dramatic sigh. "Jesus, that shit was funny." He begins putting his headset back in place, but just before he snaps the cups over his ears, he pauses. His right eyebrow arches, and he studies me for a moment. "Wait, why'd you ask me that?"

"Don't you smell that?"

He takes a deep breath and shrugs. "Smell what?" He cocks his head. "Hold up. Did you leave the lid off the nail polish remover again? April, I keep telling you, you can't be breathing in that acetone."

"No. And I haven't done that in a long time." I huff. He scrunches his face and I flap my hand. "Whatever. I swear it smells just like my nana's apple crisp. It's almost like I can taste it. It reminds me of this one time when I was maybe five or six—"

His eyes soften. "I miss her, too. And listen, you know I love your stories, but the guys are waiting. I told them I'd be on at ten, and it's almost five after." He bites at his lip. "You know what? Fuck it. Go ahead, tell me your story." Marcus is constantly at war with himself as though he could ever be anything like his father. I wish he'd stop worrying about that, but then again, who am *I* to tell someone not to worry?

I rest my hand over my mouth and tap my fingers one by one over my lips. "No, it's fine. But this is weird, Marcus. I'm totally smelling cinnamon and apples."

He rubs at his chin. "Maybe it's Mona?"

I chuckle. "Yeah, maybe." This old house creaks and groans, especially when there's wind. Marcus and I started referring to the sounds as a ghost, and we named her Mona. And now, whenever we hear anything strange, we blame it on her.

Laughing, he begins gliding back into the room but

stops. He snaps his fingers. "I bet it's that smart diffuser thing."

"Smart diffuser thing?"

"Yeah." He rolls back into the hallway and points into our bedroom. I turn and notice an elegant copper inverted cone resting on a hammered patina base sitting on a little stool in the corner. There's a steady flow of thin vapor coming out of the tip. I'm not sure how I missed it. "You remember. They're a new sponsor, so they sent over a few of those things. They're supposed to be able to adjust to whatever smell they think you might enjoy, or some shit like that. I put one in our room, one in your studio, there's also one in the bathroom, and one in the kitchen." He crosses his arms and eyes me carefully. "Baby, we talked about all this."

I don't remember, but to be honest, there have been so many sponsors lately it's hard to keep up. I just nod, and he swivels back into his cave. Before he closes the door, he calls out, "Don't forget to take your vitamin." I groan, but he shakes his head. "Oh, come on. They can't be that bad. Besides, these sponsors are our bread and butter, baby!" He chuckles as he slides the door closed.

"They *can* be that bad," I mutter. When Marcus first told me about Hemply Simple, I agreed to take them mostly because I know vitamins are important, and I've never been great about taking them in the past. I have a bit of an aversion to pills of any kind, and after what happened to his mom, Marcus does, too. But since these are gummies, I figured I could give it a shot. Unfortunately, they have got to be the worst tasting things I've ever had the misfortune of eating. They're formulated to taste sour, and I suppose if I were someone who enjoyed sour candy, I'd be on board with that. But I happen to loathe it. One bite and I'm immediately transported back to sophomore year when Walker Dolan—in one of his many attempts to woo me—left a bag of sour gummy worms on the floor by my locker. They were wrapped in a giant red bow with a note for all to see, proclaiming, "April, without you, my world is sour." Ugh. My mouth twists just thinking about it.

I stand in the hallway, taking one last deep breath of cinnamon apples, missing my nana. Then I let it all out and head to the kitchen to feed Clyde.

A FAINT PLUME of steam wafts out of the copper cone on the kitchen windowsill, making the whole room smell of fresh strawberries. I close my eyes, and suddenly I'm sifting back through childhood memories, remembering the days my nana and I would collect the sweet fruit right off the wild vine behind our house. So far, this new smart diffuser is two for two.

Clyde circles my feet as I stroll to the pantry and pull out his food bin. As soon as the lid is off, he shoves his wrinkled face into the container, mashing it deep into the brown pellets. He munches away as round bits of food fall from his lips onto the floor. I place a hand on his barrel chest and give him a playful shove. "Dude! I know you're hungry, but you have to be patient. Jeez. You act like you're starving." I survey his burly little body and shake my head. "And it's pretty obvious you're not, buddy." I sift out a generous scoop and fill his bowl. He doesn't hesitate, diving into it like he hasn't eaten in days.

I should take this disgusting vitamin and get it over with. I snatch the jar off the counter and pluck out a blue gelatinous disc. They don't even look appealing. But they promise shiny hair, clear skin, and nails for days. I've only been taking them for a week, so the jury is still out on whether or not they work, but if they deliver on their promise, I guess I can overlook the way they taste and feel in my mouth. I chew and swallow with rapid speed and attempt to chase away the aftertaste with a tall glass of water. Whispers of Walker Dolan's shy smile flicker in my head, making me shiver. Marcus told me Hemply Simple is only asking me to take them for two months and then make a video on the results I've experienced. So far, the only thing they've done is force me to relive a particularly awkward time in my life. Hopefully, I can find the strength to get through these next two months and put this, and Walker, behind me for good.

My eyes flit around the room and land on my espresso maker. It's a true sight to behold. I half expect it to be bathed in a warm glow while angels sing in the distance. I glide across the room toward it like there's some magnetic pull. This beast of a machine is similar to what you might find in a Starbucks. It was a gift from me to myself after I hit five million subscribers on YouTube last month. Before this, I was either dependent on Marcus to go out and buy me a latte every morning, or worse—forced to drink drip coffee. A shiver rolls down my spine. Nothing compares to a rich espresso made with beans that are ground fresh for each cup.

Coffee is the one thing about me that's truly high maintenance.

Okay, maybe not the one thing, but it's the most obvious thing.

All right, it's not even that. Whatever. I'm having this argument with myself in my own head. Like I need any convincing.

Knowing full well that's not true, I flap my hand with a "Pssh," dismissing myself.

I hear the tinny clank of Clyde's bowl to my right as he laps up the remnants of his food. With a satisfied snort, he rolls out of the room to take his first of approximately eighteen naps of the day.

Steaming latte in hand, I breeze into my studio and survey the space. It's a mess from the try-on haul I filmed yesterday. Clothing is laying in a heap on the floor, and the top of my desk is strewn with jewelry and hair accessories.

I bend down and begin collecting all the disheveled clothes. Ahh, the glamorous life of an influencer. I grimace. I hate that word. Mainly because of what it represents. I'm just a twenty-seven-year-old college dropout with a camera and a ring light. I barely leave my house, and yet millions of people all over the world watch my videos every week, hoping to glean some intel on the hottest trends. No one should have that kind of power. Least of all, someone like me.

What started as a hobby five years ago somehow morphed into a full-time job. I'm not even sure how it happened. The first video I filmed was of me organizing my nail polish collection. I had been putting it off, and it was getting out of control. We lived in a tiny apartment, and Marcus wasn't home, so I propped up my phone and hit record while I sorted and purged nearly one hundred bottles. The only reason I even uploaded it to YouTube was so a few of my friends could watch. I've always been a bit of a hoarder when it comes to makeup and beauty products and I knew they'd be proud of me for whittling down my vast collection. The final video was eighteen minutes long—too large to text, and I assumed no one else would be interested, so I didn't bother to make it private. Turns out they were. It didn't happen overnight, but slowly more and more people watched that video, leaving comments asking for more. And now here I am, just a girl who puts on makeup and talks about her life on camera. I have no formal training, no special schooling, no business telling anyone my opinions. But my subscribers disagree, and I'll never understand why.

I hear the opening chords of *The Golden Girls* theme song from somewhere underneath a heap of clothing. "Oh, shit. I must have left my phone in here again," I mumble as I toss a mustard slouchy sweater aside. The song gets louder as I continue burrowing through the clothes. I reach the bottom of the pile and find my phone wedged into the sleeve of a flannel button-down. On the screen is a picture of my best friend, Emma, stuffing an impossibly large taco into her mouth. I tap the phone to answer as I roll onto my bottom, letting my legs splay out on the floor.

"Hi, Em," I wheeze.

"April? Why do you sound so out of breath? Wait, don't tell me you're locked outside again. Is Twitch boy in the cave? Do you need me to come rescue you?"

I shudder at the memory of that day. It wasn't my finest moment, and it most definitely wasn't Marcus's either. "No, no, it's nothing like that. I just couldn't find my phone and thought you'd hang up before I found it."

"Of course, that's what happened." Emma chuckles fondly.

"I bet I know why you're calling," I say through a wide, toothy smile.

"I bet you don't," she singsongs.

"Whatever. Let me guess." I pause for dramatic effect and Emma adds to the dramatics with a theatrical sigh. "You wanted to tell me that you've decided to come over today and film a chatty get-ready-with-us video! Am I right? I'm definitely right. Right?"

"Yeah, no. That's not at all why I called." I groan, but she's quick to respond. "Oh, don't give me that. You know I hate the way I sound on video. Plus, my roots are a half-inch long. I'm nowhere near camera ready."

I shake my head. "Listen, you need to let all of that go. No one cares. Besides, Marcus deletes all my negative comments anyway. You'd never see them."

"Oh, wow, that makes me feel so much better," she deadpans. "Listen," her voice lowers to barely above a whisper, "do you remember Walker Dolan?"

The coffee I was sipping sprays out of my mouth like a whale's blowhole. "Is that a serious question?" I ask as I pick up a pair of distressed mom jeans that are now marbled with coffee stains. Walker was in our class at Shermer High, and for all of freshman year and a portion of sophomore, too, he had a massive, embarrassing crush on me. He was a nice enough guy, but it wasn't a love connection, at least not for me. I haven't told Emma about the gummies and how they remind me of Walker, but it's really odd that she's bringing him up at a time when he's been on my mind. Glancing at my arm, I notice goose bumps speckling my skin. I rub a hand over them.

"Yeah, I know. How could you forget? Right? Anyway, well ... it's a crazy thing, but he actually died."

I sit upright, gripping the phone tightly. "What? When?"

"Yesterday. Word is he had a massive heart attack while eating a Shorti hoagie outside Wawa, and he just dropped over."

I shake my head. "A heart attack? At twenty-seven?"

"Crazy, right? And I feel so bad for his sister. Apparently she was with him and was the one to call 911."

"That's nuts. Wow." I stand and begin pacing the room. It never felt small to me before, but right now, it's like a coffin. I shiver. Bad analogy.

I think back to those days when I had entertained the

endless barrage of notes in my locker and winks in the hall-way, hoping he'd eventually get bored and move on. And he did move on, but not until the talent show in tenth grade when he performed an off-key rendition of Foreigner's "I Want To Know What Love Is" that ended with him down on both knees holding a sign that said, "Will you go out with me?" It was mortifying. Everyone in the gym was staring at me with bated breath, waiting for my answer. So I did the only thing I could do in that situation. I ran. I'd say I felt bad for Walker, but he didn't need anyone's pity. After that stunt, girls were practically throwing themselves at him, desperate for a grand romantic gesture of their own. And now he's just … gone. He and I, we're the same age. If it could happen to him, it could happen to —

"April," Emma chastises. "Get out of your head."

"I — I'm not in my head."

Her voice is low and calm. "Sweetie, yes you are. You're probably walking in circles right now as we speak, aren't you?"

I look down at my feet as they take me round and round the cramped room. I stop so fast, I stumble. "No." I try to sound confident, but the lilt in my voice gives me away. Not that it matters. Emma can smell my bullshit from a mile away.

"Listen to me. This was a total freak occurrence, okay? And it's completely unrelated to you."

I sigh. "I know."

"And yet, you're Googling heart attacks in people our age right now, aren't you?"

I glare at the screen of my laptop as it loads the results of my search. It's irritating when someone knows you as well as Emma knows me. She chuckles softly at my silent admission.

"Okay, fine. I'll come over and film with you."

I suck in a sharp breath. "You will?"

"Yes, but only because I know if I don't come over there, you will obsess over Walker all day."

"That's not true." But we both know I'm lying. I am just about to type his name into the search bar, but her words get to me, and instead, I snap my laptop closed. "Whatever. Listen, I have an appointment with Dr. Lesser at eleven. How about you come by at noon?"

"Wow," she croons. "That's some perfect timing right there. You should definitely tell her about Walker."

I lift my eyes to the ceiling. Dr. Lesser doesn't need to hear about a boy I knew in high school. Sure, his death is unnerving, but it's nothing compared to nana's and she's usually the person I talk about the most in our sessions. "I'll see you soon."

I'm about to hang up when she says, "Oh, and April?"

"Yeah?"

"Pull out all of your Charlotte Tilbury. If I have to put on makeup while on camera with my dark ass roots, I'm using the good stuff."

I KEEP my eyes fixed on the screen. I'm early for our appointment and waiting for Dr. Lesser to start our Zoom call. I still can't believe she's willing to do these sessions remotely. She accepts how difficult it is for me to leave the house, but I'm surprised she isn't trying to push me more. I'd just assume, as my therapist, she'd be pressing me to make more of an effort to get out. But so far, she seems content with me living as I am now. Or *not* living, depending on how you look at it. Maybe that's why I keep her around. She doesn't force me to do anything. I guess you could question how she's really helping me, but it's enough just to have someone impartial to talk to.

I tap my finger on the edge of my desk and fidget in my chair. It squeaks as I shift my weight from one side to the other. At eleven o'clock on the dot, the screen goes dark, and just as quickly, Dr. Lesser's face appears. I would put her in her mid to late fifties with sleek shoulder-length gray hair and kind eyes. She smiles wide when she sees me and I smile in return. I've been seeing her as often as needed for years, but it became more regular after Nana died. I've always struggled with anxiety, but when I lost her, it was as if my life totally collapsed. Despair, grief, sadness—all of the words that usually applied to deep loss couldn't even touch what I was feeling. I was broken. I couldn't sleep; I barely ate; I couldn't get out of bed. Poor Marcus. He didn't know what to do, and after what he witnessed with his own mother, he panicked. It was the look on his face that finally convinced me to call Dr. Lesser.

Now, here we are, a year and a half later, and sure, I don't leave the house, but inside these walls, I'm functioning pretty well.

"April," Dr. Lesser hums. "How have you been?"

"I'm okay." She leans in close to the screen and I clear my throat. "I mean, I'm good."

She smiles. "You don't have to pretend with me, you know. In fact, it doesn't work if you do." She narrows her eyes slightly.

I clasp my hands together on the desk and her eyes zero in on them. I release them and rub my palms along my leggings. "Oh, it's not that I'm pretending, it's just … well, I've been thinking about Nana, but what else is new, huh?" I chuckle, but she doesn't join me. She studies my face and doesn't say a word, which is code for her wanting me to say more. I tell her about Nana's apple crisp and how I realized I'd never have it again. I swipe angrily at a few rogue tears as they glide down my face.

"April, I don't think it's the apple crisp you're worried about."

I shake my head. "No, of course it isn't."

"It's just a catalyst for your grief over losing your nana. And not having her apple crisp again means not having her again either."

I bite my lip to keep my emotions at bay. She's right, but I hate when she says things like that. It isn't her job to dance around my feelings, but when she's blunt like this, I can't escape reality. And escaping is how I cope.

I started retreating into my home soon after Nana died. Over time, I left the house less and less, and for close to a year, I haven't left at all. Dr. Lesser knows I'm a homebody, but I haven't been very forthcoming about the extent of it. It's all part of the façade. If I put on a happy face and continue being productive, it gives me the appearance of being well.

Our session continues with me talking about my day and how excited I am to film with Emma. I maneuver our conversation away from Nana and talk a bit about my crazy vivid tornado dream.

"That's your anxiety at play, April. You are co-existing with your fears as though they are a living, breathing part of you. Perhaps you should try and give yourself some new challenges."

"Challenges?" My voice cracks on the word.

"Sure, nothing too grand, at least not at first. But maybe you should try to get out of the house once a week, even if it's just a short trip to the grocery store." She widens her eyes. "Don't think I'm not aware of what's been going on. You never talk about anything outside of your house. In fact, I think it's been months—maybe even a year—since you mentioned leaving home. That's something we need to unpack. You know," she taps at her chin, "a colleague of mine runs a retreat that might help."

I break into a cold sweat and my hands start to shake as she continues to explain this program she wants me to consider. We've always been on the same page, or at least I thought we were, but now I feel exposed and attacked. I'm perfectly content in this house. And I've been doing so well and making improvements. Sure, I don't leave, but I'm functioning just fine. Why would I want to disrupt that? My throat feels like it's closing and my breath is constricted. I start to cough and reach for the glass of water sitting beside me.

Dr. Lesser pauses, watching me closely. "Of course, I'm not going to push, April. This has to be your decision. For now, though, I'd like to see you more often. Let's go back to weekly sessions at, least for the time being."

"You know what, you've given me a lot to think about. Thanks, Dr. Lesser."

"Of course. While I have you, shall we set up your next appointment?"

"Um, actually, I need to check over my schedule, uh, how about I just give your office a call tomorrow?"

She links her hands together, resting them on the table in front of her, and her eyes narrow slightly. "April, I'm on your side. I hope you know that."

"Mm-hmm." I nod. "I'll be in touch. Talk to you soon." I wave goodbye and end the call, sitting back in my chair. I don't know how I can continue anything with her. Not after this. We had this unspoken arrangement. I talk about my grief and she listens and councils me through it. We don't spend time worrying about how I don't leave my house. But now, she turned on me and I know she's not going to let this go. It feels like a betrayal. I'm safe here in my house. Within these walls, I have control, and right now, I can't even think about altering that. I'll leave the house on my own terms when I'm ready.

"OOH, WEE." Emma whistles as she eyes the spread of over-priced, high-end cosmetics. She nods approvingly. "I still can't believe they send you all this for free."

My cheeks flush, and my shoulders slump. "I know, but only because they hope I'll review their products." I steal a glance at her. Her eyes widen as she mentally tallies up the price of each item. "You can take it all with you if you want," I quickly add.

Her head whips up, sending her wheat-colored locks cascading down her back in effortless waves. She studies my face, her jade eyes holding mine captive. She places a reassuring hand on my arm. "Sweets, you know I'm not judging you, right? You don't have to give everything away just because you feel like you don't deserve it. This isn't a job that just *anyone* could do, you know?" She waves her arm around the room. "I've only filmed with you a few times, but each time, I feel sick to my stomach when I think about all of the people who will watch and criticize every little thing about me."

I open my mouth to argue, but she lifts her hand. "Marcus isn't always so quick at removing the negative comments. I've read enough, and it serves me right for look-ing. I know better. But, April, you do this all the time and you do it with ease. It's really time you got out of your own way. You're humble and self-deprecating and it's impossible not to love you. I'd say it's all part of your brand, but that would mean it's intentional, and none of it is. It's just who you are. And, you know what? Everyone can see you're truly a kind soul. That's why you have so many subscribers. It's why your channel is so successful. Your milkshake brings *everyone* to the yard, girl."

We both burst into happy laughter. Leave it to Emma to give me a pep talk five minutes after she gets here. She's my own personal cheering squad, and when she hypes me up, I almost believe her.

"Hey, that reminds me," I say, reaching for a shoebox stashed under my desk. "This company wanted me to test out their new hybrid flats."

"Hybrid flats?" Emma's forehead scrunches.

"I know, weird, right? Apparently, they have the look of flats, but the feel of an athletic shoe, so you're supposed to be able to tolerate wearing them for longer periods of time. Anyway, I won't get much use out of them and since we wear the same size, I figured maybe you could give them a try and then join me for a video talking about them?" My eyes widen and my lips part slightly.

"Oh, April," she croons. "What's stopping you from trying them out yourself, huh?" She eyes me closely and then sighs. "Fine. Hand them over."

I grin. "Thanks, Em."

What a strange job this is. I spend most days sitting in front of a camera talking to no one, and yet, according to my analytics, I'm actually talking to an average of one hundred and fifty thousand viewers per video.

That's an insane amount of people. If you had told me a few years ago that I would be doing this for a living, I would've laughed and then immediately felt paralyzed with fear. It would probably surprise people to know that I'm one of the most socially awkward people on the planet. I despise talking to a stranger, let alone hundreds of thousands of them. It's why I keep my circle so small. But when I'm making a video, it's just me talking to myself. And that's something I do all the time, so the fact that a camera is turned on to capture it isn't all that strange to me. It's the idea that there are people willing to watch me that's so hard for me to believe.

Surprisingly, the majority of influencers are like me, at least in some way. You almost have to be in order to stomach the idea of sitting in a room alone talking to yourself. I'm pretty lucky that this type of job exists and even more lucky that I have viewers who like my content.

YouTube is a finicky beast. It takes hard work to gain subscribers, sure, but it's more about luck than anything else. Personality is also a huge factor. Let's face it—this job is a twenty-four seven popularity contest. It boggles my mind that I've managed to carve out a little niche for myself because I'm quirky, nerdy, and a total klutz, but for some strange reason, that seems to be appealing to people.

I've seen comments calling me relatable. One even referred to me as a delight. I don't know about that; I'm just being me. There's no act. No pomp and circumstance. Just a weird girl living her life and filming bits and pieces of it for the Internet.

But there's also an element of pretending, too—almost to the point of lying. I may come across to viewers as someone who has her shit mostly together, but they couldn't be more wrong. I also barely have a life to film, but I do what I can with what I have.

"So, slight problem here," Emma says while riffling through foundation bottles.

"What's that?"

"Since you're as pale as Casper the freaking ghost, I'm going to have to bronze the shit out of my skin to make any of these shades work. You need to get out more, girl. Get yourself a tan or at least a base color." She smirks.

Her chiding reminds me of my session with Dr. Lesser. I roll my eyes and tug on the gauzy sleeve of her shirt. "Come on, let's get started."

"HI, guys! Welcome back to my channel. And if you're new here, hi, my name is April, and I'm so glad you're watching. If you like what you see, please give this video a thumbs-up and subscribe if you want to see more content from me. I upload every Monday, Wednesday, and Friday at twelve p.m. eastern time." I glance at my friend next to me. "Today, we have a super special guest! Back by popular demand, my bestest friend, Emma, is joining me for a fun, chill, chatty get-ready-with-us."

My normally confident friend smiles sheepishly and gives a short wave to the camera. The few times she's filmed with me, she always starts out kind of rigid and robotic, but once I get her talking and she's distracted by the makeup, she loosens up.

When Emma told me she was coming over, I hopped on to my Instagram account and posted a story asking my followers to submit questions for us to answer. Within five minutes, I had over a hundred responses. It always helps to have a focus for these kinds of videos, otherwise they can turn awkward really fast.

Emma and I get to work priming our faces, and I fire off the first question. "Okay, Em, yasmin89 wants to know what our favorite guilty pleasure TV show is." My friend and I grin wickedly at each other. "Do you want to tell them or should I?"

"Let's do it together," she says.

I nod. "All right. On the count of three. One … two … three."

"*Sister Wives*!" we yell in unison and then fall into a fit of laughter.

"Em and I never miss an episode, and we always watch while on FaceTime with each other," I add.

"Speaking of—spoiler alert—how do you think Kody is going to get himself out of this one?"

I shake my head. "Em, that's not a spoiler. 'Kody in the doghouse' is literally the plot of every episode."

"Truth," she speaks without any hesitation, earning a chuckle from me.

We continue, taking turns answering questions while simultaneously discussing the makeup we're using. Viewers love to hear a creator's thoughts on whatever product they're trying, whether it be makeup, or electronics, or clothing. They're tuning in because they want to be sold— either for or against something.

Emma is discussing her must-have taco toppings while I apply my lip color. I let my mouth fall open slightly as I skim the wand around in circles. I catch a whiff of pineapple and pause. I've used this lip cream before, but I don't remember it having a scent. Still, as I hold it up to my nose and inhale, the smell seems to intensify. I close my eyes as the unique aroma fills my entire body, penetrating every part of me. Suddenly, I'm no longer in my office.

Nana was in the kitchen of our old house on Windsor Street. The aged floorboards creaked beneath my feet as I tiptoed into the room. Cold linoleum greeted my toes and forced them to curl as I stopped in the doorway and watched her. A cast iron skillet warmed on the stove. The flame below burned low and steady. My nana dropped a wad of butter into the pan, and even though I couldn't see it, I could hear the sizzle and smell the nutty perfume. She plunked a large spoon full of brown sugar into the butter bath and stirred the two together. Once she was satisfied with the texture, the burner was turned off, and I tiptoed in close to watch my favorite part. Rings of pineapple were arranged inside the pan to form a spiral, and each center was dotted with a maraschino cherry. Nana retrieved a stain-less-steel bowl and dropped dollops of batter to rest on top of the pineapple design. She smoothed out the top with the back of a wooden spoon and then deposited the skillet into the oven. It was my mom's birthday, and pineapple upside-down cake was her favorite.

"Wow, April, you really went off on a tangent there."

I blink a few times and find myself sitting in my high-backed chair in my office. The room is bright and warm from my studio lighting.

I look over to find Emma staring at me, an expectant look on her face. I lift my hand to cover my mouth. I've always been olfactory sensitive. The slightest hint of a scent can instantly take me back in time to a memory from my past, but I've never had it happen so vividly before. "Did I say all of that out loud?" My gaze widens as I stare at the blinking light on the camera. It's still recording.

Emma's eyebrows draw down, and she opens her mouth to speak, but stops. Her eyes dart around the room and she nods, collecting her thoughts. "You didn't know that?" Her voice is quiet, tentative.

I chuckle, hoping to erase the worry from her eyes. "I guess I was too caught up in the past to notice."

She wraps an arm around me, gripping my shoulder. "I won't argue there. So, what made you take that little trip down memory lane?"

I hold up the tube of lip cream. "This stuff smells like pineapple, and as soon as I caught a whiff, it reminded me—"

"Of your nana's pineapple upside-down cake." Her mouth curls into a wry grin.

"So, I really went into a lot of detail, huh?" I blow out a slow breath.

Emma nods, still smiling.

"What did I say exactly?"

"Well," she begins. "You started huffing makeup and then you—"

I scrub my hand down my face. "You know what, I'll just catch it when I play back the footage." My gaze slides to the camera. "Since we are still filming."

Emma chews her lip and tips her head. "We are, but … you *could* just edit it all out, right? Maybe right up to the moment before you time traveled?" She shrugs, pressing her lips together to keep from laughing.

I give her arm a playful shove. "Careful now. I am a master at editing. I can always dub some unflattering commentary over your parts, you know."

She blows a raspberry with her mouth. "You wouldn't dare."

"Of course I wouldn't." I chuckle. "You know I've always got your back."

Over the next half hour, we answer more questions and finish applying our makeup. When we wrap up the video, I walk Emma to the door.

"So, did you tip Marcus off that I was coming? Because he managed to stay locked in his room the whole time." She squints at me.

"Actually, I never said a word. I didn't have to seeing as he had a full day of gaming planned." I shrug, wrapping my arms around myself. Marcus's excessive gaming is a huge bone of contention for Emma, but I wish she'd let it go. When he's in his game room, I'm working on a video— either filming or editing. Our lifestyle works and I've never complained to her about it. Thankfully, she doesn't press the issue, but she *does* press another one. And I'm not sure what's worse.

"Hey, there's this new Cuban restaurant that just opened. Flare. Have you heard of it?" I shake my head, and she continues. "It's supposed to be really good. Want to check it out later? Maybe for dinner tonight?" There's a hopeful lilt in her voice.

My smile wavers, but I try to mask it by feigning an itch on my lip. "Where is it?"

She stalls, scratching at her forehead. Her shoulders tense. "Not far. Just over in Willowton."

I frown and she clocks it, matching my downturned lips with her own. She already knows what I'm going to say, but I need to say it anyway. It's like a well-oiled machine—this dance we do where she asks me to do something and I politely turn her down. But Willowton is over forty-five minutes away. I can't even wrap my head around all that could happen in that amount of time, but even still, my brain forces me to try. It shows me pictures of cars piling up on the interstate, Emma's hatchback flipped on its roof, both of us screaming as we're trapped inside, the pungent smell of gas as it leaks from the tank, the fear in our eyes as we realize the severity of the situation just as the car bursts into flames. And that's not the only possible scenario. Hell, *possible* isn't even the worst of what I see. I envision a meteor falling from the sky, zeroing in on Emma's car like there's a target on the roof.

I wasn't always this way. I mean, sure, I've always dealt with anxiety in some form or another, but it wasn't crippling. Not like it is now. I used to enjoy living a full life and traveling any chance I could. I even spent a summer in Spain the year after I graduated high school. The change wasn't sudden, and while Nana's death definitely didn't help, it wasn't the direct cause, either. It happened gradually, evolving over the years. I stopped traveling out of state, and then I stopped traveling farther than five miles from my house. I no longer felt safe driving and barely felt safe when someone else drove. With the wonders of online shopping and grocery delivery, I really didn't have to leave. And what we can't order, Marcus picks up, alternating between using his truck and my car just to keep both in working order.

Dr. Lesser told me anxiety doesn't need a traumatic event, but sometimes if one occurs, like losing my nana, it only serves to further our mercurial beliefs. We view it as proof that our fears are valid.

I haven't left the property in months, and I know if I don't force myself to do it soon, I may never leave. But I don't want to rush it. My home is my safe haven. In here, it feels as though nothing can harm me, and those warm and cozy thoughts keep me bound inside these walls. After Nana died, it made it even easier for me to give in to my chronic fear of catastrophic events, and I guess in a lot of ways, it's kept me a prisoner in my own home. Though, I don't feel much like a prisoner. I could leave, but I also can't. I know how ridiculous that sounds. Whenever I voice any of my erratic concerns, I hear the words as they come out of my mouth, and I want to shove them right back inside. But I can't force myself to just power through it. It isn't a bad mood I need to conquer. It's the way my brain works. It's misfiring, and I don't know how to make it stop. I've done hours and hours of research, reading every article I can find. There are so many treatment options, some more traditional than others. I've even considered hypnosis, but at the end of the day, I'm just not ready to move forward. Because the hard truth—the one I can't share with anyone —is that I'm not in any hurry to "fix" myself. My agoraphobia is an inconvenience to the people who love me, but to me, it's easy to manage if I just accept it for what it is. And the only time it bothers me is in situations like this one where I've clearly disappointed someone I care about.

Emma's shoulders slump, and a sigh escapes her mouth. She keeps trying, and I know she'll never stop. But I wish she would. My answer won't change, no matter how many times she asks. "You know what, I'd like to, but I need to edit this video so I can post it tomorrow. You go and let me know how it is. If it's any good, maybe I'll send Marcus for takeout later this week." I watch as the remainder of hope melts off her face. There's no letting her down easy. I'm just letting her down.

She nods solemnly, tapping her fingers on the door. The light is gone from her eyes, and it's my fault. I'm the kind of friend who bleeds people dry. I don't mean to, but intentional or not, it's what I do. Most of them have given up on me, and rightfully so, but not Emma. "Okay, then, I should get going. Let me know if you change your mind about dinner." I won't and she knows that, but this is all part of our routine right down to the part where I smile and nod, promising to call if I can join her.

Her smile is kind as she slips out the door. I watch her leave, holding on to the entryway as though it might help keep me in place should a violent windstorm choose that moment to strike. The engine of her car roars to life, and my fingers curl, my nails digging into the molding. She waves and then backs out of my driveway as I retreat inside and close the door.

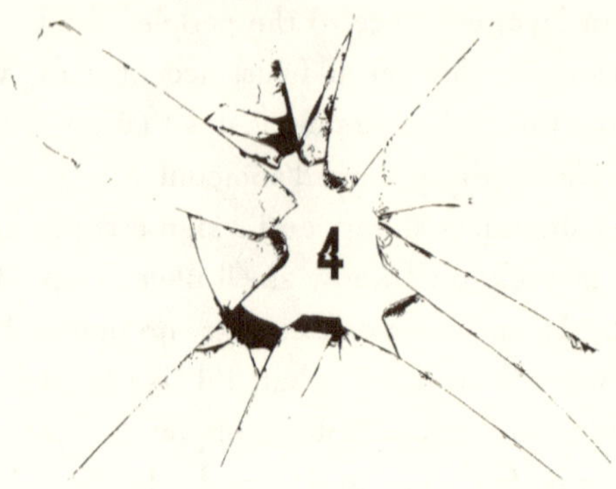

4

THE DIFFUSER in the corner emits a pleasing lavender scent. It reminds me of my laundry detergent, which makes me think about my clean bed sheets, and I yawn for what feels like the eight-hundredth time. For the past three hours, I've been holed up in my office. First, I needed to edit the Petal Pout review and now I'm working on editing the footage Emma and I shot earlier today. I cut out the section where I went off on my weird, out-of-body tangent about pineapple upside-down cake, but for some reason, I can't seem to get the sound to line up with the video during the last few minutes.

A resounding knock startles me, and I look up to see the door of my office push open. "Are you *still* working on that?"

I look down at my hands limp on the keyboard and back up at my husband. My answer comes out as a sigh, long and low.

Marcus steps into the room, plunging his hands deep into his pockets. "I keep telling you, you gotta stop with the iMovie. No one uses that anymore. Final Cut will take some time to learn, but you can take an online class or something."

I meet his gaze, but I'm too tired to speak and too frustrated to argue. He *does* keep bringing it up, and he's right. But the idea of learning something new—changing what I'm used to—terrifies me.

The skin around his eyes seems to soften, and he takes another tentative step toward me as though I'm a stray dog that he's been trying to catch. "You know, I get offers all the time from people looking for a part-time gig. They're fresh out of college and already know how to use the program. Why don't you let me hire one of them to edit for you?"

I'm shaking my head before the words finish leaving his mouth. He may have me cornered, but this dog still has some bite left. "No way. I've been editing my own videos since I started my channel. I have a style, and I can't change it now."

"Can't or won't?" He arcs a challenging brow.

"Does it matter?" The words come out in a rush, and there's an edge to them.

He tips his head back and mutters something under his breath. I don't bother asking what it was. It'll only serve to further upset me. His finger taps out a rhythm on the edge of my desk. "Let me know if you change your mind."

"I won't." I fight the waver in my voice. I want to sound strong even though I feel far from it.

He pulls his lips into his mouth and presses them together, nodding several times. "I know." He turns to leave, his socks shuffling across the hardwood. When he gets to the door, he looks back over his shoulder. "I'm beat. I'm gonna get some sleep. Don't stay up too late, okay?"

My eyes find his like I'm a tiny boat lost at sea and he's the beacon guiding me home. "I won't," I say again, giving him a small smile laced with guilt. I shouldn't have barked at him. He was only trying to help.

When he's gone, I turn my attention back to the screen. I can't be the only one who's had this problem. I open my browser and type *sound and video not lining up in iMovie* into the search bar. I'm instantly rewarded with dozens of question-and-answer pages discussing this very issue. Within a few minutes, I have it all figured out.

I sigh in relief and take a moment to work out a thumbnail. All that's left is the caption. The dreaded caption. I always make it a point to list and link every item I use or talk about in my videos. I know from a viewer standpoint it's extremely helpful, but from a creator's standpoint? It's a royal pain in the ass. But it's all part of the job, so I just have to suck it up and get it done. While I was editing, I simultaneously jotted down all the makeup we used on a Post-It Note, so I just need to gather my links and type it all out.

I'm in the middle of typing *Charlotte Tilbury Hollywood Flawless Filter* when I hear the familiar creak of the pantry door. Marcus said he was going to bed and that was—I glance at the clock on my computer—almost an hour ago. I shrug. Maybe he got hungry and decided to grab a snack. It wouldn't be the first time. Or maybe it's Mona. I chuckle. Moving into this home, I never realized how many creaks and groans old houses make. At first, they terrified me, but once I understood it was just the sounds of the home settling and the wood structure expanding and contracting, I got used to it. I even find it comforting—like my home is reassuring me it's here to protect me.

I direct my attention back to my task, but after a few minutes, I hear the creak again, followed by a package crinkling. A slow smile overtakes my face, and I tilt my head, staring at the open door. I've been at this for so long I've barely moved. Earlier, Marcus was in the middle of a boisterous game that he couldn't walk away from, so I made him a grilled cheese for dinner and delivered it to him. I was still feeling out of sorts from letting Emma down and didn't really have much of an appetite, so when I was making his food, I tossed a handful of chips onto his plate and threw a few into my mouth, calling it dinner. That was over six hours ago.

I lift myself out of my chair and stretch my arms overhead. After spending so much time in the same position, I feel like I'm twenty-seven going on fifty-seven. My bones creak, and my muscles fight against the pull. At my age, elasticity should be on my side, but instead, my body feels rigid and unyielding.

My bare feet creep along the chilled hardwood, and when I reach the hallway, I swear I hear humming. I know this song. I close my eyes. "Will You Still Love Me Tomorrow" by The Chiffons. It was Nana's favorite, her go-to song whenever she was hard at work. She sang it under her breath whenever she was concentrating. With my eyes still closed, I see her bent over the kitchen counter, her back curved like a candy cane, working her hands into flour-dusted dough. She made the very best blueberry pie. She's been gone for almost two years, and I haven't touched a slice since — nothing will ever compare to hers.

It's odd, but I can almost smell it now. Hers had a distinct hint of lemon that became very fragrant as it baked. I swipe at the moisture pooling around my eyes. I hadn't even realized I've been crying. I don't let myself think about Nana often. When I do, my thoughts shift from loss to death, and it's there that I dwell. My mind conjuring up a host of horrific ways that my own life could end. I may only be twenty-seven, but so was Walker.

A warm, faint glow wafts out of the kitchen, spilling into the hallway. I turn my head, shifting my gaze toward our darkened bedroom. The door is open, and I blink a few times, confused. The room is pitch-black save for the single stripe of moonlight cutting through the darkness. It's positioned perfectly so that it highlights Marcus's prone form shifting beneath the blankets. Clyde is curled up beside him, keeping my spot warm.

From the kitchen, I still hear someone rooting around in the pantry. An empty ache settles deep in my gut. Something hits the floor, making me jump. The noises from my kitchen are starting to sound frantic. Or maybe that's just my heart thrumming inside my chest.

Marcus moans softly as he rolls over onto his side. I should wake him up, but my feet seem to have other ideas. They're propelling me forward in the direction of the bandit. Plastic crinkles and cans clank. But it's that song that calms the pounding behind my ribs and the buzzing inside my head. The humming is feminine and familiar as I stand still and listen. Lyrics flow into my ears, and my body soaks them in. It takes me a moment to realize they're coming from me. I'm singing the words, but the melody is in the air as the gentle hum continues. This is not a solo performance. It's a duet.

My feet move quickly now as I reach the kitchen. The pantry door is cracked, and as I near it, I breathe in deep. I can smell her. Soft cotton and honeysuckle. My hand rests tentatively on the knob, and I close my eyes in preparation. "Nana?" I ask with a meek voice.

The rustling stops abruptly, and my muscles tense up. I'm now acutely aware that I may, in fact, be confronting a burglar, and I've just given myself away calling out for my dead grandmother.

I scan the room. The knives are too far away, but I spy a teal ceramic dove perched on the shelf next to me—a wedding gift from my uncle Miles. I grasp it, fully aware that it won't do anything to protect me aside from maybe buying me some time. I suck in a breath and fling the door open.

A strangled cry erupts from my mouth as my brain races to make sense of what I see.

There's no one there.

A box of pasta lays open on the floor, and little bowtie-shaped noodles are scattered everywhere. That must be what I heard, but it's odd that it fell on its own. Odd, but not impossible.

Within seconds, Clyde is at my side. He waddles into the pantry and starts lapping up the fallen pasta, crunching it between sloppy lips.

"April," Marcus calls from the hall. His voice is heavy with sleep. He comes up behind me, surveying the mess over my shoulder. "Whoa. Did you have trouble findin' something?"

I'm reminded of what I thought I might find and shiver. I've been staring at a screen for way too long, and I think it's starting to affect my imagination. "I, uh, I'm not sure what happened exactly. I heard a sound and when I came out to look, I saw the box dumped all over the ground. I guess it wasn't sitting quite right on the shelf and it just fell."

He crinkles his nose. "Huh. Maybe. Or maybe it was … nah, never mind."

"No, what were you gonna say?"

He raises his eyebrows and shrugs a shoulder. "I don't know. It could've been a mouse."

"Not again." I groan. We've had a few mice in the past, but only in the basement.

He rests a comforting hand on my elbow. "I'll call Zach tomorrow and ask him to come take a look at things."

"Marcus." I sigh. "You called Zach last time we had mice. You think maybe we should call an *actual* exterminator this time?" Zach is the king of odd jobs. He's what my dad would call a Jack of all trades and master of none. I love Zach and I get that Marcus wants to support his friend, but sometimes you just need an expert. And if there's a mouse in our living space, I'd feel much better if we hired a professional.

"It's fine. Zach will handle it. How about you? You doing okay? You scared the shit out of me with that scream. Thought someone was in here murdering you." He chuckles, but his laughter dies quickly when he notices I'm not amused.

"If you thought I was in trouble, you weren't moving super fast to save me." I cross my arms and glare at him.

He shakes his head. "Oh, come on, baby. You know I'm down for the count when I'm sleeping. I thought maybe I dreamed that shit."

I huff, but he reaches out and pinches my side, eliciting a yelp from me. Then he rests his hands on my arms and rubs them. "I really am sorry. Why don't you come back to bed? You've had an exciting night confronting an intruder." He stops abruptly, scanning my face with questioning eyes. "Why *did* you think it was a good idea to come out here alone, anyway?"

My ears feel warm, and I cast my eyes down, avoiding his. "Well, see, at first, I thought it might be you I was hearing."

He nods, accepting the rationale behind my answer, and I wish I could stop there. But I knew it wasn't Marcus or Clyde, and yet I came out here anyway. I hold up my hand, letting him know I'm not finished, and he takes a step forward, closing the space between us. His hand grips my chin, lifting my face so I can't look away. "Go on." It's just two words, but they're heavy in the air between us.

I suck in a breath. "But I saw you and Clyde sleeping in our bed, and yet I swear I heard the noise again—and then there was that song."

His face scrunches. "What song?"

I tell him about Nana and how she hummed whenever she baked. His forehead creases with worry. "April, did you think your Nana was in there?" He tips his head toward the pantry.

I shake my head fervently. "No, of course not." But there's no conviction in my voice. "I mean, I *knew* it wasn't her and yet, I also thought it could be. Or maybe I just hoped it was." I close my eyes. "It's late and I'm wiped and it's all just messing with my head."

He chews on his bottom lip. "You sure you're okay?"

"I'm fine."

He lets go of my arms and peers into the pantry, shaking his head. "Fucking mice, man. Let me grab a broom and get this cleaned up."

I back away and realize I'm still holding the dove. I settle him onto the shelf and turn my head to find Marcus watching me. He squints as if it might help him better understand my motive. "What's the story there?" he asks, jutting his chin toward the ceramic bird.

I shrug. "Protection?" I offer the word as a question, even though it's exactly what I was thinking.

He barks out a laugh. "What am I gonna do with you, huh?" He resumes sweeping, chuckling under his breath.

I smile, knowing how ridiculous I must sound and feeling grateful it can all be explained away.

"Oh, hey, baby?" Marcus glances back at me, scratching at his chin.

"What is it?" I ask, letting the words out slowly.

"Um, now probably isn't the best time to tell you this, but your mom called earlier. She says I'm supposed to 'get your butt over to their house for dinner.'" He puts the phrase in air quotes.

"And what'd you say to that?" I've been putting my

mom off for months, only seeing her and my dad when they come over here.

"I told her I'd give you the message." He shrugs and continues cleaning.

I scrub my face with my hands. This night just keeps getting better and better.

Clyde chuffs at my feet, and I bend down to scratch behind his ears. His body grows rigid, and the hair on his back stands on end. He lets out a low whine, and that's when I hear it. The faint remnants of the song I was singing earlier.

I strain my ears, desperate to hold on to the melody, but it's gone. The air is still. The room is silent, apart from the *swish* of Marcus's broom.

"It was only a mouse," I whisper to myself. But I only partly believe it.

THE GENTLE PATTERING of rain on the downspout pulls me out of my slumber. I despise the phrase "slept like the dead," but that's exactly what I did. It's what I've *been* doing for the past few nights, and it's only noticeable because it's not the norm for me. My sleep is generally of the toss-and-turn variety—waking several times throughout the night, checking Marcus's breathing, and resting a comforting hand on Clyde's rising chest before I can go back to sleep. But for the past week, I'm out as soon as my head hits the pillow, and I stay that way all night. It's been refreshing, even though I'm sure it's just a fluke and won't last.

I've had a lot on my mind since that last appointment with Dr. Lesser. Her office called me a few days after our Zoom call, but I ignored the call and haven't returned it. And I'm not sure I will. Usually, if my mind is preoccupied with something, I find it difficult to sleep, but I feel strangely okay about taking a break from therapy. That may be why my sleep is improving. It isn't like Dr. Lesser can force me to do anything I don't want to do. I chose a psychologist on purpose because I didn't want a doctor who could prescribe me medication. I know Marcus isn't keen on that either. But I thought with her as my therapist, we'd keep up our monthly sessions where I'd talk and she'd listen, offering up some advice here and there. It was relaxed and I knew what to expect. Our last appointment shattered my comfort, and in some ways, I feel like I've taken back some control by not returning her call.

I stretch my arm and grab my phone from my nightstand. It's a quarter past nine, and I'm alone in the bed. Marcus is probably already settled in for a full day of gaming. I click my tongue against the roof of my mouth. His lifestyle is so monotonous. It doesn't seem healthy. It also doesn't seem much different from mine, so who am I to judge? At least he leaves the house from time to time. I, on the other hand, rarely go outside, much less leave the property.

The darkened sky flashes with light, and the low rumble of thunder follows almost instantly. I enjoy a good rainy day, but a thunderstorm is an entirely different story. I rise from my bed and peer out the bay window in our room. The towering pines that line the front of our house sway and creak from the wind. They could fall in several different directions and completely avoid our home, but naturally, my mind focuses on the one way in which they wouldn't.

I close my eyes, and even though I don't want to, I start to envision the tallest one bending from the wind. *I feel the jolt as lightning slices through the sky, and I hear the crack as it connects with the old pine, slicing it in half. Like the peel of a banana, the trunk splits open and the largest half sails through the sky, crashing right into the bay window. Exactly where I'm standing right now.* My eyelids spring open. All the pines are still upright. I wrap my arms around myself. My body quakes beneath my hands as I slowly step back.

I've always had a bit of a fascination with death. No—fixation is more accurate. And Nana was the first person close to me who passed. Losing her was devastating. Her death turned an already lit flame into a bonfire, and now, death consumes me.

God, I wish I could stop doing this to myself. The last thing I want to do is think about the worst possible scenario, and yet it's exactly what happens, every time. I imagine it's similar to the sudden inspiration an artist may glean from their surroundings, except nothing good can come from this. It's unwelcome, albeit persistent. The moment I get a spark of a bad thought, it takes flight, twisting and turning until it's transformed into a nightmare.

In the confines of my mind, I have lived through the deaths of everyone I love more times than I can count. And me? Well, I die nearly every day in some tragic and highly unlikely way. But my brain doesn't care about the "highly unlikely" part because even though something may have less than a one percent chance of occurring, my psyche zeros in on that minuscule percent. I am always the exception. It's debilitating and completely exhausting. And if Dr. Lesser hadn't turned on me, I'd still have her to talk to about all of this. I groan.

I rub my eyes, ridding them of sleep and haunting images. My elementary school principal used to say, "The sun isn't shining outside today, so let's make sure the sun shines inside." It's funny, the things that stick with you. Most of us were only half listening to her morning announcements, and yet those words resonated. Now, whenever there's a rainy day, I hear her voice.

I call out to Alexa, determined to get my day started, and within seconds I'm trying to "walk on sunshine" even though there isn't any to be found. It works. By the end of the song, I'm dressed, and my attitude has shifted. And then, as if on cue, a growl of thunder cuts through the calm, reminding me that, positive outlook or not, I still have demons.

The door to Marcus's game room is ajar. I peer inside and find it empty. He's not in the kitchen, either, but there's a note on the counter.

Hey baby, I had to run to Trevor's for a bit. His Wi-Fi is all jacked up. Clyde wanted to come with me. Don't forget to take your vitamins. That video is due soon. I'll be home this afternoon, but in case I'm not there when he comes, Zach is stopping by later to take care of Jerry.

I want to smile at the cute nickname he's given the mouse, but I'm frowning. I know Clyde isn't much of a guard dog, but I still trick myself into thinking he'd try to protect me if the need arose. Now I'm completely alone in this house. During a thunderstorm, no less.

Marcus made sure to leave the offensive vitamins next to his note. I wonder how much they're paying us for this sponsorship. From the way he's pushing them, I'm guessing it's substantial. Might as well get it over with. I throw one into my mouth and shiver. Saliva builds from the sour taste, bringing with it thoughts of Walker. Poor dead Walker. I had a tough enough time taking these when they made me think of him in high school, but now knowing that he died, I don't know if I can continue. I need to look over the contract and find out what Hemply Simple expects from me. If there's an out, I may need to take it.

My stomach does a little somersault thinking about how far I've strayed. When I first started my channel, I vowed to never take on any sponsored products that I didn't whole-heartedly believe in. And I always wanted to speak candidly about anything I tried. When that super expensive hair dryer first launched two years ago and everyone was raving about it, I was one of the first to tell my viewers not to waste their money. My channel was based on honesty. *Was.* Now it feels as though it's more about the bottom line. It's not necessarily Marcus's fault. We just have different ideas when it comes to accepting sponsorships. He accepts most of them, because to him, this is a job, and a job is about making money. He's not wrong, but it used to be about making a difference, too. Even if the difference I made was saving someone the trouble of paying an exorbitant amount for something that wasn't worth it. I still felt like I was helping in some way.

I'm vlogging today for a video I'll post next week. As an avid watcher of YouTube videos, I've learned that it's fun to see your favorite content creators *behind* the camera. You already feel like you know them just by watching their videos, but when you get to catch a glimpse of their everyday lives, it makes them more real. These are my favorite types of videos to watch, but my least favorite to film.

I try to post a "day in the life" vlog twice a month. You would think it wouldn't be that hard to film since I'm just taking the camera along with me for a day. And maybe it wouldn't be that bad if I actually *had* a life. But since I never leave the house, it takes a lot of work to make it interesting enough for people to want to watch. I wonder if any of my subscribers have noticed that I'm always home, but I don't check the comments so I wouldn't know if they had.

I start by filming some B-roll of my coffee brewing and then of me taking the first sip. I'll dub some music over it when I edit, which will tie it all together. I take my coffee into my office and open my planner. According to Marcus, my viewers have really responded well to watching me plan out my day, so I set my iPhone up on my portable tripod and aim the camera at my desktop so that it's focused on my hands. I jot down some notes about what I'm planning to film throughout the week and add a few cute doodles in the margins to coincide with what I've written.

Once I finish, I turn the camera back on my face as I position my body into the oversized chair that lives in the corner of the room. My hair is piled on top of my head, twisted and held into place with no less than thirty-five bobby pins. I haven't put in my contact lenses yet. I'm dressed in black leggings and an oversized cream-colored sweater that hangs off one shoulder. It's a natural contrast to the dark gray microfiber chair. I stare, fresh-faced, into the camera, giving my tortoise-shell glasses a small shove to stop them from sliding down the bridge of my nose. I hold my coffee and take casual sips as I share pieces of "behind the scenes" info. I tell my viewers all about my mouse mishap (but leave out how I thought that it might be my dead nana snooping around in my pantry). "So, oh my God, you guys, there I was, holding this ridiculous ceramic bird as if that was going to protect me." A laugh bubbles out of me. "I'm a disaster, but you all know that already. And get this, Marcus has decided to start calling our little friend 'Jerry' after the *Tom and Jerry* cartoon." I shake my head, shifting in the seat. "His friend is coming over today to take care of the situation, but after he gave this little mouse a name, there's no way I'm going to let anyone hurt him. No way. This guy can catch him and then we can release him in a field somewhere." I snap my fingers. "Maybe I can get it on video for you guys!"

I continue talking this way, so relaxed, so conversational, as though I'm chatting with a close friend. It feels so natural, like I'm surrounded by people who genuinely care about even the most mundane of things.

I go about my day, taking the camera with me as I put on some natural makeup, take out my bobby pins, and try out a new waving iron. "I don't know, guys. It works fine, but I'm not sold on it. I don't think it's any better than my twenty-dollar one. You could really save your money and grab the cheaper option, and you'd be just fine."

Turning off the camera, I reach for the schedule that Marcus made for me. He has all my sponsorships listed, and as usual, there's one planned for today. I'm filming a spot for Hearty Harvest, a food delivery service based here in Pennsylvania. They provide a dinner recipe and the ingredients. This kind of meal service has been super popular for a while now, but this company claims to be different because they only use organic, locally sourced ingredients.

I drum my fingertips on my chin as I read over what's expected of me. Cooking on camera is more fun for my subscribers than it is for me. I've had to do that a few times, and it always ends up a disaster. A disaster that brings in a ton of views.

"ALRIGHTY, WHAT ARE WE MAKING TODAY?" I clap my hands, looking over the recipe card. All the ingredients are splayed out on the counter before me, and my phone is secured on a tripod, capturing everything. "Hmm, looks like we're preparing Cajun Blackened Chicken and Rice Bowls with Lime Crema. Doesn't sound too bad." With my hands on my hips, I look into the eye of the camera. "Famous last words, right?" My mouth splits into a cheesy grin.

"Hang on a second," I say, grabbing at my hair and piling it on top of my head. Once it's secured into a top knot and my hands are washed, I get to work prepping and chopping, and almost immediately, I encounter my first blunder. How many times must I cut up a jalapeño pepper before I remember not to touch my face? My left eye is a partially closed, watery mess. I curse under my breath and then remember I'm on camera. I'll have to bleep that out. "So, yeah, if you're new here, welcome to the world of April, where mishaps like this happen all day, every day." I chuckle even though my eyeball is on fire.

Holding a cold compress against my face, I continue dicing one-handed, which goes about as well as expected. I end up hacking a poor red pepper to death until it resembles a stewed tomato. I scrunch up my nose and look at the camera. "I'm not sure this is what they had in mind when they said dice the pepper, but hey, technically it's chopped, right?" I shrug, hamming it up for the video. "How do I still have a channel, you guys?" I joke.

Despite the rough start, it's beginning to smell pretty good in here. It actually reminds me of one of the last times I ate in a restaurant. Marcus and I went to Pedro's for Taco Tuesday. We were pretty regular there, enough that, Sam, the owner, knew us both by name. I breathe in deep.

A server carrying a tray of half empty water glasses bumped into a chair, and I watched in horror as the cups jostled and knocked into each other. Not one glass fell, but I still jumped. I had been anxious and fidgeting nonstop since we left the house. I couldn't even open my eyes during the ten-minute drive there. Marcus was talking, and I nodded, but I didn't hear a word over the roaring of the ceiling fan. It swiveled unnaturally and clicked with every pass, and was it possible for it to come crashing down on us as we sat there eating tacos? I was certain it was, enough that I stood up. Marcus asked me what was wrong, but all I could do was gesture limply to the spinning propeller on the ceiling.

I blink rapidly and find myself back in my kitchen, staring at the camera like a deer in headlights. Fortunately, I can make that weird moment disappear during editing. Unfortunately, I have to do that often.

"Okay, now it's time to blacken the chicken." I grin from

ear to ear. "Hey! Betcha I won't mess this part up." My laugh turns into a groan the moment I notice the camera isn't recording. *Seriously?* It was working fine, and now it randomly stopped. That's been happening far too often lately, too. I have my regular camera that I use for filming in my studio, but for vlogs, it's easier to use my phone. Looks like it may be time for a new one.

I'm about to take a closer look when there's a knock at the door. My movement stills and my stomach drops. I glance at the clock on the stove. It's just after two thirty in the afternoon. Marcus isn't home yet, but he warned me that Zach would be coming by. I relax, realizing that's who it must be.

Another knock sounds, this one a little more frantic than the first. I hear the rain coming down outside, though the thunder and lightning have thankfully stopped. Poor Zach is probably desperate to get out of the rain.

I give my hands a quick wash in the sink and scurry toward the front door. Just as I'm about to reach it, he knocks again. "Hang on, Zach! I'm coming," I call out, though I'm not sure he can hear me through the pelting rain and wind.

I unlock the deadbolt and fling the door open. "Sorry, but I—"

My mouth falls. There's no one there.

I STAND, frozen. My eyes ticktock over the empty porch. "Hello?"

What the hell? Someone was literally just knocking. My mind works overtime trying to come up with a logical reason for the current situation. It *has* to be Zach. But where is he? Maybe something caught his eye and he scurried off to the side of the house to check it out.

I take a tentative step outside. I haven't gone anywhere in months, but I do try to spend some time in my yard—just not on a rainy day, and definitely not when I'm unsure of who could be lurking out here. I shiver but press on, taking the steps slowly as they descend to the walkway. As I move along toward the driveway, I notice the rain has slowed to a light drizzle, and there's a breeze. A loose tendril falls from my topknot, and the wind whips it into my face where it gets caught in my eye. I reel back from the assault and bat my hands furiously at my face. The hair is gone, but now my vision is blurry. First the jalapeño mishap, and now this. My poor eyes are taking a beating today.

I blink a few times, and movement near the spot where the driveway meets the backyard catches my attention. That must be Zach. I walk in the direction of the activity, still rubbing at my eye. "Hey, Zach. Sorry I didn't get to the door right away. I was in the kitchen and had a bit of a mess on my hands." My vision clears, and once again, there's no one there. I swear I saw something moving. Maybe it was a bird or something.

A sheen of sweat glazes my forehead, and my breathing becomes shallow. I spin around in a circle, surveying my surroundings, but there are no cars in the driveway. The wind picks up, rustling the leaves on the large maple tree in our side yard. It sounds like a whisper, but I can't make out the words. "Hello? Is anyone out here?" I call out, my voice punctuated with desperation. I know I heard knocking. I'm certain of it. And it can't be explained away. It wasn't a branch that blew against the door or a bird that wasn't watching where it was flying. It was blatant, and it happened more than once.

But now, as I take a long look around, it appears I am completely alone. Yet I swear I feel eyes on me. I glance at my front door longingly. I should run back inside. I should shove that door closed and lock it up tight behind me. And that's exactly what I do, my bare feet smacking against the cold, concrete steps as I race toward the door. I run like I'm being chased—and I might be. I make it to the door and twist the handle. In an instant, my lips begin to tremble, and my knuckles, still wrapped around the knob, turn white. The door is locked.

"No-no-no-no-no-no," I murmur like the revving engine of a car. How could I be so careless again? We've been having trouble with the lock on this door, and now I'm stuck out here. All alone. Or worse.

I think someone is behind me. If I stand perfectly still, I can hear their erratic breathing. I spin around fast, ripping the Band-Aid clean off. But just like before, there's no one there. I bend in half, sucking in a deep breath as relief floods my insides. If anyone could see me right now, I'm sure it would be entertaining. Luckily, our closest neighbor is a half a mile down the road.

Wait! Our smart doorbell! I whip my head around and examine it. It usually starts recording when it senses movement. I wonder if it picked anything up earlier when I heard knocking. If only I had my phone. I could call Marcus or Emma to come rescue me and also check the footage on the doorbell app. But it's inside, still on the tripod. Wait, there may still be a way for me to contact Marcus. If I ring the bell, maybe he'll get a notification and answer it using the speaker. I give it a quick press and hope for the best.

In the meantime, I need to find our spare key. After the last time this happened, Marcus hid it and reassured me history would never repeat itself. The key is out here somewhere, but the location is eluding me. I close my eyes. *Think, April.* I take myself back to that day.

Marcus was in the midst of a game when I interrupted to ask if he wanted a sandwich. While I was in the kitchen making it, I heard a knock at the door and assumed it was Amazon with the new foundation I was planning to test out. But when I bent down to retrieve the package from the porch, Clyde took off running after a squirrel. I gave chase and eventually caught him in the backyard. Unfortunately, when we attempted to get back inside, the door was locked. I tried everything to get Marcus's attention—even banging on the window outside of his game room. But nothing worked. We were rescued two hours later when Emma stopped by for an impromptu visit. Giving her a spare key was one of the best decisions I ever made.

I blink away the memory and stare hopefully down the long and windy private road that leads to my house. If only Emma were here again with her spare key to save the day. I was so lucky she decided to drop by on a whim. As soon as the door was unlocked, I sped through the house and burst into Marcus's game room only to find him exactly where I left him hours before. He thought it had only been minutes since I asked him if he was hungry. And his guilt over not hearing me led to a self-imposed gaming detox. At first, I was happy he was taking a break, but without his game to fill his time, he didn't know what to do with himself. He was trailing me around the house like a dog in heat, and as much as I loved the extra attention, I realized I also appreciated my alone time. So four days later, after prodding from me, he was back in his game room dodging virtual bullets.

But first, he hid that key …

I tap my bottom lip as I recall following him to the back of the house. Letting the faint whispers of my memory guide me, I rush down the steps and follow the driveway as it wraps around our home. At least it stopped raining. Thank goodness for small favors.

I remember the key was wrapped in tinfoil because Marcus said it would keep it from getting rusty. I knew he had it all wrong. You wrap your car's key fob in foil to prevent theft, but I didn't bother correcting him. He was proud of his ingenuity. He talked about several possible hiding spots before landing on the one, which is why I'm having such a hard time remembering where it is now.

"I could put it under that planter over by the garage, but that's an obvious spot, isn't it?" He didn't wait for a response. It must've been a rhetorical question. "I know! What if I bury it in the dirt inside the pot? But no, then you'd have to get your hands dirty, and I know you don't like that."

I pinch my lips together as my eyes bounce around the yard like a wayward tennis ball. I'm only remembering the places he *didn't* hide the key. I veer off toward the back door, hoping something will jog my memory.

A flash of movement stops me in my tracks. Something

dashed around the side of the house. My eyes are clear. I know I saw it that time. If only I could find the key. I could race inside and lock the door behind me.

I don't want to investigate any of this, but maybe I'm making a big deal out of nothing. We *are* in the middle of the woods. It could just be an animal. It was too big to be a squirrel, but maybe it's a deer? I tiptoe around the back of the house toward the side yard where I last saw activity. As I creep around the corner, I walk straight into a rigid mass. Jumping back, I scream, holding my hands out in front of me.

"April! Jesus! What are you doing out here?" Zach stands before me, canting his head and making strong eye contact.

My entire body sags and I clasp my hands to stop them from trembling. "Oh, thank God, it's you."

He leans in slowly, resting a hand on my shoulder. "Are you okay?" His eyes scan the perimeter of the yard behind me.

"I am now, but … wait, how long have you been out here?" I pull back, recoiling slightly from his touch. His palm slides off my arm and his forehead creases with severe lines.

"I don't know, maybe a half hour or so. April, you're acting kind of weird. What's going on?"

"You tell me," I snip.

His eyes widen and he scratches his temple. "Uh, I'm just looking for places where a mouse may have gotten in. Didn't Marcus tell you I was coming?"

"He did. And I heard you knock, but then you weren't on the porch. I called for you, Zach. Why didn't you answer?" I lift my chin, studying him.

He points at the earbuds in his ears. They're small and I hadn't noticed them at first. "I had my music playing pretty loud and honestly, never heard you. But—did you say you heard knocking?"

"Uh-huh. And when I answered, you weren't there."

"April," he leans forward, "I never knocked. I figured I'd start out here first. I've been walking around the outside of the house."

This doesn't make sense. I know I heard knocking. I tug at my lip, looking off in the distance. Then I spin around, surveying the driveway. "Where's your car?"

When I face him, he shrugs. "I parked along the side of the garage. I'm surprised you didn't see it when you walked over here."

I retrace my steps until the side of the garage comes into view. Sure enough, his black Honda Civic is parked right where he said it would be. I must have been so focused on finding the spare key, I totally missed it.

"Huh," is all I can say.

"Why are you back here anyway? If you heard knocking and didn't see me, why wouldn't you have just gone back inside?" He eyes me carefully.

Before I can answer, a familiar voice bellows from behind me. "What's this? Havin' a party without me?" Marcus strolls up beside me, looping his arm around my neck and pulling me close. His eyes zing back and forth between us. "What'd I miss?"

"Me getting locked out again." I sigh.

"Why didn't you use the spare key?"

I lift my hands. "That's what I was back here looking for, but I couldn't remember where you decided to hide it."

His shoulders sag. "Seriously? Even after that great clue I came up with?"

My face scrunches. "Clue?"

"Yeah, you don't remember?" He's walking toward the little succulent garden we planted near the dogwood. He bends over, lifting one of the bricks we used to make a little border. The glint from the aluminum foil catches my eye. He pinches it between his fingers and holds it up proudly. "You'd have to be a prick to go digging around a cactus." He chortles.

I shake my head, giggling, and Zach joins in. "Okay, now I remember." I look around the yard and then back at my husband. "Where's Clyde?"

"He's inside, probably already snoring somewhere."

I nod, anxious to get back inside myself.

"How'd you make out?" he asks, looking at Zach. "Find any holes?"

Zach shrugs. "Not that I could see. I was actually gonna head inside, but then April saw me and we started talking." He glances down at me and something flashes in his eyes. It's like he's silently asking me not to give Marcus any more details, but why?

Marcus seems satisfied by Zach's explanation, which is mostly true, aside from the part where he scared me half to death. "You ready?" He glances at his friend and Zach nods. Marcus replaces the key in its hiding spot and links his hand in mine. He motions for Zach to follow and we all stroll back toward the door. "Why were you out here, anyway?" He tips his head to look at me.

"I heard knocking earlier and thought it was Zach, but when I opened the door, no one was there. I figured maybe he was inspecting the outside of the house, so I went to look for him and got locked out again."

"Hold on a second." He squints at me like he's trying to see through fog. "You thought the door was locked?"

I frown. "I didn't *think* it was locked. It was."

"April, when Clyde and I got home, the door was unlocked."

I stop and tug my hand out of his hold. "No, that's not possible. I tried to open it and the knob wouldn't budge."

He grips my shoulders. "Baby, I fixed the lock after you were trapped out here last time."

My palms grow damp, and I rub them against my sides. "Marcus, I'm telling you the door wouldn't open."

"Listen, I believe you. Maybe the knob was stuck and if you were frantically pulling at it, it jammed or something." He gives me a small smile, but I know what he's trying to do. He showed his hand with the "or something" he added at the end.

"Marcus," I whisper-shout. "What if someone's in there?" I point at the house with a trembling finger. I've been so focused on Zach, but maybe it was someone else entirely who knocked. What if they slipped inside while I was out here?

But he just shakes his head. "I already looked in every room when I got home."

"You did?"

"Well, sure. I called for you, and when you didn't answer, I checked everywhere. It's only when I couldn't find you that I came out here and saw you with Zach."

I rest my hand on his forearm. "I'm sorry if I scared you."

"Don't worry about it. I wasn't necessarily scared. Concerned is more like it. And besides, I've been lifting a little. If someone even thinks about laying a finger on you, I could take a punk-ass bitch out." He flexes his bicep, eliciting a chuckle from me. "Come on," he says, tugging my hand. "I saw the food spread out in the kitchen. I'm starving."

"I was filming for Hearty Harvest. This is perfect, actually. I can get you and Zach on camera tasting everything." I wink.

"As long as I get to eat, I don't care what I need to do." He winks back.

"Did someone say food?" Zach sidles up beside me, rubbing his stomach.

I lift my eyes to the sky and smirk. "Perfect."

Just as we cross over the threshold heading inside, Marcus stops, leaning out over the porch. "Baby, why would someone knock when there's a doorbell?"

DOORBELL! That's right! I dash inside, snatching my phone from the tripod. My palms begin to sweat as the app loads. As I scroll through the activity, my body deflates. Nothing was detected and it's even worse than that. It appears the doorbell battery is dead and needs to be charged. I can't believe this. Actually, I can. We are forever forgetting to charge that thing. But of all the times for that to happen, why did it have to be now?

"Any luck?" Marcus stands behind me, lowering his chin onto my shoulder.

"Nope. Turns out it's dead. Again." I press my palm to my forehead and drag it down over my face.

"You know," Zach chimes in. "You really shouldn't let that happen. You guys are out here, away from the rest of civilization. It really isn't safe to not have a working camera."

I glare at him. I know he means well, but stating the obvious isn't helping. He looks away, wandering over to the counter and snatching a pepper remnant off of the cutting board.

I feel so disappointed. If I had confirmation that someone was out there, maybe I wouldn't feel so …

No. I won't say it, and I'm definitely not going to think

it. Sure, the odds feel stacked against me here, but I heard knocking. I know I did. And just because there's no video evidence of it, doesn't mean it didn't happen.

I need to talk this out. But first, I make quick work of dinner and get Marcus and Zach on camera raving about the meal. As I straighten up the kitchen, Marcus and Zach begin looking around inside, surveying any potential spots where a mouse may be hiding.

A few minutes later, I breeze out of the kitchen and down the hall, where I hover in front of Marcus's game room. By the sounds emanating through the door, he and Zach gave up on mouse hunting and are engaged in a lively game. I lift my eyes to the ceiling. This is why I wanted to hire a professional.

I'm holding my phone, so I tap my number-two favorite and waltz into my filming room, shutting the door behind me.

"Hey, you," Emma croons into my ear.

"Hey, yourself," I say, plopping onto my recliner with a sigh.

"To what do I owe this honor?"

I scoff. "What? Can't a girl call her BFF just to say hi?"

Her laugh sounds tinny through the line. "Not *my* BFF."

She knows me too well. "Whatever," I snip. "All right, fine. So I'm calling because this weird thing happened today. Well, actually, it started last night—"

"Hold on! I need to prep for this. Let me grab my coffee and go sit on my porch." I hear her bare feet smack against the wood floor in her house, followed by the creak of her screen door. She lets out a long sigh, and I imagine her settling into the large Papasan chair on her porch, tucking her feet underneath her and balancing a mug of coffee on her knee. "Okay, I'm ready."

I start by telling Emma about the pantry and how I thought I might find the ghost of my nana.

"Wow. That's a lot to unpack there."

My mouth sets in a grim line. "I know. And it's weird because in the moment, I was so sure it was her, and honestly, I was almost hoping it was."

"That's not weird."

My face scrunches. "It's not?"

"Well, I mean, sure, it's weird that you thought your nana—who's been dead for nearly two years—was snooping around your pantry, snacking on chips. But it isn't odd for you to want to see her again."

"I don't like to think about it too much, but I do really miss her." More now than ever.

"Of course you do. And maybe suppressing those feelings is what made your mind go there last night."

I chuckle, trying to disguise my shock, but Emma's words have me rattled. There's a lot of truth in them. "Well, look at you, Dr. Emma."

She laughs. "That's right, bitch. And for you, the doctor is always in. Now, tell me what else is going on."

I open my mouth, and all the day's events come tumbling out. Hearing it out loud, it's easy to see the holes, and I'm starting to doubt myself. "Look, I know how this sounds, but Em, I heard knocking. I swear."

"I don't doubt you did."

I cover my mouth with a trembling hand and close my eyes. My resolve was beginning to splinter, but her words smooth every rough edge. "Really? You believe me?"

"Listen, sweets, who do you think you're talking to here? I'm always Team April. If you say you heard knocking, then you heard knocking. I don't need every detail to line up perfectly."

"I love you."

"Right back at ya." I hear her take a sip of coffee. "I can't believe you actually went outside to look for someone."

"I know, I know. It's way off brand for me, but I really thought it was Zach. I was so sure of it, but he swears it wasn't, and why would he lie?" Zach's behavior was a little off, but then again, so was mine. Besides, he's family. Marcus even lived with him for a bit after his mom died. If he isn't trustworthy, I don't know who is.

"True. That doesn't sound like him. And if it wasn't Zach, then who was it?" Emma muses.

Suddenly feeling warm, I roll my shoulders, shrugging off my cardigan.

She hums into the phone. "Not to freak you out, but is it possible you've got a little stalker situation on your hands?"

My throat instantly feels like it's wrapped in a corset that's cinching up tight. Breathing is nearly impossible, and my forced attempts send me into a coughing fit.

"April? Honey, try not to panic."

"A little late for that," I wheeze between bouts of hacking.

"That was a poor choice of words. I'm sorry. I was just thinking out loud."

"I get what you're saying, Em, but Zach was out there. I know stalkers can be bold, but wouldn't they have seen him?"

"Not necessarily. I mean, you didn't see him at first, right?" She continues talking through theories, but her voice becomes white noise drowned out by my own dark thoughts.

It isn't something I like to think about, but it's not unusual for content creators to find themselves victims of stalking. I experienced it a little myself a couple years ago. I had around two hundred and fifty thousand subscribers at the time, and one of them turned out to be an overzealous supporter. Kimmie_kiwi92 started out by commenting on every video and quickly moved on to commenting on every comment someone left on a video. At first, everything was positive and supportive, but when another viewer was critical of the lipstick I was wearing in one of my videos, kimmie_kiwi92 became confrontational, threatening violence. The comment section got out of hand fast and turned in a very dark direction. I turned comments off for that video and blocked kimmie_kiwi92. After that, Marcus took over monitoring my comments in case they showed up again under a different username. I have no idea if they ever tried. Marcus never said anything, but I doubt he would, even if they did come back. He wouldn't want to worry me. But now here I am, worried anyway. And this is far more serious than a rogue commenter. If I have a stalker and they've found out where I live, I can't stay here.

My eyes dart around the room. It feels smaller somehow.

"Hello? You still there?" Emma's voice is like my morning alarm jolting me awake.

My bottom lifts off the chair and my hand flies up to my chest. "Sorry, Em. I was just—"

"Overthinking."

I bite at my lower lip. "Yeah, that."

"You know, I'm sure there's nothing to worry about, but maybe you should look into a security system."

I lower my chin and lean in closer to my phone. "You think?"

"I do. For what it's worth, I think it'll really help you relax just knowing that you have that extra protection."

I nod. She has a point. Marcus and I talked about security when we first moved in, but we're so far away from everything, it didn't seem necessary. But maybe that's exactly why it *is* necessary.

"You want me to call a few places for you, or can Super Mario handle that?" Even without the nickname, it's impossible not to notice the disdain in her tone.

"I'll talk to him. I think he was a little freaked out today, too, you know. I'm sure he'll agree." Marcus loves me. It's exhausting having to defend him all the time, but I'll never stop.

She lets out a long breath. "Honey, it's all going to be okay. You know that, right?"

"Mm-hmm," I lie, knowing she'll see right through it. I'm never convinced anything is really okay.

"Oh, April. What am I gonna do with you, huh?"

"If you figure it out, let me know."

"Ha ha," she chimes. "Know what you need?"

"What?"

"A glass of wine and David Rose."

"Mmm," I hum. "That sounds simply the best."

We chuckle as we say our goodbyes.

I sit in stillness and ruminate over what we talked about. If we had a security system, maybe those cameras would've captured whoever knocked on the door. I shiver thinking about a possible stalker lurking outside. I need to talk to Marcus and see if he's noticed anything odd in the comments section of my videos lately, but in the meantime

...

I flip open my laptop and navigate to one of my recent posts on YouTube. It was an "empties" video where I shared all the products I've used up in a month and give my thoughts on them. In other words, I show my trash to the Internet. It's a classic video style, and at two hundred and nine thousand views, it's clearly still a favorite.

I haven't looked at my comments in a long time. Marcus

always hops on for an hour after I post, liking comments and keeping track of video requests. If a subscriber asks a question, sometimes he'll share it with me, and I'll dictate a response for him to type. And if someone leaves a nasty comment, he wipes it from the page. It may seem like a copout, but it's in the best interest of my mental health that I stay far away from the space that I'm currently scrolling.

Let's see, misty1515 says, *Love your content, girl! Keep it up!* That's so nice!

And jenni_loves_coffee doesn't like that body wash, either. *The smell was way too strong.* Yep, totally agree, Jenni.

As I continue to scroll, most of the comments are similar to those two, but one from tulipdaisy1 is different, and it catches my eye. I pause my finger to read. *Anyone else think April's videos are getting a little stale?* My stomach drops, and my heart feels like it's beating outside my chest. No one likes to hear something negative about themselves, but when you put yourself out there, it comes with the territory. There are no comments underneath tulipdaisy1's post—either for or against what they said—but there are twenty-one likes. It isn't the worst thing anyone has ever said about me, but it still hurts to think that twenty-two people think my content is stale.

What makes it sting even more is they aren't wrong. I've had my channel for five years now, and I haven't really changed a thing. I recycle the same few video formats, sprinkling in some vlogs here and there. And yet, my channel has grown exponentially. People know what to expect from me, and they like that. But tulipdaisy1 and her posse of twenty-one "likes" don't agree. And that bothers me.

I wish they would've offered suggestions. If my videos are boring, what would they rather see? What can I do to keep them entertained? It's like I'm the "dance monkey" in that song by Tones and I. I want to roll my eyes, but how can I when this is how I've chosen to make a living?

I try giving myself a pep talk. "You can't please every-one, April. You know that." I do. I've always known it, but sometimes knowing it isn't enough if you can't feel it. I slam the lid of my laptop harder than I mean to and spring to my feet. That's enough wallowing for one night. I'm heading down a dangerous road, one that leaves easy scars that are hard to get rid of. The sag in my shoulders and the frown lines on my face are proof of that.

I SMELL her before I see her. Clean cotton mixed with honeysuckle and something else —something I've never quite been able to put my finger on, but it's unique to my nana. She's standing ten feet in front of me, but there may as well be an ocean between us. She's trying to speak, but no sound reaches me. "Nana? I can't hear what you're saying." I don't think she can hear me, either. The wind is less of a howl and more of a scream. I can barely make out my own voice as it passes through my lips.

The sky is a sickening shade of green, and the blackened clouds above are starting to spiral. It happens faster than I've ever seen before. The swirling mass lowers behind my nana and blows the ground apart as soon as it makes contact. The sound is deafening. And yet, her lips keep moving. I wonder if she can hear the chaos all around her. She makes no move to look behind her.

I step toward her, but the wind makes it nearly impossible to move. Every step takes effort. My hair whips all around me in a frenzied mass, but Nana's gray pin curls stay fixed in place. In fact, nothing about her appears to be affected. Her blue dress —the one with all the tiny white flowers —barely registers a breeze, much less the cyclone and gale force winds out here.

And where exactly is out here? I grab my hair out of my face and spin my head around. We're in an open field, and it could be anywhere if not for the weeping willow that sits back and off to the *left of the old farmhouse. This is the field behind my grandparents' house. The same place I spent hours exploring as a kid. I used to roll down the hill, only to climb back up and do it all over again.*

But it's the willow that pulls at my memory. The tree has a split in its trunk that served as the perfect reading nook. I'd lean back as it cradled me, tucking my arm behind my head. I watch now as the tree's leaves sway like a stage curtain preparing to open. An ear-splitting crack fills the air as the tornado rips the limbs off the old willow as though they were made of cardboard. A branch somersaults through the air and soars right over Nana's head.

I cup my hands around my mouth, calling out, "Nana! You need to move!" But the wind makes a mockery of my efforts, trapping my words and holding them hostage.

She's going to get hurt. And for a fleeting moment, I wonder if a ghost has the ability to feel pain, but I push it away. She's standing before me looking more flesh and blood than specter. I have to get to her. I force my legs to move, pushing my feet into the earth. I keep my eyes focused on my movement, afraid if I look away, I'll lose my grip on my progress.

"April." Nana's voice is calm and quiet, like she's trying to rouse me from sleep. I can hear her so clearly now. I must be getting close. I look up, but to my horror, she's even farther away.

"Nana?" My throat is hoarse from screaming.

"It's okay, sweet pea." Tears well in my eyes at the endearment. I hadn't realized how much I missed hearing it. Sweet peas are the birth flower for the month of April, and Nana has called me that for as long as I can remember. "It's going to be okay. It will. You're strong. You've just forgotten how much, that's all."

My eyes snap open, and I bolt upright in my bed. My heart is racing, my breathing ragged. I flit my eyes around my bedroom in search of my nana, but all that remains are her words. They swirl inside my head like the funnel cloud in my dream.

From the window, I can see the light of dawn beginning

to break. Marcus snores quietly beside me. I close my eyes and breathe in deep; the faint scent of Nana still lingers slightly. Imagination is a powerful force. But something about that dream feels like more than just my imagination running wild. Tornado nightmares are commonplace for me, but I'm always the sole participant. This is the first time someone has joined me, and the fact that it was Nana seems significant. That's twice in the last few days that I've had a strange encounter—for lack of a better word—with her. And if it really is her trying to communicate with me, I wish I had more time.

I shake my head like I'm trying to clear away a storm, but my attempt is useless. On a deep sigh, I push myself up off the bed, accidentally nudging Clyde's leg in the process. He startles, glaring at me. I hold out my hands. "Sorry, sorry. Jeez." He grumbles and rests his head back against the mattress.

As I head into the bathroom, I stop myself from turning on the light. I don't want to disturb Marcus, and the illumination from the nightlight is sufficient for a quick potty break. When I'm finished, I wash my hands, catching a glimpse of myself in the mirror. I stare deep into my own eyes and mouth the words Nana said. "You're strong." But I don't feel very strong. I feel more like a fragile vase that's been dropped one too many times. The fractured pieces have been glued into place, but the cracks are too numerous, and the vase is beyond repair.

I reach for a towel and swipe at the moisture on my hands. I glance out the open door and into my bedroom. The morning light has pushed in through the slats of the blinds, but it's still too early for existential thoughts.

If I'm awake, I may as well get ready for the day. My toothbrush is still in the charger from last night. I pull it out of the base and slide the brush head underneath running water while reaching down to open the cabinet drawer. I look down for a split second to grab my toothpaste and my toothbrush shifts. Water bounces off the bristles and sprays the front of my shirt. I grab the faucet and turn it off, slamming my toothbrush on the counter. My hands fist the hem of my shirt as I hold it out in front of me. I look like I was caught off guard on a water ride at an amusement park. I flap my hands in an attempt to dry my shirt, but my effort is futile. I shrug. I guess I'll just get dressed while I'm at it, too.

I unscrew the cap of the toothpaste and squeeze some out onto the bristles. As I raise it near my mouth, I notice the minty aroma smells different this morning. It reminds me of the fresh strawberry mint salad my mom used to make. It was her signature dish whenever we had a gathering to attend, but she hasn't made it in years. I reach for the tube and flip it over, checking to see if it's a different brand than I remember. The Crest logo stares back at me. It's the same tube of fresh mint plus whitening that I've been buying for years. In fact, the last time I left this house was to run to Target to pick some up. I don't even know how long ago that was, but if I had to guess, I'd say almost a year. That drive is one I'll never forget.

Black dots like tiny pinpricks started to form around the edge of my vision almost as soon as I left the house. I backed out of the driveway, and for a moment, I nearly blacked out entirely. I had no business driving, and the only thing that kept me going was the little voice in my head telling me how ridiculous I was behaving. People go to the store every day. It's a simple errand. Things were becoming more dire for me. My agoraphobia was always present, but up until that point, I was still going places, though it was happening less and less.

Somehow I made it to the parking lot, but once I found a spot, I couldn't turn off the engine. I was afraid of the silence that would greet me, followed by the need to get out of the car. My breathing started to become shallow; short puffs became shorter until I was practically gasping. Tightness wound around my throat. I couldn't swallow. My vision dimmed, and then it left me completely. Minutes passed, although it felt like hours. Marcus. I needed to call him. He'd know what to do. Once his name flitted across my thoughts, I grabbed it, holding on for dear life. In my head, I began repeating his name like a mantra, and eventually, my breathing mellowed, and my throat cleared just enough for me to call out to Siri. I've never been more grateful for hands-free dialing. Marcus picked up on the fourth ring. "Baby? Everything okay?"

"No," I rasped. "At Target. In the parking lot. Please come."

"April, you're freaking me out. Are you safe?"

"Yeah, but I need you."

He showed up fifteen minutes later. I slid across the console, and he hopped into the driver's seat. We never talked about logistics, but we didn't need to. Later that afternoon, Zach drove him back to Target to pick up his car.

I haven't been anywhere since. Dr. Lesser told me I had a panic attack. All I knew was I never wanted to experience one again, so I never put myself in a position to have one. Thankfully, that was the worst of it and it hasn't happened since. I feel a moment of relief, followed by a wave of nausea. *See? Not very strong, Nana.*

I finish brushing my teeth and wash my hands. Looking up at the mirror, I catch my gaze once again. I look far too serious. I raise my eyebrows at myself and stick out my tongue. Chuckling softly, I'm about to turn away when my reflection winks.

My eyes widen. I didn't wink, and yet, according to the mirror, I did. I take a step back, never taking my eyes off my reflection. Frozen in place, I just stare, blinking rapidly to rid my eyes of the sleepy haze that obviously must be the issue. Because to consider the alternative would be madness. Reflections do exactly that; they echo what's in front of them, mimicking movements in a synchronized harmony. They don't act independently.

I raise my arm slowly, and the April in the mirror does, too. I wave and she waves back. I close my eyes and quickly open them, meeting my own gaze. Everything seems to be as it should, but then again …

"Baby, what are you doing in the dark?" Marcus's voice sends a ripple of shock through my spine. I cry out just as warm light floods the room. I'm still standing in front of the mirror with my arm raised, only now I have an audience.

He arcs a brow. "You okay?" I don't miss the concern in his inflection. Hell, his worry was already warranted before, based on me thinking a mouse was my nana and hearing unexplained knocking on the front door. Now here I am, standing in the dark, waving at my own reflection. My mind scrambles to come up with a logical explanation.

I start nodding even before I speak, as if that alone has the power to extinguish the distress that's beginning to spark. "Oh, I'm totally fine. I mean, you scared me half to death." I feign a glare at him, and he tilts his head the same way Clyde does when he's confused. "It's just, well, it's a little embarrassing. I thought I saw a piece of popcorn in my hair, but now with the light on, I can see that it's noth-ing." I'm babbling; even I hear it, but I hope it's enough to convince my husband that everything is fine. And, I mean, everything *is* fine. Isn't it? Sure, I thought I saw my reflec-tion move independently of me, but it was dark, and I had just woken up from that awful dream. I *had* to be seeing things.

"Popcorn, huh? Well, maybe next time you should turn the light on instead of standing in the dark like a weirdo."

I roll my eyes and huff. "Gee, thanks. I'll keep that in mind."

He reaches out and takes hold of my hand, tugging me into his arms. His finger traces the side of my face, tucking a piece of hair behind my ear. "You're a mess, you know that?"

"I am, but that's why you love me so much." I wink at him and instantly feel a chill. *Get a grip, April. It was just your imagination.*

Marcus notices my tremor and pulls me closer. "It's true. It's one of your best qualities." He gives me a sly smile, but it drops just as fast. He tips my chin up with his finger. "You sure you're okay?"

I'm not really okay. I haven't been for quite some time, and Marcus knows that. But he also knows I'm the first one to plaster on a smile and pretend—no sense in changing things now.

"Who, me?" I arc my thumb at my chest. "I'm better than okay." I lean against him, the muscles of his arm twitch beneath my cheek. He holds me, and I allow myself to feel what I'm always chasing. The one thing that always seems to elude me. Peace.

I know it was just a dream, but I keep going back to what my nana told me. She said everything would always be okay—and also, I seem to have all this strength I've apparently forgotten about. Man, I wish I could've had more time to talk to her. To me, dreams sometimes feel like a portal. Either to an untapped place in our minds or maybe even to another realm. I'm not entirely convinced the spirit of my nana visited me last night, but I'm also not ruling it out.

I settle into Marcus's arms and think back to how things were before I became a recluse. It wasn't that long ago, but then again, I've been like this, in one form or another, for a while. I may have left the house before, but that doesn't mean I was happy about it. I've always been a homebody, but once Marcus and I moved two years ago, everything changed. This home is the embodiment of a warm weighted blanket. Its effect on me is instantly calming. Inside these walls, I feel safe and secure in a way I'd been lacking for so long. For as long as I can remember, I've struggled with the "what ifs" in the outside world, but in here, I can almost pretend I'm in a bubble, padded and protected from everything. Why would I ever want to leave that?

"Hey, could you eat pancakes?" Marcus's sudden subject change pulls me from my thoughts.

I lean back and squint up at him. "Are you hungry?"

"I'm always hungry." He pats his stomach, grinning.

I crane my neck to see his alarm clock behind him. "It's only six thirty. Are you sure you don't want to go back to bed for a little longer?"

"Hey, now that's not a bad idea." He lowers his eyelids and tilts his head, attempting to smolder. He's failing so badly, I can't contain my laughter. He swats at my backside. "Oh, whatever. You know you want it." I laugh even harder, and he shakes his head. "Fine. Let's go get you some pancakes." He takes hold of my hand and practically drags me to the kitchen.

"I don't remember agreeing to pancakes."

He stops short and turns, resting a hand on his hip. "Baby, don't even try that. You want pancakes *almost* as much as you want me."

I bite my lip. "I do love a good pancake."

OUR PLAYFUL BANTER continued throughout breakfast and was the perfect distraction from my disturbing morning. But now he's in his "cave," and I'm sitting at my desk staring at my laptop. I should be editing my latest video, but I can't stop thinking about the odd occurrence in the bathroom earlier.

I didn't wink. I'm positive of that. As sure as I am that I heard knocking the other day and the faint sounds of my nana's favorite song several nights ago. I'm certain I didn't imagine anything, and yet, there's doubt. It's a sneaky little bastard hiding out in the shadows. It's sometimes easy to overlook, but it's there. Now, as I sit here mentally listing all the strange things that have happened, I start to wonder what's real and what isn't. Is it possible that I'm imagining things? Or worse—hallucinating?

I shiver and reach for the old gray cardigan on the back of my chair, pulling it up around my shoulders. I can't be hallucinating. It's bad enough I'm living with a crippling fear of catastrophic events. If I have to add in delusion, I'm not sure I'll be capable of functioning. I'm on precarious ground as it is.

No. I brush my hands together. That's enough of that line of thinking. I need to get back to this video. I tested out a new skincare line, and the brand is expecting a proof video in their inbox tomorrow. Looking over the notes Marcus printed out for me, I double-check it against the video, making sure I hit all the talking points. It's an honest review, but since the brand sponsored the content, they still expect me to speak about specific ingredients and product claims.

I'm struggling to concentrate so I try a different tactic. "Alexa, shuffle my chill playlist." Seconds later, a playlist of my favorite relaxing music fills the air. I breathe in deep and catch a whiff of lilac. Mist rises from the diffuser in the corner. "Nice choice," I commend. Shaking my head, I sigh. "Great. Now I'm complimenting inanimate objects. Next thing you know, I'll be asking that chair over there if it has plans for the weekend."

Don McLean's voice flows from my phone as he sings about a long time ago. I glance at the screen to find my mom trying to FaceTime me. I groan and then still my expression as I answer.

"April? Is that really you? Jesus, Mary, and Joseph, I thought you died!" My mom has always had a flair for drama.

My dad shouts from another room, and I can just barely make it out. "Cut it out, will ya, Grace? At least the kid answered."

"Pssh," my mom chastises. "You'll stay out of it if you know what's good for you."

Without even seeing him, I know Dad is in the living room with his feet propped up on his recliner—navy blue sweatpants, a Philadelphia Eagles T-shirt, and his tan moccasin slippers. The TV is on full volume and tuned to a Jeopardy rerun. I very clearly just heard a man say, "I'll take Bats in the Attic for five hundred, Alex."

My mom is alone at the kitchen table with her hair

perfectly curled and a pound of makeup caked on her face. There's a half-smoked cigarette resting on an ashtray in front of her. The ash is nearly an inch long. There's a haze of smoke hovering around her. If I close my eyes, I can almost smell it through the phone line. The peppery burn tickles my nostrils. She's always promising me she'll quit, but after all these years, I don't think she ever will. This is one of the reasons why I've struggled to visit them. It's not the smell (oddly enough, I find the scent of cigarette smoke comforting—chalk that up to me attaching sentimental value to everything from my childhood). My problem is what the habit is doing to her and what the second-hand smoke does to my father and me. Not to mention that she's forever leaving lit cigarettes lingering in the multitude of ashtrays stashed all over the house. I swear, their home is a twenty-four seven fire hazard.

"So, Dad is still refusing to watch new episodes of *Jeopardy*, huh?"

"He says Alex will never be replaced." She sighs.

"Can't be done," my father yells from his chair.

"I can't argue with him there," I agree.

"It's so nice to see you, even if it is through a screen," she quips. Her eyelashes look like spikes, all clumped together. And the severe set of her drawn-on brows gives her a permanent scowl. Don't get me wrong, my mom is beautiful. However, makeup is meant to enhance beauty, but with her technique, it detracts from it. I've tried to give her some advice and even point her in the direction of some helpful tutorials, but she's content with her methods. As soon as she sees me, she beams—and it's contagious. I smile right back at her, but the moment I do, she frowns. "April?"

"Yes?" I respond through gritted teeth. I can feel a dig coming.

She leans in so close, I can see every pore on her nose

despite the caked-on foundation. When she sits back, her brow furrows as her eyes continue to scrutinize me. "Yep. I knew it. You're looking too thin. Are you eating enough? Is Marcus taking care of you, or is he just off playing games like a twelve-year-old?"

Five minutes in and already she's criticizing my husband. Like it's his job to make sure I eat. I'm an adult, for Christ's sake. Of course, I can't say that to my mom. I may be an adult, but the kid in me is still terrified of her, and without Nana here to referee, I mostly just grin and bear it. It's best just to take the route that's easiest—deny and deflect. "Who, me? Nah. I'm eating just fine, and Marcus is always helpful." I notice her not-so-subtle eye roll, but I ignore it and press on. "You look great, by the way! Have you been using that skin serum I gave you?"

She looks down, letting out a heavy sigh. "Oh, yes, I sure have, and it's ... really something."

"Don't listen to her! She's full of shit! She tossed it into the trash as soon as she smelled it. Said it reminded her of dirty diapers." Leave it to my dad to spill the tea. He never was one to mince words.

My mom presses a hand to her mouth in embarrassment. I almost feel sorry for her. But it's kind of fun to watch her squirm for once since I'm usually the one in the proverbial doghouse. The difference is I'm not as ruthless, so I don't let her sit in discomfort for long. "Yeah, some skincare is like that sometimes. It's great at what it does, but it doesn't always smell the best."

"Uh-huh, and that's why you gave it to me in the first place, isn't it? You couldn't stand the smell, so you passed it off to your poor mother."

I shake my head. "Mom, it was unopened. I've never even tried that serum before."

My words are useless as she rants a little longer about

how I need to remember how sensitive her nose is. I tune her out after that. How she can sit in a cloud of cigarette smoke all day and yet still complain about the scent of a skin serum is beyond me.

She moves on to her favorite topic—trying to convince me to come visit. She's listing off reasons on her fingers when something behind her catches my eye. Now it's my turn to lean in. I squint as I look over her left shoulder. I swear I just saw something—a shadow maybe—move, but there's nothing there. Maybe it was just my dad.

"Mom?" I'm interrupting her, and I'm sure there will be hell to pay for that, but the need to reassure myself is stronger than my fear of her wrath.

"What? What is so important that you felt you needed to talk over your mother?"

"Is Dad in there with you?"

"He's here in the house, but he's not in the kitchen. He only comes out here when he's looking for food, and I already told him the kitchen's closed until supper." She yells that last part loud enough for him to hear, and they launch into a back-and-forth about snacking before meals. I keep my eyes glued to her shoulder, and right as I start to move back, I see it again. It was fast, like a wisp, but I'm almost certain I caught a glimpse of a familiar blue dress with tiny white flowers. Just like the one from my dream.

"There it is again," I shout, pointing at the screen.

She jerks her head back. "There's *what* again?"

I stay completely still, watching the screen for movement, but nothing else happens, making me wonder if my eyes were just playing tricks on me. Or maybe it was a bug flying around her. It can't be what I think it was.

It can't.

I bite at my nail, trying to choose my words wisely. My mom is a chronic worrier, and being an only child, I've always borne the brunt of that worry. Over the last several months, as I've become more withdrawn, her concern has increased.

"It's nothing, I just … is there someone else there with you and Dad?"

Her face pinches. "If there is, it's news to me. Jeff?"

My dad sighs. "What now?"

"Who's in this house right now?"

"What the hell is this? Some kind of test?"

She groans. "Just answer the damn question, will you?"

"No one else here except me, you, and the man in the moon, baby." He chuckles because if he doesn't laugh at his own terrible jokes, no one will.

"There. See?" She gestures toward me. "Told you it's just us."

I nod. I must've just imagined it.

"Why?" she asks through pursed lips.

I pause, collecting my thoughts. "Oh, no reason. I just thought I saw something move behind you, but you know what? It was probably a fly or maybe just a bad connection."

"Hmm …" The crease on her forehead becomes a gully, but she doesn't press me further. Neither one of us speaks for a moment, and then she claps her hands. "So! As I was saying before I was so rudely interrupted"—she draws out the last word and glares at me—"when can your dad and I expect a visit from you?"

I massage the right side of my jaw. I didn't realize I was clenching it, but the ache I feel tells me it's been a while. "Um, well, actually, why don't you guys come here?" She opens her mouth, but I hold up my hand. "Wait a second. Just hear me out. Marcus has been talking about setting up a table and chairs out on our patio. You know how nice the yard is here and, well, the only one that ever uses it is Clyde and he's not doing much out there so—"

"April, you're rambling."

I sigh. "Sorry."

"Don't be sorry unless you've done something to be sorry about." She leans in toward the screen, and when she speaks again, her voice is quiet and contemplative. "Listen, you know how I worry. I'm your mother; it's my job. But I hate to see you live this way. Live isn't even the right word. You're just existing. And I knew this would happen. I predicted it, remember?"

"I know," I say on a sigh. "And I'm trying, but—"

"I wasn't finished," she scolds. "I know you're seeing Dr. Lesser." I bite my lip to keep myself from blurting out the truth—that I haven't seen her in a few weeks and I'm not sure I'm going to see her again. My mom continues, "I want you to get the help you need, but only you can do that for yourself. Or maybe Marcus could if he were up to the task." She huffs.

"Mom."

She waves her hand. "Fine. I won't push the issue. For now." She arcs her artificial brow. "If the only way we can see you is if we come to you, well, then, tell me what day and we'll be there."

I lean back in my chair and let my shoulders sag against the smooth leather. "Thanks, Mom."

She smiles without an ounce of pity, and I love her for it. "You're welcome. Now, talk it over with that husband of yours and let me know when you want us. I'll bring a cheesecake."

"Sounds perfect. Talk to you soon."

"Is that a promise?"

I roll my eyes dramatically and smirk at her. "Yes, that's a promise."

"Good. Now go get something to eat. And April?"

"Hmm?"

"I love you."

I let her words wash over me like they're bathing me in protection. She doesn't say it often, so when she does, it holds an even deeper meaning. "Love you, too, Mom."

I set my phone on my desk and lift my hands, shaking them out. My wrists crinkle and pop like bubble wrap. I think I need a change of scenery. Maybe my mom was right. I should eat something.

I pad out to the kitchen, and what I find on the counter stops me dead in my tracks.

WHEN NANA MOVED in with us after my grandfather died, she transformed the small flowerbed in front of the house into a gorgeous rose garden. She would snip off the roses, keeping the stems long, and gather them together in a milk glass vase. Fresh cut flowers adorned our dining room table so often, I barely noticed them.

Roses very much like the ones currently sitting in the center of the kitchen island. The smell hits me the instant I walk into the room. I close my eyes, inhaling deeply. And when I open them, I zero in on the vase housing the roses. Sure enough, it's milk glass. I take a few timid steps forward until I'm a foot away from the flowers. They've only just begun to bloom. These roses were cut very recently.

I focus on the petals, so dark they appear almost velvet. I haven't seen anything like them since the day we buried Nana. Admittedly, I thought red was a bit inappropriate for a funeral, but my mother insisted. They were Nana's favorite. I used to have a similar variety growing in my yard, but without Nana's help, my tiny rose garden has died off.

Who would send me flowers? The obvious answer

would be Marcus, but other than prom, I don't think he's ever brought me flowers.

I move in closer and brush my hand through the stems in search of a card, but I can't seem to find one.

"Whoa! Holy shit, man!" Marcus's voice carries through his game room door and down the hall into the kitchen. Every so often, I can hear him shouting, but most of the time, it stays trapped in his room. Based on the clarity I just heard, his door must be open.

I stroll down the hall, and sure enough, it is—more than a crack, actually. I peer inside and spy Clyde asleep in his bed in the corner. Chances are, he pawed at the door until Marcus let him in and then shoved his round body into the room, leaving the door ajar.

I step inside and am about to speak when Marcus calls out, "Hey, yo! Watch it, bruh!" I roll my eyes so far back I think I see my brain. It's not the game playing that bothers me; it's how obnoxious he is while playing.

I sigh loudly, even though I know he'll never hear me. But Clyde does. He lifts his head laboriously and hoists himself up onto his short legs, waddling over to me. His stubby tail gyrates as I lean down to pat his head.

Marcus clocks the activity and slides off his headset. "What's up?"

"Hey. I saw the flowers." I tip my head toward the kitchen. "Any idea where they came from?"

He flicks at his nose absentmindedly as he puts his thoughts together—a habit I used to find endearing; now, it's just kind of gross. "Some dude dropped them off when you were on the phone with your mom."

My face scrunches. "They were delivered here? I never got any notification."

"Well, yeah, about that," he rubs at his chin. "I never

did bring in the doorbell battery to charge it so there was no notification."

I cock my head, pursing my lips, and he smiles sheepishly.

"It is a little weird though, right? They were dropped off by Bella Flowers, and before you ask, there was no card. I checked." He looks down at his hands resting in his lap. "I've got to admit, I don't love the idea of someone sending you flowers, but maybe it's from someone we know."

I rest a hand on his shoulder. "Yeah, I considered that, and it's definitely a possibility, but who?"

He places his hand on top of mine, threading our fingers together. "You don't think you have a secret admirer or something, do you?"

I frown. "Let's not go there. Don't even think it."

He grins, and his eyes twinkle with mischief. "Right, because if we think it, well, then it must be true. Isn't that what you're always saying?"

My face is at war with my emotions. I'm feeling so many things at the moment, but I can't fight the smile, especially when he's looking up at me so earnestly. He squints at me like he's trying to read my thoughts. "Go ahead. Lay it on me."

I wrinkle my nose. "Huh?"

"Come on, April. You have theories or fears or whatever you want to call them. Just tell me where your head is at right now."

I sigh. "Well, you know red roses were Nana's favorite."

He nods. "Uh-huh. I remember." His head continues to bob, and then he adds, "Wait. You're not suggesting ..."

"No, no. Of course not." I sound so sure, but am I? I shake my head, trying to cast aside my own doubts, but all it does is enhance Marcus's frown lines.

"Okay." He speaks slowly, deliberately drawing out the

word. All his misgivings live in the parts he doesn't say. "Could it be from a brand?"

"Maybe. Actually, that's probably the most logical answer, although, wouldn't they just send them to the PO box?"

"Most likely, but some brands—the ones we've worked with many times over the years—have our home address."

"True," I say, tapping my finger to my lip. I remember a question I had a few days ago. "Hey," I whisper. "Have you noticed any strange activity in my comments section lately?"

"Other than the usual opinions, it's been calm." His tone is so blasé—like he's discussing the difference between black and dark gray. Marcus doesn't care how other people perceive him. He is who he is, and he's completely unapologetic about it. I envy that kind of freedom.

I bite my lower lip. "Now, when you say, 'the usual opinions,' what do you mean, exactly?"

"You know"—he shrugs—"just those people who think they have all the answers." He flaps his hand back and forth.

"Marcus?" I place a hand on either side of his face and force his eyes to meet mine. "I'm gonna need you to be more specific."

He sighs and tries to look away, but I don't let him. "Why do you do this to yourself?"

"Do what?"

"You know."

I do. There's a reason why I put him in charge of my comments. I not only obsess over what people say, I let it consume me, but this is different. If there's a mystery admirer or worse—a stalker, then I need to know what I'm up against.

"Okay, fine." I huff. "Maybe don't tell me about the

nasty ones, but … is there anything I should be concerned about?" My thoughts drift to tulipdaisy1. Her comment wasn't exactly nice, but if that's as bad as it gets, I can handle it.

He grips both my arms and rubs his hands up and down. "Listen, April, your channel is fine." I bristle at the word, and he backtracks. "More than fine. Your subscribers tune in because they like you. And your regular content is comforting to watch."

"Comforting?"

"Sure. Think about it. Every day, people go about their lives with little curveballs thrown at them. But when they watch you, they know what to expect. One viewer even said you were like a warm blanket on a cold day. What more could you ask for?"

He's got a point. If I'm bringing people comfort by talking about winged liner, well, then I really can't complain.

"I check those comments every day, you know that." I nod and he continues, "You have nothing to worry about. I'm pretty sure if you had a stalker, I would know."

"Yeah, you're right. It's just weird that there was no card attached."

"It could've just fallen off, you know? Why don't you give the flower shop a call and see if they have a record of who sent them?" He grins, proud of himself.

I tap him on the nose. "You're so smart."

He pulls me down on his lap. "What would you do without me, huh?"

"Good thing I never have to find out." I lean in for a quick kiss, but Marcus lingers a moment longer.

My eyes drift around the room, landing on an intricately folded piece of paper on a small end table. I lift myself off Marcus's lap, and he lets out a grunt. I recognize the note as soon as it's in my hand, even though it's been years since I've seen it. "Is this what I think it is?" I ask, smiling widely.

He lifts his shoulder in a half shrug and smiles sheepishly.

I unfold the origami-esque paper, revealing Marcus's barely legible handwriting.

Will you go to Prom with me?
Yes or No
(circle one, but only if it's yes)

I had found this shoved halfway into one of the slats of my locker after seventh period senior year. We'd been dating for almost a year at that point, and I had assumed we'd be going to prom together. But Marcus wanted confirmation and was too nervous to ask me to my face.

I chuckle, remembering those carefree days. "Where'd you find this?"

"I was cleaning up a few drawers the other day to make space for some new equipment Zach gave me and I found it shoved behind an old keyboard." His smile is wistful. "Feels like forever ago, right?"

I turn to face Marcus, considering his question for a moment, then I nod. "It does, but also it doesn't. Does that make sense?"

"Nothing you say makes sense, but also it does." He laughs, and I join in because he's right. I take quirky to a whole new level. It's what made him fall in love with me, and it's also what drives him crazy. But isn't that always the way? The things we love most about a person are, at times, the very things that infuriate us.

I sigh. "Okay. I've taken up enough of your time." I tip my head toward the screen where scenes of war and carnage continue to play. "I'm gonna go see if I can figure out who sent the flowers."

"Let me know what you find out," he says as he slides his headphones back into place.

As I walk past, he takes hold of my arm. I swing my eyes to his face, and he smiles. "I'm glad you said yes."

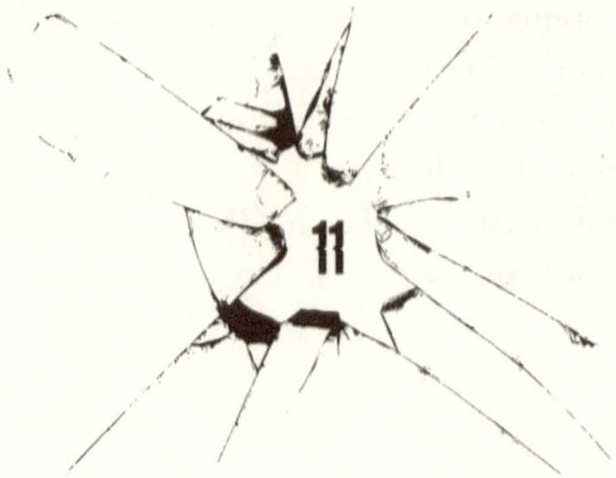

I MOVED the roses to my office. It's been three days since they mysteriously arrived, and I'm no closer to finding out who sent them now than I was when they were delivered.

I called the flower shop, but the guy who answered wasn't all that helpful. He struggled to find the paperwork and then hastily told me there wasn't a sender listed. I doubt he was even looking at the right order form.

Then I called my mom. I'm not sure what I was thinking. Even though I had already talked to her that day, I still lost another hour on FaceTime with her. She didn't send the roses, though she said she'd call around and ask family. She wanted to see the flowers, and as soon as I flipped the camera, she said, "Oh, Nana would've loved those!" She texted later, letting me know that no one she talked to had sent them.

Emma didn't send them either, though she, too, tried to push the secret admirer narrative. I squashed it quickly, even though it was beginning to take root.

I checked my business email yesterday, hoping maybe a brand sent them and followed up, but I came up empty-handed. So I took the initiative and sent out my own emails. I contacted a few brands and heard back from most of them —none were responsible for sending the roses.

I turn my head, looking at them. All the blooms are open now. They're disarmingly beautiful. I wish I could fully appreciate them, but without knowing who sent them, I'm left with an uneasy feeling. Still, it doesn't stop me from moving them to the long, narrow table behind where I film.

I'm about to record a monthly favorites video, and with the flowers in the background, I'm certain there will be comments. Maybe one will contain a clue. It's a bit of a long shot, but it's my only option at this point.

I arrange all the products I plan to talk about in front of me. Most of them are makeup, but a few are skin care. There are some candles, books, and even music thrown in to balance it out. My videos are planned to an extent, but I'm far from organized. I've been doing this for so long, some of it is second nature. And the rest is just me. I don't have an online persona. It never even occurred to me. Since the beginning, I've never changed. As my dad always says, "If it ain't broke, don't fix it." Maybe I should ask him what to do if it's "stale."

I stew for a few more moments and then stand, shaking my entire body from head to toe. Preschool teachers are always telling kids to "shake their sillies out." Well, I've found it works for more than just "sillies," and it's also not exclusive to three-year-olds.

"Baby, what the hell are you doing?"

Marcus's voice startles me so much, I jump. My hip bangs the side of my table, sending all the arranged products flying. I pat at my chest and feel my poor heart beating wildly. I close my eyes and try to get my breathing under control.

When I open them, Marcus is on the floor swiping up all the fallen items. He lifts to his knees with a tube of CC cream in one hand and a vial of rose hip seed oil in the other. "What even is all of this stuff? It looks like it belongs in a scientist's lab."

I open my mouth, but he cuts me off. "Actually, don't answer that. Instead, tell me why I just caught you flailing around like Aly Sheedy in *The Breakfast Club*."

I lift my eyes to the ceiling. "First, you didn't *catch* me doing anything. That would imply I was doing something wrong that warranted catching. Second, when I'm stuck inside my head, sometimes it helps to just shake it out, literally. You should try it sometime. And third, excellent movie reference. I'm impressed." I smirk, and he grins proudly.

"Whatever you say. It's a little weird, but I guess if it works, then cool."

Nodding, I lean forward and take the products from his hands. We continue working that way as a tag team. It doesn't take long before my table looks the way it did moments ago.

Marcus stands, dusting off his hands on his pants. "So, I found out who sent the flowers."

My eyes snap to his. "What?"

"Those roses," he says, jutting his chin toward the vase behind me.

"Yeah, I know what you meant, but, well, who was it?"

He chuckles. "Damn. This mystery sure has you all twisted up."

I glare at him, and he holds up his hands. "All right, all right. Don't shoot the messenger."

"Marcus," I practically beg.

His face folds like a house of cards. "Sorry, baby. I know this stuff gets you rattled. I was just trying to lighten the mood."

"I know you were, but right now, the only thing that will actually help me is to know where these came from." I arc my thumb behind me.

"Right." He nods, resigned. "So I was just in there putting some new sponsor dates on the calendar when I saw one of those new email notifications pop up. Actually, that reminds me … I never finished working on the calendar." I think my eyes must be bulging out of my head because one look at my face has him scrambling. "Yeah, so, like I was saying, the email was from Hemply Simple."

"The vitamin company?" I sent them an email yesterday but hadn't heard back right away.

He nods. "Yep. They mentioned you emailed them, actually. They were checking on the timeline for the video, and at the end, they said something like, 'Hope April loved the roses.'"

"Huh. Interesting." Interesting and a little strange. If a brand sends me any type of gift, it's usually after I post a video and it's sent as a thank you.

"Is it?" He shrugs. "I don't know. I guess it just seemed nice to me."

I look at him pointedly, and he rolls his eyes. "Okay, I guess it also kind of looks like they're buttering you up."

"Mm-hmm, or bribing me." I press a finger to my mouth and bite at my nail. This whole situation makes me feel uncomfortable, especially since I haven't spoken to anyone from the company. So far, Marcus has handled all of the interactions.

He balks. "Oh, come on, April. It's not that underhanded. Loads of other brands have sent us stuff over the years."

"That's true, but usually not before they've heard how I feel about their product. Unless … wait a minute, how'd they get our home address? A few of our OG brands have it, but Hemply Simple is new." I narrow my eyes.

Marcus's gaze drops to his feet. He nudges the instep of his shoe with the toe of his other one.

"Marcus?"

He quirks his brow, but his eyes never lift to meet mine.

"Seriously?"

"What? They've been really great to work with and they told me they'd rather send vitamins directly to a person and not to a PO box. I don't know, it made sense to me, I guess. And as for how you feel about the vitamins, I didn't tell them anything that wasn't true." Now he's looking at me, but all I see is guilt.

"I don't believe you," I say, shaking my head. "We've talked about this. I let you handle sponsorships, but when it comes to my opinion about the products, you can't speak for me. It's bad enough that I'm testing so many things. I, at least, need to feel like I have some integrity left. And you should have told me you gave them our address." I cross my arms over my chest.

"I know. I know. Listen, all I told them is you've been taking them every day."

"And?" I tilt my head, challenging him.

He shoves his hands deep into his pockets. "And I maybe told them you liked the taste."

My palm meets the center of my forehead with a loud *smack*. "You're unbelievable." I haven't told Marcus the Walker Dolan connection my brain has made, but he knows how I feel about sour things.

"What? I know sour candy isn't really your thing, but you can't fault them for that. I mean, if you were talking to someone who liked sour things, you'd probably tell them they'd like them, right?"

"Marcus, the point of me giving my opinion is that it's *my* opinion. If I were to make a video and talk about the taste, I'd have to be honest. I can't speak for anyone else. Those vitamins repulse me and that's the truth." I flail my arms, narrowly missing the table. Marcus chuckles, but I level him with a steely glare, shutting him up quick.

"Look. I'm sorry. I fucked up. It's just, this guy, Troy, he's really nice, and I think this connection could be good for us, you know?"

I sigh. "I know you were only trying to help, but please don't talk to brands about my thoughts without talking to me first, okay? It's really important to me."

"You got it."

"Thank you. And you're right, it was nice of them to send these." I turn and pinch a petal between my fingers. "At least now I can enjoy them without constantly wondering who they're from."

He smiles. "Hey, what if I head over to Panda Garden and pick up some Rangoon? What do you say, huh?" He raises his eyebrows.

"Now who's trying to butter me up?"

"It was just a suggestion, but if you don't want it, well then —"

"Hold on. I didn't say that. Do you think maybe you could pick up some dumplings, too?"

A triumphant grin fills his face. "As you wish."

"Wow. You're really trying to make it up to me." I laugh. "First, with my favorite takeout, and now, you're quoting my favorite movie."

"Well?"

My face scrunches. "Well, what?"

"Is it working?"

I pluck my cardigan off my chair and toss it at him. It sails through the air, landing unceremoniously at his feet. We both laugh. "Okay, just go bring me my food." I cross my arms.

He throws me a cheeky grin before strolling down the

hall. A few seconds later, I hear the door open and close, followed by the sound of the engine as he starts his car.

I finish arranging everything for my video and then shuffle over to my camera. As I'm looking over the settings, movement to my left catches my eye. Clyde meanders into the room and settles onto his bed in the corner.

"Okay, buddy, you can stay there as long as you promise not to emit any explosive bodily functions." He sniffs, turning his head to face the wall. Dogs can't understand complex conversation. Logically, I know that, but a larger part of me—the part that believes in unexplained phenomenon—thinks he knows exactly what I just said. And he also knows he can't make that kind of promise.

I get myself situated at my table and begin the video. About ten minutes in, a hint of lemon catches my attention. There's a perfume on the table in front of me that has notes of citrus; it must be coming from there. It sends me off on a tangent about a time in my childhood when I made a battery out of a lemon for a science fair project. My poor viewers. I talk way too much—*ramble* is actually a better description. I like to think it's an endearing trait that makes me relatable—and it is, but not to the extent that I do it. I'm not even halfway finished discussing all the products in front of me, and already I've been filming for nearly thirty minutes. The average length of my videos is between sixteen and twenty minutes. I'm going to have my work cut out for me when it comes time to edit this.

My phone vibrates on the table. It's been doing that nonstop for the last five minutes. I peeked at the screen a few times and saw it was only Emma. She's on a TikTok kick right now and loves to send me the craziest videos she can find. It buzzes again, and I decide to take a break. My camera is probably close to overheating, and I'm sure the battery needs to be charged. "Where's a lemon when you need it?" I chuckle.

Phone in hand, I settle into the recliner in the corner. Within seconds, I'm watching insane videos of people playing practical jokes, falling down in the most dramatic ways, and singing spectacular parodies. Each one is more hysterical than the one before. By the time I reach the last one — some guy burps, hits his head, and falls down — I can't even see straight through the tears.

At first, no sound comes out of my mouth as I bend in half, convulsing. A few wheezes escape as I struggle to catch my breath. I swipe at my watering eyes. Once I can see clearly again, I fire off the skull and "rolling on the floor" laughing emojis to Emma. She sends them right back, and it's enough to set me off again. Peals of laughter bubble out of me and my eyes well up.

"Hahaha," I hear a near-perfect echo of my own laughter.

My entire body seizes up, and I grasp the arms of my chair with both hands. My head jerks toward the door. It sounded like it came from my bedroom. Is that even possible? Maybe it was just an echo or something. I look around. There's a large throw rug in this room. There are curtains on the windows and plenty of things hanging on the walls. This isn't a room that echoes. And yet, I heard myself. My laugh circled back, assaulting me.

I look over at Clyde. He's sprawled out and snoring blissfully, completely undisturbed. His relaxed behavior has me doubting what I heard.

I sit frozen in place for at least five minutes. The silence is deafening, and yet my ears are hyper-sensitive, picking up all of the minute sounds in the house. Every creak and groan is amplified. Finally, curiosity gets the better of me. I wobble as I push myself to standing, but my feet propel me forward. My determination to settle the mystery outweighing my fear.

My steps are tentative and small, but I hear them. The light pound of my feet mimics the pounding in my head. This is the kind of silence that almost hurts. Your whole body quiets as you strain to hear everything and anything. But aside from my footsteps and labored breathing, I hear nothing. As I enter the bedroom, I crane my neck, peering into every nook and cranny. The room is empty, as it should be.

As I turn to leave, my eyes trip over the bathroom door. It's slightly ajar, which isn't odd, but my mind snaps back to the morning when I thought my reflection winked at me. My breath picks up but gets lodged in my throat. I sputter out a cough, keeping my gaze locked on the door as though someone will jump out.

There's a stillness in the air—ominous, foreboding. I could be injecting my own fears into the situation—I'm sure I am—but I can't deny the chill that creeps up the back of my legs and continues up my spine.

I know what I *want* to do—pretend I never heard someone laugh, someone who sounds a lot like me. But even as I replay it over in my mind, I can't shake the feeling that what I heard was real. Though it makes no sense and I have no explanation, I know what I heard.

"What am I doing?" I whisper as I creep in slow motion toward the bathroom. My hand makes contact with the door faster than I anticipated.

I jump into the room as though I'm trying to catch an intruder off guard. But no one is there. My bathroom is vacant. At least, I think it is.

The shower curtain is closed, and I've watched enough horror movies to know it makes the perfect hiding place. I grab a bit of the curtain, balling it up in my fist, and jerk as hard as I can. Nothing but bottles of shampoo and body wash stare back at me. The *pat-pat* of the dripping faucet provides a dismal soundtrack.

I bend over, grabbing my knees as a huge rush of air expels from my mouth. "Careful, April. You're starting to lose it," I mutter.

I stand slowly, avoiding the mirror. I'm not looking for a repeat of the other morning. Mulling over what just happened, I start to feel a little silly. I actually thought that someone who sounded just like me was hiding out in my bathroom, mimicking me. Another laugh bursts out of me, but this time it's directed at my own actions. My laughter fades into soft chuckles. I'm being ridiculous. I glance up at the mirror and smile wide at myself and then relax my face, feeling the edges of my mouth sag.

My eyes widen at my reflection. Even though I've stopped smiling, the version of me in the mirror hasn't. And as I stare in stunned horror, her smile continues to grow.

I COVER my face in my hands, shaking my head. This isn't real. It can't be happening. As I slowly pull my hands away, everything is as it should be. My mirror is back to reflecting like it never skipped a beat. And it didn't, did it? Even just considering it, my heart picks up its pace, and my palms start to sweat.

Plunging my fingers into my hair, I rake at my scalp as though I'm attempting to claw the memory from my mind. If only that were possible.

I race out of the room and begin pacing near the front door. A track in the carpet forms after a few minutes. I obsessively check the tracking app to see Marcus's location. Right now, he's about five minutes from home. I have no idea what I'm going to say to him when he walks through the door. But something is off inside this house. I can't put my finger on it, but strange things keep happening. And it's a strange that goes beyond our "Mona" joke. These aren't just typical old house sounds.

In my feverish pacing, I fail to notice Clyde as he waddles into the hall. I catch sight of him when I'm inches from tripping over him. I veer to the right and hip check the small table by the door. I stumble and flail until I land in a heap on my backside. I cast a sideways glance at

Clyde and find him glaring at me, annoyed that I disturbed him.

And that's exactly where Marcus finds me when he pushes the front door open seconds later. He quirks a brow and tilts his head. "April?"

"Yeah?"

"What are you doing on the floor? Did you fall again? You know, you should consider auditioning for *America's Funniest Home Videos*." He chuckles.

I look around, imagining how this must look. Not exactly a great segue into the other news I was planning to share. "It's a long story that started with me almost tripping over Clyde and then falling anyway." I pinch my lip and squint upward, shrugging. "Actually, I guess it's not a long story."

He snorts, shaking his head. "Need some help?"

I nod. "Please."

He sets the bag of food on the table I ran into and extends a hand. I grasp it eagerly, and he tugs me back to my feet. Instead of letting go, he pulls me toward him, and I can tell by the smoldering set of his eyes, he's starting to get ideas. I wish I could be spontaneous right now. It would be so freeing to let go of all my worries and give in to his advances, but my mind is fixated on the apparently haunted mirror in the bathroom. And with ghosts on the brain, there really isn't room for much else.

I have no idea how to communicate any of this to him without setting his worries on fire and sending him into a tailspin. Fortunately, he speaks first, giving me a reprieve. "Baby, you're shaking. Are you cold?" He runs his hands up and down my bare arms. The gesture is meant to be soothing, but the friction only heightens my nerves. It takes everything in me to calm the frenzy that's brewing just below the surface.

"A little. Please tell me there are dumplings in there," I say, pointing at the bag of food.

He grins. "Hell yeah, there are."

I LET Marcus direct the conversation while we eat. He talks about a system upgrade or a new headset or ... honestly, I have no idea. I rarely do, but I listen and bask in his excitement, soaking it up like a sponge. It doesn't matter that I don't understand. Right now, it's the perfect distraction from all of my worries, and I'm not about to interrupt that.

I know I should tell him what happened. He would want to know. But the more time I put between me and the girl in the mirror, the easier it's becoming to doubt whether it even happened at all.

"April?"

I look up from my plate to find deep-set eyes focused on me. "Huh?"

Marcus's forehead creases. "Sorry. I keep going on and on, and this must be boring the hell out of you."

"No, no." I shake my head. "I like seeing you so happy."

His expression softens. "I know you do. But I talked enough. Now it's your turn. Tell me about your day. What kind of trouble did you get into while I was gone?" He tilts his head.

I'm taking a huge gulp of water and launch into a coughing fit. Marcus jumps into action, patting me on the back, which does little to stop the spasm in my throat. After a little more sputtering, I'm able to get my breathing under control, but I've made a mess of the table and myself.

I jump up and grab the dish towel off the counter and begin mopping up the water. Marcus snatches a few paper towels and dabs at the spots across the table. "Shit. That really went everywhere." He bends down to clean a small puddle on the floor.

"It was a pretty big sip." I'm aware of what I'm doing. This is avoidance at its finest. But I could bring it back around if I wanted to—confess to my husband that his wife heard laughter and watched her own reflection move separate from her. Except I'm not quite sure what that would solve aside from terrifying him and forcing him to relive the worse parts of his childhood. It took him years to get over what happened to his mom. I can't do that to him. He worries enough about me as it is.

I've already made it this far without telling him. And maybe that's a mistake. It probably is. I've seen the movies and read the books—I know it's never a good idea to keep secrets from the people you love. But what if it's in their best interest? Are there ever any exceptions?

"Here, why don't you hand me that towel," he says, reaching his hand out. "You go change your shirt, and I'll throw everything in the dryer." I smile at him and stroll out of the room, leaving words left unsaid.

I'm a little apprehensive to walk into our bedroom after what happened, but Clyde is sprawled out on our bed and it helps ease my fears just a bit. I scratch behind his ears. "You don't think I'm crazy, do you, buddy?" He snorts and rolls onto his back, giving me access to his belly. "I didn't think so." I chuckle, patting his rotund stomach. I wonder if he heard the laughter, too. He didn't react, but that's pretty on-brand for him. If it isn't something to eat, he barely acknowledges anything. I sigh. "Sometimes, I wish you could talk."

"Almost done, April?" Marcus calls from the laundry room downstairs. I forgot he was waiting for my shirt.

"Be right there!" I spring from the bed and dash to my dresser. With my damp shirt halfway off, I tug open a drawer and sort through the disaster, grabbing one of my dad's old concert tees. I run my hands down the front, smoothing out the vintage decal. The cover of Pink Floyd's *The Dark Side of the Moon* is emblazoned on black fabric. It's one of my dad's favorite albums. To this day, anytime I hear a clock chime, I'm immediately transported back to my childhood.

A few years ago, my mom made him clean out his dresser and told him it was time to part with the collection of concert T-shirts he amassed over the years. Our love of music is something we've always shared, and Dad couldn't handle the thought of his beloved shirts going to strangers. So instead of taking the shirts to Goodwill, he drove straight to my house with a trash bag full of memories. He told my mom he donated them, and technically, he wasn't lying. To me, these shirts are on par with precious heirlooms.

I lift the shirt to my nose and inhale. It's been washed a few times, but if I catch it at just the right spot, I can still smell the faintest trace of my dad's musky Soap on a Rope. This time, I find it just beneath the stitching around the collar. One whiff feels like a hug and makes my eyes well. I wish I could get over my fear. I'd jump in the car right now and get a hug from my dad in real life. I swipe at the moisture under my eyes and slide the shirt over my head.

I scoop my wet shirt off the floor and stroll down the hall toward the basement door. It's closed. That's odd. Marcus just yelled up to me, and his voice was so clear.

With a twist of the knob, I tug the door open. Darkness greets me with a faint glimmer of light coming from around the corner at the bottom of the stairs. It's an almost eerie glow. I hated this room when we moved in, and I still hate it. If it weren't for our laundry room, I'd never go down there. As it is, Marcus does most of our wash. In the past two years, I could probably count on both hands the number of times I've been down here.

Our laundry room is in a closet hidden by bi-fold doors. I always turn on the overhead light before I come down here, but Marcus likes to run down in the dark and only use the light over the washer and dryer. He says he's not scared of the dark. *Well, dear husband of mine, I am. Without a doubt.* I flick the switch, and the room is instantly illuminated.

At the bottom of the stairs, I spy the open closet door, but Marcus isn't there. "Where'd you go?" I ask as I amble toward the dryer. It's still open and the wet towel is inside, so I toss my shirt in along with it and start the cycle. Then I spin on my heel, surveying the space like I'm afraid something is hiding down here. I may be twenty-seven, but I'm not above thinking the Boogie Man is still lurking somewhere in the dark. And this would be the perfect place for him to hide.

When we bought this house, Marcus and Zach had grand plans to make it a man cave. I scoffed a bit at the idea, but Marcus said, "Don't worry, baby. I want to make a home theater, too. Then you can watch your movies in surround sound." I had to admit, that idea was appealing. But, since Marcus hired Zach instead of an actual carpenter, the space is only half-finished, and I'm not even sure I'd call it that.

The stairs split the room. The right side has a sprawling, plush area rug and the left bare concrete. The carpeted portion has off-white painted drywall and houses a tan sectional sofa and a coffee table. A white screen hangs on the wall with a projector sitting on a shelf across the room. This is the closest we've come to a home theater and the sound system only works half of the time.

The other side is cold and dark, even with the light on. Gray cinderblock walls and chipped concrete give it an almost dungeon-like vibe. And the hole in the back corner is right out of a horror movie. This house has a sump pump, and the access is down here, but unlike the rest of the home upstairs, this part could use updating. Marcus said he and Zach would take a look at it, but this is beyond their capabilities.

Rows and rows of boxes in haphazard stacks fill the room. Most contain blankets, clothing, a few things from my childhood, and Nana's belongings that I couldn't bear to part with. I promised Marcus I'd go through them eventually, but only when I absolutely have to.

I turn my head back and forth between the two spaces, but I don't see my husband anywhere. "Marcus?" My voice wavers. Maybe he went back upstairs. That would explain the closed door, although I'm surprised I didn't hear him come back up. The basement door creaks—another thing I hate—and I never heard it when I was changing in our room.

"Are you hiding? You know I hate that." He hid from me once when we first moved in. I still can't understand how he managed to wedge himself under our bed. I must've walked around that room ten times before he reached out and grabbed my ankle. You'd think after the way I stomped on his hand, he'd never try that again, but this is Marcus we're talking about.

"All right, you've had your fun. Come on out now." I tiptoe over to the sofa and peer around. The back is pressed up against the wall so there's no place for him to hide there. This side of the room is barely furnished, offering no easy hiding spaces. My eyes skim the space and land on the concrete side. I glance up at the ceiling and shake my head. If he's hiding down here, he has to be over there.

I study the maze of boxes before me. Kids playing hide-n-seek would be thrilled with this space. For me, it's much more sinister. "Marcus, if you even think about jumping out at me, I swear I won't be held responsible for what I do." A fury begins to rage inside of me. It's small, like a smoldering fire, but as I move toward the dank storage side of the basement, I feel the burn begin to travel from my gut to my extremities. "Damn it, stop this!"

I pause among the first few boxes, straining to hear a breath or a snicker, any sound at all. It's completely silent. The kind of quiet you feel.

It's like water on an open flame—my insides are all but extinguished, and I'm left with a feeling of cold dread. The room is bathed in light, but there are places on this side where it will never touch. Shadows loom, and an eerie stillness lurks behind every stack of boxes.

I turn, glancing longingly at the stairs. I'm reminded of the day I was stuck outside moments before I realized I was locked out. The same feeling overwhelms me now. The urge to run is so strong it's as if my legs are being pulled by an unseen current. I could race up those steps and be away from all this in seconds. But what am I running from? The longer this goes on, the surer I am that Marcus isn't down here. He's an ass when it comes to practical jokes, but he'd hear the agitation in my voice and stop right away.

This is *my* house. Just like it was my yard the other week. I am afraid of most things in the outside world; if I start to fear my own home, I don't know what that'll mean for me. A memory of my reflection smiling at me flashes in my head, and my entire body erupts in tiny bumps. I'm not sure what to believe anymore, but I don't think there's anything down here with me, and I need to prove that to myself.

My feet shuffle in half steps around the perimeter of the room. The left corner is empty, nothing but a few boxes of Strawberry Shortcake dolls. The next stack is my baby clothes. Around the same time my mom made my dad clean out his T-shirts, she also boxed up all my old clothing and told me if I wanted them, it was "now or never." As if I even had a choice.

Walking around this room is getting a little easier. My anxiety quells with each new stack of boxes I approach. There's nothing down here except remnants of my childhood. The nostalgia begins to outweigh the fear.

There's another group of boxes in the far-right, darkest corner. I think of my phone lying on my nightstand. If I had it with me, I could use the flashlight. I take a deep breath. *It's just one more spot, April. You can do this.* I take a few tentative steps, keeping my eyes trained on the boxes. There's another reason why I avoid this part of the room, and it's the only one that really matters—these boxes belonged to my nana. Inside there are a few articles of clothing, some photo albums that probably don't belong in a dark basement and her recipe cards are somewhere in there, too.

As I walk on shaky legs toward the boxes, a faint hum drifts through the air. The same one I heard in the pantry not so long ago. My mouth opens and I find myself singing about giving love so sweetly. Tears pool in my eyes, and I let them fall. The room feels as though it's suddenly bathed in warmth as Nana hums her favorite tune. I can't see her, but I can feel her.

I lean forward, hoping to catch a glimpse of her gray curls, but before I have a chance to focus, a hand wraps around my bicep.

I SCREAM and tug my arm out of Marcus's grasp. "Are you trying to scare me to death?" I sputter, bending at the waist as I try to catch my breath.

His hands fly up to shield his face. This isn't the first time he's been the unfortunate recipient of my impulse reactions when I'm caught off guard. "Jesus! Didn't you hear me calling you?"

"Huh? You never called me." I poke his sternum with an accusing finger, but then my face softens as I recall what I *did* hear. She was here. I know she was.

"April ..." His voice is low and even, like he's trying to talk me off a ledge. "I've been calling you for a little while. I heard you start up the dryer and then you never came upstairs. What were you doing down here?" He glances around the room. "Wait! Are you finally going through these boxes?" He sounds like a kid trying to guess a surprise and hoping it's a puppy.

I shake my head vehemently. "No. That's not what I was doing."

He studies me closely. "Well, then, what *were* you doing?"

I sigh. I don't want to tell him I was tiptoeing around the room looking for the ghost of my nana. I look over at the stack of boxes. The warm glow and the melody that was there moments ago seem to have vanished. I deflate a little. This keeps happening. I hear or see something, and then I don't. Marcus hooks a finger under my chin and forces my eyes to his. "Hey, what's going on in there?" He taps at my temple. Marcus may not always know what I'm thinking, but he keeps trying to understand. I love him for that.

My lip curves in a half-smile to soften the blow of what I'm about to say. "Well, I *was* looking for you. I never heard you come back up after you called me, but I guess I must have missed that. And then ... I thought I heard something. Something that definitely *wasn't* you."

His eyebrows squish together. "What'd you hear?"

"Well, I'm not sure exactly." I shrug, feeling a little guilty for lying, but in a way, it's also the truth. I thought I heard Nana, but I can't say for sure.

"And you were just over here like a little detective trying to figure it out?"

"Yep."

"Again? By yourself?"

My lips pinch together. "Yes, by myself. Listen, I'm an independent woman, okay. I'm capable of doing things on my own." While I may be capable, I'm actually kind of shocked that I made it this far without completely losing my shit. Especially considering all that's been happening lately.

His eyes widen and he shakes his head. "Baby, I know you are. That's not what I'm saying. It's just ... well, lately, you've been ..."

I put my hand on his mouth. "I know. I've been a bit of a mess." He smirks and I glare at him. "Fine—more of a mess than usual. But I came down here and somehow ended up among Nana's things and now that I'm here, it's not so bad." I shrug.

He grins. "Well, look at you!"

My cheeks heat, and I look away, a small smile playing on my lips.

"So, what happened?"

I tell him about thinking he was hiding from me. His nostrils flare. "Seriously? Come on. Give me some credit. I like to play jokes sometimes, but I know better than to hide from you." He flexes his fingers and mutters, "I learned that the hard way."

I grimace. "Yeah, I figured as much. I knew even if you were hiding, you wouldn't continue to do it once you heard the panic in my voice." He takes my hand and squeezes it. "Anyway, once I was over here, I decided it was silly to be afraid of my own house. So I made myself walk around this side." I continue the story right up to when I approached Nana's boxes. "And that's when you came down and scared me half to death." I glance up at him, but there's no menace in my eyes. "I must've been so focused on what I was doing; I never heard you calling for me."

He nods. "Where'd you hear the noise?" he asks as he walks over toward the boxes.

"It was over there, but I don't hear it anymore. I was having kind of a nostalgic moment, and I think I imagined it." I hear the words as they come out of my mouth, but I still don't completely believe them.

"Well, we should check it out just to be sure it's not another mouse or something."

I nod and follow in step behind him.

"I think I found the culprit," he declares.

"You did?" I ask, my voice tripping on the words.

"Yep. And I was right!"

I narrow my eyes at him. "What do you mean you were right?"

"It *is* a mouse. Take a look." He moves off to the side

and motions me toward him, but after hearing the word "mouse," I have no intention of coming any closer.

"Will you come here? Trust me, will you?"

I huff and plod over beside him. There's a box on the floor behind the stack. The flaps are wide open, and the backside of my Mickey Mouse doll is protruding out of it.

I give his arm a playful shove. "Hahaha. Very funny."

Marcus smiles wide. "Okay, now that that's settled, what'd you say we go upstairs and relax?" He waggles his eyebrows, making me laugh.

I want to join him, but Nana's recipe cards are just over there in that box. I should grab them while I'm down here. And I don't know—maybe it's odd—but I felt her in this space only moments ago. I guess I'm just not ready to let that go. "You go ahead. I'll be right up."

"You sure?" He tilts his head, studying me.

"Yeah. I think it's time I bring Nana's recipes up to the kitchen. I'm not sure why I left them down here so long."

"I can wait while you do that."

"No, it's fine. I'll grab the stuff out of the dryer on my way up, too. It's gotta be dry by now."

He eyes me warily, but if there's a question in his mind, he doesn't voice it. He just gives my shoulder a squeeze and heads upstairs.

Once I hear the floorboards creak overhead, I spin around and face Nana's things. On a sigh, I peel open the flaps on a box and sift through the contents. My hands stop short when they brush against something familiar. It's soft and willowy. Gripping it between my fingers, I lift it from the box. It may be dark down here, but there's just enough light to make out the intricate white flowers that I remember so well. I don't think this was Nana's favorite dress, but it was mine. I can't recall ever putting it in here.

A chill moves across my shoulders. "Nana," I whisper. "Are you here?"

I stand statue-still and wait. Minutes pass, and then I hear it. That song. Nana's humming. Only this time, it's not swirling around me, hitting me from every angle. It's more concentrated and it's coming from the back corner. Dropping Nana's dress back into the box, I tiptoe in the direction, and as I move closer, it becomes louder and more urgent.

When I reach the spot where the hum is located, I pause, thinking I must have it all wrong, but I can't argue with what I'm hearing. The humming is coming from the ground. It's wafting out of the uncapped sump hole. It's hard to reconcile my nana's voice pouring out of that dark, seemingly endless pit. Why would she be down there?

My entire body tingles with fear that leaves my extremities numb. I gasp and sputter out a single word, "Nana?" The humming stops and the silence that remains is louder than any song. I manage to speak again; my voice splits the sentence into short staccato. "Are … you … there?"

I wait in terror for an answer that never comes. There's no music. No reassuring voice. No residual warmth. I'm left feeling bereft—and something else. Something sinister. My eyes zigzag around the perimeter of the room, bouncing from the sump hole to the walls and every corner as though something may jump out at me.

It's as if this house is keeping secrets and revealing them to me in tiny terrifying increments. I've had enough. Whipping around, I bolt up the stairs. My feet pound against each step, or maybe it's the sound of my blood pounding in my ears. I don't look back as I reach the top stair, but as I grasp the knob and attempt to turn it, I'm horrified when it won't budge. The lock on the outside of the door. Someone used it to trap me down here. Someone or some *thing*. "No, no, no, no, no," I shout, banging on the door with both fists. "Marcus! Marcus! Let me out!" I sob and shake as I pound against the wood. I hear breathing; it's breathy and erratic. Maybe it's mine. Or maybe it isn't. I have to get out of here. "Help," I cry out.

The door flings open and I fall at Marcus's feet. He squats down beside me, gripping my shoulders. "Baby, what the hell happened?"

It takes me a moment to find my voice, but when I do, a sickening thought flits into my mind. What if Marcus locked me down there? "The door was locked," I stammer. "D-did you do that?"

He reels back as though he's been slapped. "Of course I didn't. How could you even think that?"

At that moment, Zach strolls into the hall from the kitchen. His hand is buried in a bag of Doritos and he stops short when he sees us on the ground. "Whoa, am I interrupting something?"

"Zach?" My gaze snaps to his. "How long have you been here?" I'm mentally calculating the time I spent downstairs after Marcus came back up. I don't want to suspect Zach any more than I wanted to suspect Marcus, but nothing makes sense right now.

He shrugs, looking at Marcus. "I don't know. Ten minutes, maybe?"

"April thought she was locked down in the basement, but, baby," Marcus squeezes my shoulders, getting my attention, "the door wasn't locked."

Not this again. I tried that knob multiple times and it didn't move. "But it was. Marcus, you have to believe me. I tried opening it and nothing happened. I was trapped down there." I fling myself at him, wrapping my arms around his shoulders and burrowing my face into his neck.

He rubs small circles on my back while whispering, "Shh."

Zach struts over to the open basement door and grips the knob. He twists it a few times before looking down at us. "It seems to be working okay, but I'll take a look at it while I'm here."

"Thanks, man." Marcus nods before turning his attention back to me. "How're you doing? Think you can stand?"

I feel a bit ridiculous and small sitting here on the ground, but I also feel immense concern. For my mental well-being, but also for the state of this house. I'm feeling more and more convinced that my home is starting to turn on me. Even though I'm aware of how completely bizarre that sounds, I can't shake it. I need to talk this through, but not here and not with Marcus. His eyes are filled with his own fear and that's my fault. He doesn't need me to pile on my own fears as well. He's a rock, but more like one of those soapstones. The kind that appear tough but can easily be marred with the scrape of a fingernail. Marcus wears enough scars from the time he spent with his parents. I'm not about to add to them.

He takes my hands in his and helps pull me to my feet. My legs are still shaky, but Zach shoves the basement door shut behind me and having the room closed off helps me regain a bit more strength. It hasn't solved the problem, but for now—out of sight, out of mind.

Marcus tips my chin. "Hey, baby? Your hands are empty."

"Huh?"

"Your nana's recipes. I thought you were staying downstairs to look for them. And you didn't bring your shirt and towel up from the dryer, either." He plunges a hand into his pocket.

"Yeah, uh," I lower my gaze to my feet, "the, um, shirt and towel needed more time in the dryer. And I-I guess I wasn't quite ready to go through Nana's recipes yet," I offer on a shrug.

His eyes narrow slightly. That lie was weak and so transparent, anyone could see through it, but thankfully Marcus doesn't push. "No problem. I'll run down later and grab the things out of the dryer. If you're okay," he looks at Zach and then back at me, "we were gonna go play a few rounds. But I can stay with you, if you want."

"Yeah, April, just say the word and I'll get the hell out of here," Zach adds.

I give them a small smile. "No, it's fine. I'm just gonna get some work done. You two go ahead."

They saunter off into Marcus's game room and he shoots me a wink before closing the door. Once they're gone, I sprint down the hall into our bedroom and grab my phone off my nightstand. Without even a glance at the bathroom, I skip out of the room and back to my office. Once I'm settled into my oversized recliner, I tap on Emma's face. She picks up on the second ring.

"Hey, you! I was actually gonna to call you later. What's up?"

"Nothing much." I bite my lip. My standard answer to everything is to deny there's any problem at all. Over the last few weeks, there have been multiple instances that have had me questioning my own sanity. Today was "one for the books," as my dad says. And that's the whole reason why I called her, and yet here I am deflecting again.

"Uh-huh. Let's try that again, shall we? While I'm really happy to hear from you, you never call without a reason. That's *my* MO, remember?"

"Ugh, you're right. I don't know why I said, 'nothing much.' The words just slipped out like I'm on autopilot."

She hums into the phone. "It's because you always discredit yourself. It's your default mode. But that's okay. You're a work in progress." I can hear the smile in her voice.

"That's one way to put it." I sigh. Here goes nothing. "So, Em, let me ask you, have you ever had any strange experiences when you were alone that you can't explain?"

"What do you mean? Like ghosts?"

I shake my head. "No. I mean, maybe? But I don't think that's it."

"You don't think *what's* it?"

"Do you remember when we went to Stacy's eleventh birthday sleepover, and we all crowded into her hallway bathroom to play Bloody Mary?"

She laughs. "Not only do I remember; I've still got the scar on my hip from when Meg pushed her way out of the room and knocked me into the corner of the vanity."

"Right. I forgot about that. I guess we were all in a mad rush to leave the room after what we saw."

"You mean, what we *thought* we saw."

"What's the difference?" I snip.

"April, you don't really need me to answer that, do you?"

I roll my eyes. "My point is, we were kids, but when I think back on it, I can still picture the face in the mirror."

"Well, sure you can. Just like I remember being in the air for a full minute when we would sled down the hill at school. Doesn't mean it actually happened that way. It's just the grandiose imagination of childhood."

"Look at you, all philosophical!" I chortle.

She snickers. "I have my moments. Why are you bringing that up, anyway?"

"I don't know," I lie. "I was just thinking about how our mind can play tricks on us sometimes."

"Uh-huh. And why do I feel like there's more you're not telling me?"

Because there is, but saying it out loud feels impossible now. Something shifted inside me during our conversation, and my brave resignation has been replaced with doubt and an overwhelming feeling of foolishness. She does have a point about childhood imagination, but maybe it isn't just a childhood thing. I've been inside this house for months now. It could just be that I'm going stir crazy. Still, I need to tell her something; otherwise, she won't let it go. "I just had this funny thing happen earlier where I thought I heard something downstairs. Marcus thought it might be a mouse, and then, of course, he found an old Mickey Mouse doll of mine and claims that was the culprit."

"Oh, jeez," she laughs. "You do have a lot of memorabilia down in those boxes."

"I sure do, and until Marcus says otherwise, it'll live down there forever."

"Preservation at its finest." She chuckles.

Maybe that's my whole problem. I'm trying to preserve myself. By not leaving the house, I'm left in a holding pattern of sorts. It's the ultimate pause button. Nothing bad can happen to me, but nothing good can, either. I know if I live in constant fear of all of the "what ifs," then I'm going to waste my entire life. That's not what I want, but it's really easy to just put it off for another day. When I'm living inside my home in my own controlled environment, I know what to expect. Or at least I did. Now I'm not sure what I know. Lately, it's hard to tell the difference between real and imaginary. And all of the bad that I thought couldn't reach me, may have found a way in after all.

I clear my throat. "So you said you had planned to call me. Any reason in particular?"

"Oh, yeah! I ran into Nora Dolan at Target this morning." Hearing Emma say that name steals the breath from my lungs. Nora is Walker's sister. She was the one with him when he died. I can't seem to find my voice, but thankfully, Emma presses on without waiting. "I literally ran into her. I was turning out of the deodorant aisle when my cart collided with hers. Girl, if you could've seen me! I'm sure I looked like I wanted to crawl out of my skin. Luckily, I recovered quickly and asked her how she was doing. She told me they found out Walker had an undiagnosed heart defect and that's what caused his heart attack."

"Huh." I'm left dumbstruck. I feel relieved in a weird way. A heart defect provides a logical explanation for a twenty-seven-year-old to drop dead from a heart attack. I also feel mildly nervous that maybe I might have some undiagnosed medical condition that's currently raging throughout my body. But mostly, I just feel sad. Walker was a good guy, and now he's dead.

"April?"

"Yeah?"

"Talk to me. What are you feeling right now?"

"Really fucking sad." I suck in my lips and press them together to keep the trembling at bay.

Emma sighs. "Yeah. Me, too. But, you know, Nora told me it was over so fast. He didn't suffer."

People love to say that when someone dies. Like the suffering is worse than the dead part. I'm glad he wasn't in pain, but now he isn't in anything. I'm not sure the tradeoff is worth it.

"BABY? YOU AWAKE?" Marcus's breath is hot on my cheek. I felt the bed dip when he crawled in a moment ago, and now he's perched on all fours, hovering over me. I press one hand to his chest and the other scrubs the sleep from my eyes.

"I am now." I groan. "What time is it?"

"A little after two." He leans in and kisses the spot where my neck meets my shoulder. It's his signature move and with good reason. A few seconds there and I melt faster than a stick of butter in a hot pan.

Despite some residual grogginess, my body responds immediately. My back arches and he slips a hand under my tank top, cupping my breast. His fingers skate over my nipple as his mouth makes a trail up and down the curve of my neck. A soft moan escapes my lips, and it's a green light for his revving engine. He straddles me and lifts my tank top over my head. Hooking his fingers into the waistband of my underwear, he slides them down my legs, tossing them onto the floor. Then he works his way back up my body, placing soft kisses along the insides of my legs, my knees, my thighs, and … oh, God.

To all the guys in high school who wondered why I ever gave Marcus a chance, you should've made better use of your time. You could've been perfecting your game the same way my husband has. He takes direction well and has learned a lot from my verbal and bodily cues. His tongue makes lazy laps around my center before his mouth closes over its target. He takes me to the brink several times before finally sending me over.

I barely have time to recover before he's slowly pushing inside of me. Tiny tremors reverberate through my body, and I grip his shoulders to steady myself. He leans in close and whispers, "You're so beautiful. I don't know how I got so lucky. I love you." This is my favorite part. Marcus isn't the kind of guy who wears his heart on his sleeve, but when we're this close, he doesn't hold back.

His movements are tortuously slow. He presses his forehead to my shoulder, and I tip my head to rest my cheek against him. I inhale, taking in his musky scent mixed with Cool Water. It was the cologne of choice for most guys in high school, and even now, nine years later, it's still Marcus's favorite.

My fingers dance along the ridges of his back and up to his neck where they get lost in his hair. Marcus has thick, dark hair the color of burnt umber that falls in unruly waves. He keeps it longer on top and short around his ears and neck. Next to his soulful eyes, it's my favorite trait of his. But something feels off tonight, as my fingers find more hair around his neck than I'm used to—hair that feels fine and more straight than wavy. My hands move in a circular motion as my fingertips probe his scalp. My brows lace with confusion as the hair in my hands feels nothing like Marcus's. I press my palms to the sides of his face and gasp at the smoothness. Marcus always has stubble at the end of the day, but tonight, his face is soft and almost velvety. I swear I felt his scruff between my legs earlier.

I push back against his face, but he resists, keeping his

neck bent and his face obscured. I try one more time with a little more force, and his head lifts. A thin beam of moonlight has slipped through the blinds, providing just enough light to illuminate the face above me. Piercing steel eyes meet mine and I freeze. Terror spreads through my body like lightning in a blackened sky. He smirks at my reaction, and his lips part, mouthing the same words over and over. It takes me a moment before I realize he's singing. And his song of choice is one I'll never forget. "I Want to Know What Love Is" by Foreigner.

The man above me *and* inside me isn't my husband. It's Walker Dolan.

My body and brain finally catch up with one another and I shriek, shoving Walker as hard as I can. Once I'm free, I scramble backward and huddle in a ball on my pillow.

Hands are on me fast, grabbing my wrists, attempting to pull my arms away from my face. I claw and scratch at him, yelling, "Get the fuck away from me!"

"Okay! Okay! Jesus! What's happening?"

I know that voice, and it's not Walker's.

Slowly, I uncoil my body, letting my arms fall to my sides. My eyes come last, opening in tiny increments. Walker's cold eyes are gone. But I still blink several times just to be sure. Marcus is in front of me. His skin looks ashen, and the tendons in his neck seem to protrude out of his skin. He holds out his hand, but then pulls it back. He looks lost.

I launch myself at him, catching him off guard. He wraps his arms around me, holding me tight. My mind races, trying to make sense of what just happened. But there's no sense to be made. I clearly imagined Walker, didn't I?

Of course, I did. Only … his hair felt so real. That's the part that's holding me back from fully embracing the "it's all in my head" idea. Up to this point, all these instances could be written off. My eyes and ears were playing tricks on me. But now that I've added a tactile element, it's harder to shrug off. I lift a tentative hand, letting it brush against Marcus's hair, and sigh audibly when I find the familiar thick strands exactly where they should be.

"Baby?" Marcus's voice wavers. He rests his hands on my biceps and gently pushes until there's a little space between us. We rest our foreheads together and he lets out a shaky breath. "Are … are you okay?"

I open my mouth, but nothing comes out. I don't know if I'm okay. I don't know what I am. And poor Marcus. His eyes are a mixture of shock and sadness. I can't even imagine what he must be thinking. One second we were intimately connected, and the next, I was fighting him off like a crazy person.

Am I? A crazy person, I mean. I shake my head, but it's getting harder to deny when the case against me keeps building. My body erupts in tiny bumps and I shiver. Marcus notices and rubs his hands up and down my arms.

"April? Tell me what happened." His eyes flick back and forth between mine like they might find the answer there. He sucks in his bottom lip and holds it in his teeth.

My mind swims with unsaid words. I could tell him everything. I should. But I'm afraid for him. I close my eyes, remembering the way he looked after his mom died — crippled with agonizing grief. It took him years to find his way out of it. His mom and I aren't the same. She had schizophrenia and severe depression, but the road to despair doesn't care about exact diagnoses. Marcus was not to blame for his mom's suicide, but he still struggled with guilt. Guilt for not seeing it coming. Guilt for not being there when it did. I refuse to be responsible for that kind of guilt. I can't do it to him. Maybe I can get this under control myself. If it happens again—and going off the past few weeks, it *will* happen again—I can close my eyes and remind myself that it's all in my head. It worked this time; it would work again. I nod, more for me than him. It's decided. I'll give him pieces of the truth rather than the whole thing. That way I can protect him while also being a little honest. "I'm sorry. It's just … I was asleep when you came in and I guess I was dreaming about Walker Dolan— I told you he died, right?" He tips his head, and I continue. "So when you woke me up the way you did …" I grimace, wishing I could keep this part from him. He keeps his eyes trained on me, watching me intently. "I was still half asleep, and I thought I saw him instead of you."

He leans back and his jaw drops. "You thought I was Walker?"

I shrug. I know how it sounds, and the worst part is, I'm leaving out how I didn't just *think* I saw Walker; I *felt* him.

"Hold up." He pulls away, letting his arms slide off me. "April, did you think it was Walker inside of you instead of me?" He flinches, and his eyes flash wide.

I did think that, but admitting it to Marcus would only hurt him. And it might hurt us, too. I shake my head. "No, of course not," I reply without hesitation, and his entire body seems to sag.

"Still, maybe you should talk to Dr. Lesser about this," he says. I frown and bite at my lip. "What's that look for? " He leans forward as though he's examining my face for clues.

"Uh, well, about Dr. Lesser …"

"What about her?" His voice is slightly elevated and his nostrils flare.

"I just wasn't sure I still needed to talk to her. We had a difference of opinion and I'm not convinced she's helping anyway." I cast my eyes to my lap.

His head shakes slowly. "Why didn't you tell me any of this?"

"Marcus, it's fine," I say, though I don't believe it.

He doesn't either. "April, mistaking your husband for your dead boyfriend isn't fine."

"Walker was never my boyfriend and it's not really that I mistook you for him," I lie. "It was more like I was dreaming awake. You know, kind of like I was sleepwalking."

"Hmm." He opens his mouth again as though he wants to challenge me, but then he snaps it shut. He places his hands on either side of my face, and for a moment, I'm reminded of how smooth Walker's face felt. I shiver, and Marcus wraps me in a tight embrace. "It's late," he whispers in my ear. "Let's get some sleep. Maybe we can try for round two in the morning." He chuckles, but it lacks the usual carefree sound. Despite my attempt to smooth things over, he's still rattled by what happened. And so am I.

"Sleep sounds good, and a second round sounds even better." I pull back and smile at him. He gives me a quick kiss on my cheek, and we settle back under the covers.

After a short time, his breathing evens out, but I lie awake thinking about fine hair in my hands and gunmetal eyes.

MARCUS HAS BEEN HOVERING all day. I'd tell him to stop, but I'm grateful for it. It's nearly noon and I haven't been alone for longer than ten minutes since I woke up this morning. I smile, remembering the way Marcus chose to wake me. We more than made up for the debacle I caused last night. With all of the attention he's given me, there have been no opportunities for my reflection to smile at me, or for unexplained sounds, or for ghosts to drop by. It also means I haven't had a chance to edit the video I filmed the other day, but I still have time.

I'm in my office for the first time today. Marcus asked me if I wanted some tea, and now he's in the kitchen banging away, making me wonder if he actually knows how to use the kettle.

I open my laptop and cue up the footage from my drugstore makeup video, groaning when I see it's fifty-two minutes long. Why must I talk so much?

Marcus pops his head into the room. "Hey, April?"

"Yeah," I answer, keeping my eyes on the screen in front of me.

"Looks like we're out of sugar."

"Did you check in the pantry?"

He sighs. "Of course I did."

"Okay, I can order some from Amazon. Just give me a minute."

He holds up his hand. "It's no big deal. I'll just run to the store real quick and grab some."

My eyes snap to his. "Right now?"

His expression softens. "Baby, it'll be fine. You just keep working on editing. I'll be back before you even realize I'm gone. Unless ..."

"Unless what?"

He clasps his hands behind his back and leans forward slightly. "You could come with me?" His eyes seem to shine as he watches me, waiting for my answer.

Could I go with him? I think about the question. Physically, I'm totally capable of getting into a car and going to the store, but mentally? It's been so long since I've gone anywhere. I think about Walker and how he died so young, but at least he was out living life when it happened. I can still see his face the way it was split in half by shadows and moonlight. It was only my imagination, but what if it wasn't? Do I really want to be alone here in this house in case he wants to drop by again or perhaps my nana wants to sing to me again from the hole in the basement? I shudder just thinking about it. Maybe a short trip would do me good. Before I can give it any more thought, I nod.

"Wait. You'll go?"

I smile. "Yep, I'll go." I stand, ignoring the slight numbing in my fingertips and toes. This is a big moment, but I can't think of it like that or else I'll never get in the car.

Marcus reaches for my hand and laces our fingers together. I let him lead me through the house and out the front door, never stopping to consider anything along the way.

He walks us to the passenger side of his truck, parked in the driveway. The sun's rays bounce off the anthracite exterior, making it appear to sparkle. I slide onto the black leather seat and immediately reach for the seatbelt. I exhale once I hear the click of the latch. Marcus is still standing beside me with his hand on the door. He lifts a brow and studies me. "You good?"

"Mm-hmm." My lips stay pressed together. I'm honestly not sure "good" is the right word to describe how I am. I haven't dropped over, and my heart rate is only slightly elevated. So, I guess I'm stable.

He shuts the door with a slow push and races around the back to the other side. The driver's side door flings open, and he's in his seat fast. He pulls the door shut and buckles himself in before turning to me. "How we doing? Okay?" His forehead creases and he rubs a hand on the leg of his pants. I can only nod, but it seems to appease him.

As I turn my head, I notice a pack of Marlboros in the cupholder. I knew he was smoking again. A quick glance at his face confirms him noticing me noticing the cigarettes. His eyes flick to mine and then immediately cast down at his lap. It makes sense he'd think his secret was safe in here since I haven't set foot in this truck in over six months. I should feel anger or disappointment or both, and maybe if I dig deep enough, I do. But right now, his hand is on my knee as we sit in his truck, ready to drive somewhere together for the first time in months, and I can only handle one thing at a time. So I'll file this away under "deal with later" since I'm far too hyperaware of my current predicament.

"Okay, I'm ready," I croak.

He squeezes my leg. "You sure?"

"Nope, but if we wait for that to happen, we may be here a while."

His grin is wide as he starts the engine. His hands grip the wheel. The low rumble quickens my pulse. As he backs out of the driveway, I squeeze my eyes shut and curl into myself. My body folds up like an envelope. Marcus reaches across the console and rests a hand back on my knee. My leg jolts, but he keeps his palm pressed to my skin. "You're doing great. Deep breaths. We're almost there."

Deep breaths, huh? At this point, I'm grateful for any kind of breath.

I feel the gentle vibration as the tires hum along the windy road. Marcus seems to be taking his time, which I'm grateful for. I haven't been able to open my eyes, and I keep my body clenched up tight. The air in the car is starting to feel thin. I'm beginning to hyperventilate. Marcus cranks the AC, and a cool stream of air is directed toward my face. The icy rush snakes between my fingers and finds my nostrils. I inhale as deeply as I can, feeling the air flood through my system.

"That's it, baby. You got this."

The *click-click* of the turn signal tells me we're nearly at the store. I part my fingers just enough to peek. It takes me half a second to confirm our whereabouts, and then I'm back in my comforting ball.

I'm bracing myself for our arrival, but a half-mile feels a lot longer when you're waiting for it to end. I'm just about to ask Marcus how much longer when I feel the car tip toward the right. We bounce a little as we drive into the parking lot, and then we glide into a spot.

The engine stops purring, and the keys clank together when Marcus pulls them from the ignition. "We're here now. Do you want to look?"

It's not really a case of whether or not I *want* to look. It's more that I'm not sure I can physically pry my own hands away from my face. I keep my eyes closed and focus on my breathing. Small inhales and quick puffy exhales. Marcus presses a hand to my back and rubs in a clockwise motion.

Okay, April, you made it this far and nothing happened. You can open your eyes. It's only the grocery store. I let out a deep sigh and peel my fingers away from my face. Blinking a few times, I look around. It's an odd feeling—coming back to a place you've been so many times before after being gone for nearly a year.

Only I haven't really been gone. I've just been at home. For months. Trapped in my own fears. They may seem irrational to most people, but they've felt pretty real to me. Still, I can't help feeling a little silly when going to the grocery store is considered a major accomplishment.

I've been so overwhelmed with what *could* happen if I left the house. But I never stopped to think about the odds that *nothing* would happen. For years, I just went places and did things. I didn't focus on all the horrible possibilities lurking in the outside world. I just fucking lived my life. Until I stopped.

"YOU HAVEN'T SAID ANYTHING. What're you thinking?" Marcus leans in, taking my hands in his. His eyes dance with mine.

"I …" I clear my throat. "I'm thinking you should probably grab that sugar because I'm not sure how long I have before the clock strikes twelve and I turn into a pumpkin." I do my best to give him a cheeky grin, but it probably looks more like a grimace.

He looks at me sideways. "Don't do that."

I straighten my shoulders. "Don't do what?"

"Try and make jokes. You did a brave thing. Just let yourself feel good about it."

"Pssh. You can't hear what's going on in here," I say, pointing to my head. "The celebration is so loud I can barely keep my thoughts straight." I grin at him. It's not a complete lie. Although I'm not sure I'd refer to the noise in my brain as a celebration. I'm here in body, but my mind is still back at the house trying to make sense of the impossible. The only positive is that it's distracted me from fixating on all of the potentially lethal things that could've happened to us on the drive over here.

A reluctant smile forms on his face as he studies me. "Do you want to stay here or come with me?"

"I'll stay here. I think one adventure is enough for today."

He nods. "Okay. I'll leave the keys with you and be back as quick as I can." He plants a kiss on the top of my head.

It's not until the door closes behind him that I let my body sag against the seat. I've been so tense with worry. The muscles in my arms and legs are screaming.

The back of my head slides along the leather as I let my eyes drift around the parking lot. Marcus parked a little farther away from the store, and from here, I can see most of the lot and the store front, too. It's the perfect vantage point for people-watching, but after several minutes, the only person I've seen is an older woman with blue-gray hair and an oversized lime green sweater. She's pretty hard to miss.

I let my head fall back and sigh. Maybe I should've just gone inside with him. I glance over at the keys resting in the cupholder. I could lock up the car and go join him. Closing my eyes for a moment, I try to picture what that would look like. I've been in the grocery store many times before. It shouldn't be hard to visualize.

I'm strolling up to the glass doors as they part for me. The store is cool, but only slightly uncomfortable. They always keep the thermostat a little low; maybe it has something to do with keeping the food fresh or making sure no one overheats while shopping. I'm trying to find Marcus, but instead, I see the blue-haired lady from earlier. She's trying to maneuver her cart, but one of the wheels is stuck on an end cap of canned corn. Instead of taking her time to figure out what the problem is, she's yanking and pushing with all her might. I open my mouth to yell at her to stop, but it's too late. The wheel on her cart finally breaks free, but not before loosening the display and sending all the cans on top of her. All that's visible underneath the pile is a tiny strip of lime green fabric.

I gasp, sitting up straight. The possibility of any of that actually happening is highly unlikely, but it doesn't matter. That isn't the way my brain works. It could have a .01% chance of actually occurring, and I'd still focus on that chance like it was inevitable. The images my mind just showed me felt pretty real and that's enough for me.

I grab the visor and tug it down. My reflection stares back at me. I level myself with a stern look. "Listen, April, you need to stop this worst-case scenario bullshit." I scrub a hand over my face but stop partway, narrowing my eyes at my reflection. The girl in the mirror does the same. I lean in close; she leans in close. I close one eye; she closes one eye. I shake my head; so does she. "Okay." I groan. "Get a hold of yourself."

I shove the visor back in place at the same time Marcus opens his door. His sudden arrival makes me jump.

He was sliding into the car, but he freezes when I squeal. "April? What's wrong?" He drops into the seat and tosses the grocery bag in the back. His hands cradle my face as his eyes search mine.

I rest my hands on top of his. "I'm good. I just didn't see you coming is all."

His eyes narrow a bit, and his mouth forms a thin line. He nods only once, and then he releases me.

"So," I say, gripping my hands in my lap to keep them from shaking. "How'd it go in there?"

"Fine." His answer is clipped, but when he notices me leaning in, he continues. "They moved a few things around —swapped the baking aisle with the cereal. Took me a minute to find the sugar."

"Stores are always doing things like that. Like, what was wrong with the way it was before, you know?"

"Maybe they were bored." He shrugs.

"Maybe." I can't say I relate to boredom. There's a security in knowing what to expect—a kind of comfort in the ordinary. That's the main reason for why I've been isolating myself in my house. But now that my security there has been threatened, I feel as though my little bubble has a pinhole that's slowly letting all of the air out. Right now, I would give anything to be bored.

He starts up the car, and I try to keep my eyes open as he backs out of the spot. I make it to the exit before I curl back into myself and seal my hands over my face.

The drive home is filled with mindless music and Marcus's raspy voice singing along. I'm able to tune him out, but that all comes to an end when I hear the opening notes of Foreigner's "I Want to Know What Love Is." I spring upright just as my husband slaps a hand over his mouth. "Hey, isn't this the song that—"

I turn the knob on the stereo so hard I'm surprised it doesn't come off in my hands. "I think I'd rather just have it be quiet, okay?"

He tilts his head and raises his eyebrows. "Yeah, sure, but—"

"Shh!"

He flinches.

"Sorry. I have a bit of a headache. I'm just gonna lie back and close my eyes until we're home."

"Okay," he murmurs.

I rest against the seat. I'm sure from the outside, I look relaxed, but there's a flurry of activity happening deep inside of me. A tornado of worry and frantic energy swirls within my mind.

Walker Dolan is someone I hadn't considered in almost ten years, and now it seems he's never far from my thoughts. He's even started materializing in the place of someone I love. No. I can't go there because it didn't happen. Walker is dead, and dead people don't just force their way inside of living people.

I've always been afraid of dying. Most people would probably say the same, although most people still get out and live their lives. When Nana died, it brought death into my house. It made it unavoidable. But I could still tell myself that Nana was older and had lived a full life. Then Walker died and that idea no longer applied. He was young and his life was only just beginning.

The reason I've been thinking about him so much lately is because of what he represents. Death at any age is terrifying, but at my age? It's my worst fear. Maybe that's the connection between my unexplained experiences involving Walker and Nana. Death links the two.

"Home safe and sound. You made it." Marcus pats my knee.

I sit up, feeling a little light-headed. "It felt like it took longer to get there than it did to come home."

He bites his lip. "I *did* drive a little faster on the way back." I arch my brow, and he half shrugs. "What? You seemed a little on edge so I figured you'd want to get home."

"You figured right," I say, smiling sweetly.

"Baby, you did it."

My cheeks flush. "It was just a quick ride to the—"

"Uh-uh. Don't even try that shit. You haven't been anywhere in months. This is big."

I grin. "I guess it kind of is, isn't it?"

"Damn right." He rests a hand on my head and musses my hair. "Now, come on. I still owe you that tea."

THE REST of my afternoon has been blissfully uneventful.

And after my small return to the outside world, the calm is appreciated. I thought about calling someone to share what I did, but my parents would assume I'm ready to come to their house. I don't think a short trip to a grocery store parking lot comes anywhere close to the chaos of going to my parents' home for dinner. The last time I was there, I narrowly escaped a panic attack when my mom started a small grease fire after forgetting she was simmering meatballs.

I almost picked up my phone to call Emma, but then I thought better of it. She's been so patient with me, but I know the minute she hears I left the house, she'll celebrate in a huge way. And I don't want to get her hopes up.

Sure, I managed to survive a short jaunt in the car today, but that doesn't mean I'm anxious or even ready to do it again anytime soon. It was a one-time thing, for now.

I'm listening to my Spotify chill playlist and working in my office. I just finished editing my video and am prepping it for upload now. I have it scheduled to post tomorrow morning.

"Baby," Marcus calls from the hallway.

"In here."

He struts into the room holding the bottle of vitamins. "Did you take one this morning?" he asks, shaking the jar.

I tap my chin and look up at the ceiling. "You know, I don't think I did, but it's fine. I think I'm done with those."

"What? No, April, come on. You need to take these." He strides over and plops the bottle onto my desk with a *thud*.

I squint up at him. "Why would I *need* to?"

He rubs the back of his neck. "Okay, maybe *need* isn't the right word, but they're paying us a lot and you agreed to the sponsorship."

"Did I, though? Honestly, Marcus, I haven't been

directly involved with sponsors for a while now, and it's making me a little uncomfortable."

"Uncomfortable?" He takes a step back, and when he speaks again, his voice is firm. "Listen, you asked me to help."

I hold up my hands. "I know I did. It's just …"

"It's just what?" The veins in his forearms dance beneath his skin when he crosses his arms.

"All right, let's start over," I say, keeping my tone even. He's feeling defensive, but that's only because I've never challenged him on this before. Our arrangement has mostly worked; it just needs some tweaking. "Maybe I don't say it enough, but I appreciate you. You have to know that." He swallows hard, tipping his head once. "I know this is my channel, but it's also ours. I couldn't do any of this without you. I just think maybe I should be a little more involved with the sponsorships, that's all."

"Involved how?" He runs a hand through his thick hair.

"Well, for starters, how about you check in with me before agreeing to anything?"

He snorts. "What's the point of me taking over this part if you need to sign off on everything?"

I hold up my hand. "It's not that I need to sign off on everything."

He arches a brow.

"Okay, fine, I guess I do, but only because I'm the one who's making the videos, so I feel like I should be on board with the things I'm telling people to buy, you know?"

He lets out a sigh. "That's fair. If a company contacts us, I'll make sure I run it past you before I agree to anything." He starts to turn away but spins back. His fingers graze the top of the vitamin jar. "Just think about these, okay? I mean, baby, the money they offered us … whew." He whistles.

My smile wavers. "Sure thing."

He shuffles toward the door, and my guilt gets the better of me. Before he leaves, I call out, "Oh, and Marcus?"

"Hmm?" he answers over his shoulder.

"I think you and I should have a little meeting later on in the bedroom. You know, in case you're still feeling under appreciated." I lift my eyebrows.

A mischievous grin fills his face. "I really am. You're probably gonna have to work extra hard to appreciate me."

"That shouldn't be a problem." We laugh, and he strolls out of the room.

I'm chuckling to myself when my eyes zero in on the bottle of Hemply Simple vitamins on my desk. Marcus keeps talking about the money they're paying us for this sponsorship. We aren't exactly hurting when it comes to our finances, but of course, he can't help but focus on the dollar signs. If they've offered a large amount, it almost makes me wonder why. Have they been having trouble finding sponsors?

I scoop up the jar and spin it around to read the ingredients. There are a bunch of common vitamins listed on the label like Vitamin B-12, D, and B-6. There's also potassium, zinc, and calcium, along with a few other large words I've seen before but could never pronounce. But it's what I find at the bottom that makes my breath catch in my throat. Underneath all the different vitamins and their percentages are the words, *and various other important nutrients*. It's not in bold print; in fact, it would be very easy to miss if I wasn't scouring the label.

I wonder what *various other important nutrients* they've included in these. That wording is vague, and it seems intentional.

I type *Hemply Simple vitamins* into Google and shake my

head. I can't believe I haven't already done this. This is why I need to be more involved. I used to research all these companies before ever replying to a sponsorship request, and I assumed that Marcus was, too—but I'm starting to have my doubts. Maybe that's not fair, but I see how quick he is with accepting proposals. I can't be mad at him, though. It's not his fault. I was too overwhelmed so I tossed this part in his lap without so much as an explanation. He's doing the best he can, but for him, it's more about the bottom line. If they offer the right amount, he says yes on the spot.

My search results bring up a link to the company's main website, but it's what I see listed above that piques my interest. It's a sponsored link for another multivitamin that's written like an article. The heading reads, *Are some multivitamins dangerous?* It's intended as clickbait, and it works.

One click brings up a tabloid-style article written by someone calling himself "Dr. Jeff." It's a red flag. It's hard to take a person seriously when they pair the prefix Dr. with their first name unless they're a pediatrician. Still, I continue on to the article. Despite it being an obvious ad, there's enough information peppered in to raise concern about the vitamins I've been blindly taking.

Turns out, vitamins don't need FDA approval. I'm not sure how I made it to twenty-seven years without knowing that, but it's shocking. Also, it seems the "right" concoction of vitamins can actually cause an altered state of reality. It doesn't list out the specifics, but it's enough just knowing it's possible. Suppose these "various other important nutrients" Hemply Simple has in their vitamins are the same concoction this article talks about. They could be mixing inside of me, messing with my mind and causing me to hallucinate.

My stomach drops and my palms begin to sweat. Not long after I started taking these, things started to shift. I thought my nana was humming in my pantry. I smack my forehead with a moist hand. I can't believe it hadn't occurred to me before. Here I was thinking I was losing my mind, but could it be these vitamins that were causing my hallucinations?

I back click on the browser and find the link to Hemply Simple's website. Once it loads, I'm overwhelmed by the amount of stock photos covering the page. There are more images than words and I even recognize a few of these pictures. I saw them on a popular site where I've purchased graphics in the past to use in my videos. These people may look happy, but their smiles are manufactured and have nothing to do with the vitamins.

After more sifting, it appears the vitamins on my desk are the only ones they make. There's one photo that could actually be considered factual and that's a still shot of the vitamin bottle with a few of the gelatinous discs spilling out around it. The only other thing I notice is the complete lack of supporting evidence. There are no studies mentioned. No impressive figures. No graphs. Just a repeat of the same list of ingredients I read off of the label. But as I lean in close, I notice the phrase "various other important nutrients," seems to be missing.

I eye the bottle on my desk with suspicion. These repulsive sour gummies haven't done anything for me besides force me to think about Walker every morning. It was bad enough before he died, but now that he's gone and especially after that night with Marcus, he's the last person I want to think about it. It's time for me to be done with these. I pitch the bottle across the room, and it rails against the wall with a *crack*. The lid pops off, and little blue gummy discs fly across the room, speckling the carpet.

I groan. It felt satisfying to throw the jar, but now I

have to clean all these up before Clyde eats them. I'm about to crouch onto the floor when I have an idea.

The only other option on the website, aside from the page I'm currently viewing, is a *contact us* section. I click on it and fire off a question about the mystery ingredients listed on their bottle. I'm about to type my main email address in the box when I think better of it. When my channel grew enough that I got recognized a few times, I realized it might be useful to create a separate email account as a way to hold on to some anonymity. I type in Bulldog-Mom0494@gmail.com, hit submit, and close my laptop.

THE RUMBLE of thunder is getting closer. I can't stay huddled under this tree. I need to get back to the car, but I don't remember where I parked. Marcus and I were just at the grocery store, but the parking lot looks different. I wonder if they rearranged the spaces like they rearranged the aisles.

Rising to my feet, I shake my head and blink a few times. There's a blue car parked a few feet in front of me, and I swear it wasn't there a second ago. I can't worry about it now, though. Not with the way those dark clouds are beginning to congregate above me.

Here comes the wind. It whips around me like I'm its center point and its sole purpose is to orbit my body. It smells like the moment after a summer rain, when the air is pungent and sweet as the water starts to evaporate on the warm concrete. "Careful, April," a deep voice calls out.

My eyes ping pong around the lot before finally fixating on the broad figure in front of me. His hands are stuffed into the pockets of his jeans and he's leaning back against the blue car like he's waiting for someone. His pale hair remains still while mine stands on end, repeatedly smacking me in the face. I grab at it, twisting the strands and holding them at the nape of my neck. "Walker?"

He answers with a sad grin. If he senses the storm around us, he doesn't let on. Not even when the funnel cloud spirals toward the earth and begins ripping apart the ground behind him.

The asphalt quakes beneath my feet, making it difficult to stand. I back up until my heels hit the base of the tree. Moving to the side, I wrap my arms and legs around the trunk. It's a foolish move, but I'm at a loss.

Walker shakes his head and tsks at me. The tornado seems to have its sights set on him. It stalks toward him, tossing cars and chunks of blacktop aside like they're weightless.

"Walker," I scream. "Behind you!"

He doesn't move. The tornado is only a few feet away now. I don't understand how he remains so unaffected.

It reaches the blue car and rips the side-view mirror clean off. It sails through the air. I never see it land. The car is next. It's lifted straight up, and yet, Walker barely reacts—only shifting his body at the last second.

"Are you crazy? Look out!"

He laughs. It's deep and raspy, and I can feel it more than I can hear it. "It's you who needs to look out, April. Pay attention. Now is not the time to let your guard down," he warns. The funnel envelops him, surrounding his body in thick, black nothingness. I scream his name, but no sound comes.

The dark spiral barrels toward me at a speed my brain can't comprehend. It tugs at my hands, prying my fingers off the tree one by one. I turn my face into the bark and close my eyes, bracing for the end.

I sit up like I'm spring-loaded. Sweat pools at my temples as my eyes dash around the darkened room. Beside me, Marcus and Clyde share a pillow, snoring together in a tuneless harmony. My hand rests over my pounding heart, and I suck in a ragged breath.

I've had a bit of a reprieve from these nightmares, but they sure came back with a vengeance. That one was far too violent and real for my liking. I'm also used to being the only person in them, but these last two times I haven't, and it isn't lost on me that the people who've joined me are dead.

Nana seemed to give me a pep talk of sorts. She wanted me to remember that I'm strong—although most days, I feel anything but.

I didn't get the same vibe from Walker. His was more of a warning. Phrases like "look out," "pay attention," and "don't let your guard down," are far more ominous than "you are strong."

But look out for whom? Pay attention to what? I'm sitting here trying to control my panting and feeling more confused than enlightened.

I look to the ceiling, silently cursing Walker. He keeps showing up—in conversations, in song lyrics, in hallucinations, and now in dreams. If he has something to tell me, he needs to be more clear.

As I sit here pondering the hidden messages in my dreams, daylight is starting to break. The darkness in the room has begun to fade as the light outside overtakes the last remnants of night. I'm wide awake at this point, so I might as well get some work done.

I rise out of bed, careful not to disturb Marcus and Clyde, although a high school marching band could probably parade through the room and they still wouldn't stir. I look down at them, feeling a stab of bitterness in my gut. I can't remember the last time I slept like that—blissfully unconcerned about anything. I'm not sure I've ever had that luxury.

My visit to the bathroom is punctuated by a hasty need to get in and get out. I keep my glances at the mirror to a minimum, brushing my teeth as though someone pressed my fast-forward button. So far, this is the only mirror in the house where I've had any incidents, and I hope it stays that way. I've been using the lighted magnifying mirror in my office to style my hair and apply makeup. The April in that reflection does what she's supposed to do.

In the kitchen, I make a quick cup of coffee and bring it with me as I stroll into my office, still rubbing the sleep from my eyes. I'd be surprised if I slept more than eight hours total over the last few days. Something has to give.

On the way to my desk, I step on something gelatinous. I gag as my mind begins to catalog all the possible things Clyde could have left for me to step on. Whatever this is, it's stuck fast. Hobbling toward my chair, I plop into the soft leather and rest my ankle on my knee. Pasted to the sole of my foot is a gummy vitamin I must have missed during my clean up last night. I peel it off and stick it to my desktop. It reminds me … I wonder if the people at Hemply Simple replied to my email.

Rolling myself forward, I lift open my laptop, tapping my fingers on either side of the trackpad as it boots up. It may just be my anxiety talking, but this computer seems way slower than normal. This spinning disc is enough to make me want to rip my hair out.

The screen finally transitions to my desktop, and I'm moving at warp speed as I open my secondary email. Thirty-nine unread messages taunt me, forcing me to navigate through a sea of newsletters, coupon codes, and advertisements. Smack dab in the middle is an email from Hemply Simple with the subject line *re: Ingredients*.

With a shaky hand, I move the cursor to hover over the email and press down on the pad. The opening is a copy of my question to them. *I was just reading over the list of ingredients in your vitamins and was wondering if you could elaborate on what you mean by 'various other important nutrients?'* By design, I kept it short and to the point. I didn't sign it or elaborate any further, fearing if I did, they might go down a different road and avoid my question altogether.

Their answer is buried in a bunch of code. They should have their IT department check over this mail form. Something is clearly out of whack. It takes me a moment to find what I'm looking for, but when I do, my mouth hangs open, and my eyes flare.

Good evening, April! It's so great to hear from you. Listen, we understand you're a little skeptical about our vitamins, but we can assure you, we only use the highest quality ingredients. Each of our little gummies is chock-full of superior vitamins and minerals designed to make you the very best version of yourself. We here at Hemply Simple are anxiously awaiting your video! We are excited for your subscribers to hear all about our vitamins. Thank you for reaching out to us and please let us know if you have any other questions!

It's signed *the team at Hemply Simple*, but it could be signed *Cookie Monster*, for all I care. How the fuck did they know it was me?

I used an anonymous email account, and even if it could be traced back to me somehow, why would anyone take the time to do that? I didn't accuse them of anything or attack them in any way. I simply asked a question. A question they didn't even answer. This email reads like an advertisement. It's filled with flowery, empty words.

Maybe it was the question I asked that had them on edge. It must be. Why else would they work so hard to figure out who sent the email?

Unless ...

My gaze snaps to the open door.

Unless they were tipped off.

IT'S AN ODD FEELING, being suspicious of your husband. Aside from the cigarettes, it's not a feeling I'm used to. Well, there was that one time when I suspected he was planning a surprise party for my twenty-fifth birthday. Turned out I was right to be leery of him. A flash of a smile crosses my face, but it immediately turns sour.

I don't know if Marcus contacted the vitamin people, but the timing makes sense. Last night, we had that conversation about me not wanting to take them and his reaction wasn't great. Maybe after we talked, he sent Hemply Simple an email letting them know how I was feeling, and then I sent mine about the mystery ingredients. Even though I was incognito, they may have been anticipating it and put two and two together. Although, I still don't understand how or why.

This entire scenario sounds both possible and highly unlikely—story of my life. Right now, I'm only certain of one thing, I will *not* be taking any more vitamins.

I haven't shared my thoughts with Marcus because they're completely irrational. He woke up an hour or so after me. We ate breakfast in amicable silence, each of us taking turns with brief comments on our plans for the day. His revolves around a gaming tournament—big surprise there. And mine will be wrapped up in filming and editing, as per usual. When we finished eating, he asked if I took my vitamin, and I answered with a simple "no." He frowned and told me we could talk about it later. I don't know when that will be, but I need to stand firm and let him know I will not be changing my mind.

We both retreated to our rooms, where we've been ever since. It's been a few hours since I've seen him, but despite our closed doors, I can still hear him. "Take that, you little bitch! Bruh, did you see that? These little fuckers can't keep up with me!"

I sigh and lay my head in my arms. Am I really doubting him? This is Marcus we're talking about. I think about how he behaved in the car with me the other day. So patient. So considerate. Like I'm the most important person in the world to him. And I've never doubted that for a second, so why am I doubting it now? He's the most loyal person I know. I can't imagine not being able to trust him.

But then I remember the cigarettes in his truck. I hold my head in my hands and sigh. Even if he did contact the vitamin company, he wouldn't have done it with bad intentions. He'd probably just want to give them a heads-up that I may not move forward with the sponsorship.

The same can't be said for Hemply Simple. I don't trust them at all.

How the hell did they know it was me who sent that email? I drum my fingers on my desk. Maybe they traced my IP address. I'm not very tech-savvy, but I do know that your IP address is unique to your location. Even though I used an anonymous account, I did send it from home, and Marcus has been corresponding with them as well, so it probably wouldn't take much sleuthing to figure out they both came from the same IP. I hang my head in my hands. Paranoia has laced my every thought to the point where I'm not sure what's real and what isn't.

I still think their vitamins could be to blame for my recent hallucinations. I'm going to do a little experiment — if I stop taking these and the "incidents" also stop, then I'll know what's causing them. I drum my fingers on my desk, realizing I feel hopeful for the first time in a long while.

IT'S BEEN one week without any strange occurrences. No rogue reflections in mirrors, no visions of dead people, and no tornado dreams. And I haven't had a single vitamin.

Hemply Simple, my ass. There's nothing simple about those vulgar little gummies. And there's no way I'm telling my subscribers to try them.

Marcus stopped asking me if I was taking them after I told him no and we never did "talk about it later" like he said we would. I had been hoping to avoid that discussion until after completing my experiment, but now that I know the effect they've had on me, I can't stay silent.

He's been in his game room all day. I hate going in there, but it's looking like it may be the only way I'll ever be able to talk to him. I groan as I turn the knob.

With a shove, the door flies open, and Marcus startles. His headset is already around his neck, and his hands are pressed to the armrests on his chair, poised to get up. The game's start screen is up on the monitor. "Damn, you scared the shit out of me." He puffs.

"Sorry." I shrug. "I've been waiting for you to come out and figured it wasn't going to happen."

He chuckles. "One more second and you'd have seen me. I was just gonna go grab some food."

"Perfect timing, then." I beam.

"Looks that way. Listen, come out to the kitchen with me, okay? I'm starving."

I nod and stroll out into the hallway. He moves fast in the kitchen—swiping bread from the counter and slapping lunch meat and cheese on it like he's being timed. The second the other slice of bread hits the sandwich, he scoops it up and presses it into his mouth, taking a quarter of it in one bite.

"Jeez. You weren't kidding."

"Mope," he mumbles between mouthfuls.

I shake my head. A soft giggle escapes my lips, and the last of the remaining apprehension leaves my body. I hadn't realized how nervous I'd been to talk to him about this. I just know how excited he was about the sponsorship since they promised a high payout, but he cares more about me than money. Once he hears the whole story, he'll be as done with Hemply Simple as I am.

He finishes his sandwich in under five bites. "So," he says as he wipes his mouth with the back of his hand, "what'd you want to talk to me about?" He leans back against the kitchen island, letting his elbows rest on the counter. One ankle crosses over the other, and he looks at me with a lopsided grin. The same look he gave me when I walked down the aisle toward him on our wedding day.

I give him an easy smile. "So these vitamin people …"

"Hemply Simple?"

I nod. "Yep, those people. What do you know about them?"

He scratches under his ear and presses his lips together. "Just that they make vitamins, and they are *very* generous if you're willing to talk about those vitamins." His eyebrows dance, and he claps his hands, rubbing them together.

"Aha. So it *is* about the money, huh?" I lower my chin.

"Well, I mean, sure, but that's not all." He sucks in his cheeks. "They told me their vitamins help people."

The hair on my arms stands on end. "Help how?"

"I don't know. They just help. Like, with your hair and skin and also your mood." His hands gesticulate wildly as he talks.

"My mood, huh? And how'd they say it would help that?" I tilt my head, studying him as if he were a retired CIA agent ready to spill all his secrets.

He averts his eyes to the floor. "Baby, you know you've been having a tough time."

I cross my arms and then uncross them. "I do."

"Well, I guess I just thought maybe you'd take these vitamins and, you'd, I don't know, feel better."

My expression softens. "Yeah, but Marcus, I don't think this problem is something vitamins can fix."

He nods, puffing out his cheeks. "I know, but it couldn't hurt, right?"

"Or it could."

He cocks his head. "What do you mean? Did something happen?"

I blow out a breath. "You could say that. You could also say that once I stopped taking those vitamins, nothing happened."

"I don't understand. So, are you saying the vitamins had no effect on you or … what?"

I cross the room, standing toe to toe with him. Placing my hands on either side of his face, I force his eyes on mine. "Since I started taking those gummies, weird things have happened."

He leans in. "Weird how?"

"I don't really want to get into all of that except to say that I thought I might be going crazy. Then I stopped taking them a week ago—"

"Wait, I know you told me you were thinking about not taking them anymore, but I guess I had hoped you'd give them another try. But you haven't, huh?" He pulls his head back, and my hands fall away.

I shake my head. "No, I haven't."

"But, April, how can they help you if you don't take them?"

"Are you even listening?" I huff. "*Not* taking them is helping me."

He rubs at his mouth, looking around the room. "I just don't get how vitamins could make you feel crazy."

My eyebrows scrunch together. "But yet you *do* understand how they could help my mood? Think about that for a second."

He dips his head slowly. "Good point."

"So you're not mad at me?"

His body grows still. "Mad at you? Why would I be mad?"

"Well, I mean, just last week you were upset when I told you I thought I might be done taking them."

"Yeah, but only because I thought they were helping. You never told me about any of this." He shifts his weight to his right leg and narrows his eyes.

"I know, I know, but hey, I'm telling you now, right?" I raise my eyebrows and smile.

He snickers, throwing an arm over my shoulder. "Yeah, you're telling me now."

"So, what do we do about the sponsorship?" I grit my teeth and wrinkle my nose.

He shrugs. "Not much. I never took any payment from them, and they only wanted a review if it was positive. I'll shoot them an email later and tell them it's not gonna work out. And, baby," his eyes tick back and forth over mine, "I'm so sorry."

"Why are you sorry?"

"I just, man, I gave you something to help your mood, and it ended up hurting you instead of helping. If anything ever happened to you, I'd—"

"Shh." I press a finger to his lips. "Don't go there. Don't even think it. You are *nothing* like your father, do you hear me? You were only trying to help and besides, I was in control of what I put in my body."

"Yeah, but I didn't give you the whole story." He casts his gaze to the floor.

I sigh. "No, you didn't, but Marcus, your intentions were good. Your father's were not. There's a huge difference."

His mouth presses into a thin line and he nods. "Okay." He doesn't sound totally convinced, but he'll get there.

My body sags against his, and I let out a long exhale. "Not gonna lie—I feel like a huge weight is off my shoulders." As soon as the words leave my mouth, I hear "American Pie" blaring from my phone in the other room. My mom has incredible timing.

"Looks like you spoke too soon." Marcus chuckles. I give him a playful punch in the abdomen, and he only laughs harder.

"APRIL? YOU SOUND UPSET. WHAT HAPPENED?"

I lift my eyes to the ceiling. She called me. That's what happened. And her phone calls always seem to raise my blood pressure, but I can't tell her that. "Nothing, Mom. I was just in the kitchen with Marcus."

"You weren't making dinner, were you?"

I pull my phone away from my ear to glance at the

clock. "It's only two thirty. Why would I be making dinner this early?"

"I don't know what goes on over there." She quips. "That man probably feeds you cereal for all three meals."

"Mom," I warn.

"Fine, fine. I didn't call to fight."

"Then, why did you call?" My voice still has an edge to it. I can't help it. She never misses an opportunity to put Marcus down, and I'm running out of patience.

She clucks her tongue. "April, is that any way to talk to your mother?"

It is if my mother is her. "All right. To what do I owe the honor of this phone call?"

"Oh, for Christ's sake." She groans. "I made too many meatballs again."

"You always make enough for a small country," my dad yells in the background, making me grin.

"You just keep watching your stories while I talk to our daughter." Her voice is muffled like she covered the mouthpiece with her hand, and when she speaks again, it's clear. "So how about you and that husband of yours come over here and help us eat these?"

"Um," I stammer, looking around the room. My eyes land on Clyde slumbering away on his bed. "You know, actually Clyde hasn't been feeling well today." His ears perk up at the sound of his name. Thankfully, we're not on Face-Time, so she can't see that he's completely fine.

"Oh no, that poor boy." She's always had a soft spot for Clyde. "You shouldn't leave him if he's sick."

"Yeah, we really shouldn't—"

"So it's settled then," she says.

My face pinches. "What's settled?"

"We're coming over to your house for dinner. Have some water boiling for the pasta. We'll be there at five."

I open my mouth to protest, but the line goes dead.
Shit.

THERE IS no frenzy like the mad rush of cleaning that happens before your parents come to visit. After I got off the phone with my mom, I rushed out to tell Marcus the bad news. He took it about as well as I did, maybe worse. He flailed his leg, and the toe of his shoe caught on the lip of the trashcan, scattering it and its contents across the floor. It's been chaos ever since.

It's a little after four thirty, and we're in the home stretch now. I fill a pot of water and set it on the stove. I'll turn on the heat in a few minutes. My mom will expect a rapid boil when she walks in.

Marcus is finishing up setting the table. I hear him muttering under his breath while he slams the silverware against the napkins at each place setting. "You know," he says, storming back into the kitchen, "while I appreciate that your parents are both well and in our lives, Grace is really tough to take in any dose."

"I know." I sigh. "But she means well."

"Maybe, but so what if she does? It isn't enough just to mean well when everything she says feels like an attack."

He's right—it's a moot point if we need the reminder. We should just be able to tell her heart is in the right place by her actions alone. Instead, we need to placate ourselves with a different narrative to make the pill that is my mother easier to swallow.

The water has started to boil, and right on cue, the doorbell rings. I glide up to the door and take a big cleansing breath, steeling my emotions before Hurricane Grace blows through the house. "Time to get this over with," I mumble as I tug open the door.

"Hi, Mama! Hi, Dad," I singsong.

Mom bursts in first, throwing her arms around my neck. "Hi-ya, honey. Oh, boy, you are just skin and bones. Mm, mm. This will not do," she tsks.

I catch my dad's eye as he comes up behind her, his arms laden with bags of food. We share a look. One we've perfected over the years. "Hey, sweets." He gives me a peck on the cheek and follows my mom into the kitchen.

She gets to work, bustling around the room like it's her house, not mine. It's not such a bad thing that she's so comfortable here, and it isn't like I've given her much choice in the matter. If they want to see me, they have to come here, and we've shared many dinners this same way over these past several months.

"Marcus?"

My husband looks visibly shaken at the mention of his name, but he stills his features. "What can I do for you, Grace?" he asks with a forced smile.

"Hand me that pepper mill, will you?"

He eyes the wooden grinder sitting on the counter right next to the stove. It's within reach of my mom, and yet for Marcus, it's across the room. This is another one of her tests.

I've got to hand it to Marcus, though. He doesn't question her motives. He just strolls over, scoops up the pepper mill, and hands it to her.

"Thank you, dear." She pats his cheek. He grins,

accepting the win, but he knows not to let his guard down. "Oh, and Marcus?" *Here it comes …* "I saw you set the table, but you used those little plates. Last I checked, we aren't children. Swap those out with proper plates, why don't you?"

He grits his teeth. "Sure thing, Grace."

The rest of her dinner prep goes by without issue, and soon we're all seated at the table ready to eat. My mom insists we pray first. "I know this household has some heathen tendencies, but you were raised with God, April. As long as I'm around, we will thank him before every meal."

Marcus shoots a side-eyed glare at me, but all I can do is shrug. I know he'd like me to stand up to her, and sometimes I do, but you've got to pick your battles. And this isn't the hill I want to die on.

We clasp hands, and Mom says a few familiar words about "thy bounty." She finishes it off with a booming, "Amen," and that's the green light. Dad digs in first, plopping three meatballs onto his plate, followed by a generous helping of pasta. We all take turns filling our plates, and then it's blissful silence as we enjoy our food. My mom may be difficult to deal with at times, but she's a hell of a cook, and she knows it.

"Okay, you two, give us the scoop."

I tilt my head, regarding my father. "What do you mean, Dad?"

"Oh, you know," he says, snapping his fingers. "Tell us what's new? What's shakin', Kevin Bacon? What's up, dawg?"

Laughter bubbles out of me. Marcus snorts and then immediately falls into a coughing fit. My mom doesn't laugh, but she doesn't yell, either. In fact, with the way she has her hand pressed to her mouth, it's as if she's trying to suppress a giggle. Leave it to my father to defuse the situation with humor.

I wink at him and mouth, "Thanks."

He nods and winks back.

And that's where it should've ended. Things were light-hearted and everyone was smiling. But nope. Marcus had to go ahead and toss an emotional grenade on the table.

"Oh, hey, Grace? Jeff? Did April tell you about her big breakthrough?" He grins and raises his eyebrows at me.

I widen my eyes, wishing I had telekinetic powers right about now. What is he doing?

"Breakthrough? April, you didn't say anything to me about a breakthrough." My mother narrows her eyes, making me feel like I'm twelve instead of twenty-seven.

I wave my hand. "It's nothing, really."

"Nothing, huh? Why don't you let me be the judge of that. Marcus?" She angles her body to face my husband. "Since my daughter refuses to tell us. Why don't you?"

"Um," he mutters as he dips his chin and scratches his face. I glare at him, but he won't look me in the eye. *It's too late now, buddy. You got us into this.* "Well, I don't want to step on April's toes—"

"Marcus." My mother's voice is a warning.

He swallows hard. "She and I went for a little drive the other day, that's all."

My mom's palms meet the table with a *smack*. "That's all?" She turns to me. "April, is this true?"

I nod, keeping my eyes on my plate.

"Well, then, why are we here?" She lifts her arms, shaking her hands.

"What do you mean, why are you here?" I ask.

"If you're going places now, you could've come to our house for dinner."

I shake my head. "Mom, remember? Clyde isn't feeling well."

"Wait, my boy is sick?"

Oh, my God, Marcus …

"Yes, he's been acting strange all day. I told you that earlier," I say through clenched teeth.

He nods, catching on, but it doesn't matter. My mom never misses a thing. This new development leads to a soliloquy about the importance of visiting your parents. My dad tries to interject, and it escalates into an argument.

Marcus looks up at me and mouths, "I'm sorry."

I miss Nana every single day, but even more in moments like this one. I can almost picture her sitting at the head of the table. She'd scold my mom in a tone that would get everyone's attention, though she'd never have to raise her voice. And the best part was, she'd not only calm the waters; she'd also make sure my mom knew where she went wrong. It was never enough just to change the subject. If only I could conjure her right now.

I scoot back in my chair. "I'm just gonna run to the bathroom real quick." My parents barely look up, too engrossed in their dispute. My husband watches me, a solemn look on his face.

I don't run out of the room, but as soon as I'm out of view, I practically sprint to our bedroom and into the bathroom. I shut the door, careful not to let my emotions slam it. Gripping the counter, I hunch over, taking huge gulps of air.

This is exactly why I didn't tell my mom. I knew she'd overreact and assume I was "cured." She has very little tolerance for my way of living.

I really don't like being a topic of discussion, but I need to get myself under control and head back out there.

Breathe in. Breathe out. I repeat the process over and over until I no longer need the reminder.

I stand up straight.

I may as well use the facilities while I'm in here. As I'm sudsing up my hands in the sink, the smell of vanilla fills my nose. Things weren't always so strained between my mom and me. When I was little, we used to bake cookies together. She let me crack the eggs and taught me the importance of reading a recipe first before starting. "That way you know the order of things," she'd say. I smile and feel a lone tear trickle down my face. I glance up at the mirror, making sure my mascara is still in place. When I step back, my reflection appears to step forward.

I close my eyes and shake my head. *No. Not this again. It's not real.* But when I look up, the girl in the mirror cocks her head, studying me with a wry grin on her face. I rub at my lips and find them set in a grim line—an expression she doesn't mirror.

"What's going on?" I ask the question out loud, never expecting an answer, so when it comes, I jump.

"You tell me," she says. Her voice is mine, but it's also not. It's as if I can hear her in my mind.

I grab the sides of my head and pinch my eyes shut. This isn't happening.

"Yes, it is," she whispers, throwing her head back as she laughs.

My hands clench and unclench at my sides, and my body begins to shake—small tremors starting at my toes and buzzing up through the top of my head. "Stop!" I slam my palm into her face. The mirror splinters into a fractured web beneath my hand. I see myself in fragments, split apart by the cracks in the glass.

She's gone. My shoulders sag as I let out a breath.

A drop of blood trails down my arm. I pull it back and

examine my hand. There's a small gash on my palm and a few tiny cuts on my fingers. Nothing that requires stitches.

"April?" I jolt from the frantic knocking on the door.

I tug on the knob and find Marcus's fist poised, ready to knock again. My parents stand close behind him. "We heard you scream and something break. Are you okay?" He looks me up and down. The veins in his neck jut out from under his skin.

"I'm okay," I say, wiping at my brow.

His eyes widen as they scan my face. "You're bleeding! What happened?"

I feel the trail of wetness on my forehead and silently curse myself. "It's nothing. Just a few nicks and scratches. I'll be fine." I don't believe a word I'm saying. My body is jittery and my breathing is shallow. I thought all of this was behind me.

Marcus grabs my hand, flipping it over to look at my palm. He eyes me warily like there are so many problems and he doesn't know which one to tackle first. "Come on. Let's get you cleaned up."

"April," my mom calls from the hall. "What did you cut yourself on?" She steps into the room. Despite her small stature, the room suddenly feels stifling. I suck in a breath, but before I can answer, she spies the broken glass. "Oh, my God! Did you punch the mirror?" When she looks back at me, there's something new behind her eyes. Fear. I've never seen her afraid before. I honestly figured she was immune to the emotion. But as she takes a step back and rubs at her temple, I can see how deeply this is affecting her. Her mouth rounds in an *O*.

I shake my head, struggling to get my words out fast enough. "No, no, of course not," I lie. I mean, technically, I didn't punch it, but I don't think there's much difference between palming and punching in this instance. "I just, uh, tripped."

A deep crease forms on her forehead. "You tripped? On what?"

I blink several times, trying to put together my story. "On this rug," I say, kicking the small, braided carpet beneath my feet. "I put my hand out to stop myself, on instinct, and, well, you get the picture." I half shrug.

"This is too much," she whispers, followed by a few mumbled words that I can't understand.

I open my mouth to ask her what she's saying, but my attention is redirected when Marcus brings my hand under cold running water. The sensation is both soothing and irritating. Bursts of pain, like tiny zings of electricity, pulsate under my skin. It makes me want to shove my hand farther under the water, while at the same time, pull it away. Marcus's hand encircles my wrist, holding the affected area under the stream. Clear water flows from the tap and collides with the deep red blood on my palm. As it runs off my hand, it pools in the sink, where the two mix to form a pink tinged liquid. I watch as it spirals down the drain and imagine it taking the last of my sanity along with it.

MY PARENTS DIDN'T WANT to leave after my little incident. My mom, especially, kept fretting about my hand, worrying that it should be checked out by a doctor. Between Marcus, my dad, and me, we finally managed to persuade her to let it go. But I saw the way she was acting when they left. Her shoulders were curled forward, and her chest was caved in. She dragged her feet toward the door, all the while making quiet excuses not to leave, asking if she could help me clean the kitchen, and even offering to take Clyde outside for a walk. She'll be calling me tomorrow, for sure.

I managed to wash my face with one hand tonight. The broken mirror was a spiderweb of cracks that I avoided completely. It was harder than I thought. You do something every day, and you just assume you'll be able to carry out the motions without watching yourself, but you'd be surprised.

Tossing the throw pillows aside, I grip the comforter and peel it back. Marcus trudges over to the other side and wordlessly turns it down. I watch his face, how the muscles in his jaw tic and the vein in his temple seems to pulsate. We've barely spoken since he bandaged up my hand. He told me to go get ready for bed while he cleaned up the kitchen and dining room, and he mumbled "sorry" when he accidentally walked in front of me when we were both heading for the dresser. Other than that, he's been silent— and I guess, so have I.

"Penny for your thoughts?"

He glances up at me, a slack expression on his face. "Huh?"

I swallow and scratch at my arm. "It's just a thing my nana used to say when she wanted to know what I was thinking."

"Oh." He nods, looking back down at the bedding.

I pause for a moment, but when he doesn't answer, I prod him. "So, what are you?"

His eyes snap to mine.

"Thinking, that is."

He shrugs. "Nothing. Just tired, that's all."

"Yeah, me too." Looks like we won't be talking tonight, but maybe that's for the best. We'll both feel better after a good night of sleep.

We climb into bed, each leaning over to turn off our respective lamps. The room is pitch-black, and it takes me a moment to adjust to the darkness. The bed dips as Clyde slowly climbs up. He lies in his spot at the foot at the bed, and within seconds, his deep breathing morphs into a low snore.

I lie on my back, staring up at the slow-moving blades on the ceiling fan. Now that my eyes have become accustomed to the room, I can see a bit of moonlight trickling in through the blinds. The fan blades catch it and slice it in half. Over and over, the beam is fragmented, just like the broken mirror.

"Baby," Marcus whispers.

"Yeah?"

"Before we heard the glass breaking, you screamed, 'Stop.' Why'd you say that?"

I swallow hard. I was screaming at the impostor in the mirror, but how can I say that to Marcus? "Did I say that?" I ask, stalling until I can come up with an excuse.

"You did."

"Huh, well, it all happened pretty fast, but I'm guessing I was yelling 'stop' because that's what I was trying to do. Stop myself from falling. You see how well that turned out." I chuckle, despite the growing apprehension in the pit of my stomach.

"Yeah, maybe that was it." His voice has a funny lilt. He clears his throat like that might help, but we both know it won't. He leans over, pressing a kiss to my temple. "Get some sleep, okay?"

He rolls onto his side, and I roll onto mine. Our backs face each other while a forest of unsaid words rests between us. I wish I could tell him all that's happened. He seems to know there's more I'm not saying, but if I say it out loud, it'll make it too real. I don't want my problems to become Marcus's. That may seem unfair. He'd want to know everything, but once it's out there, I can't take it back. He's already been through all of this. Sure, it was in a totally different capacity, but I don't think it matters. And I'm not ready to find out. For now, it's just this thing that I'm experiencing and doing my best to manage. I think of the splintered mirror in the bathroom and shiver. Okay, maybe I could've managed that better.

After several minutes, his breathing evens out. But not mine. It becomes more erratic as my eyes roam the room, imagining something skulking in the shadows. Hours later, exhaustion finally wins out, and I close my eyes with visions of leering dark figures hovering over me.

MY EYES slowly peel open and glide around the room. From the way the light is hitting the bed, I can tell I've slept later than normal. I reach my arms above my head and stretch out my body like a starfish.

The covers on Marcus's side are thrown back, revealing his empty spot. I place a hand where he slept, but it feels cool. He's clearly been awake for a while.

I sit up, mindful of my head, which feels like it weighs as much as Clyde. It's an odd feeling, waking up from a sound sleep. I feel disoriented, like I'm rousing after anesthesia.

Pulling back the comforter, I swing my legs around the side of the bed. My feet search out my sherpa-lined slippers. I let out an "ahhh" when I find them, reveling in the comfort of the memory foam inserts. Lifting my toes, I spy the pale pink microsuede.

These slippers were a Christmas gift from Marcus last year. When I opened them, I fell into a fit of hysterical laughter. Marcus thought I didn't like them, at first. It took me a bit to regain my composure, but once I did, I explained that I loved them. It was just the idea that *he* bought me slippers; it seemed like such an adult gift coming from the guy who once gave me a Philadelphia Eagles T-shirt—not because I'm a football fan, but because he is. When I asked him why he gave me slippers, he just shrugged and said, "Your feet are always cold."

He's not wrong, and these slippers definitely help, but what struck me most about his reason was that it proved he was paying attention. It wasn't necessarily a surprise; it was more of a reminder. Marcus is the most dependable person I know, even if he is a giant kid most of the time. He's perpetually living in a virtual gaming world where there are always hard battles to be fought—battles he sometimes wins and sometimes loses. But really, when you think about it, life outside of his game room isn't much different. Except, the battles out here are harder to identify and even harder to win.

Marcus knows something is up with me. I can't pretend that he doesn't. His behavior is one thing, but just like those slippers he knew I needed, he's always watching and listening.

I either need to get a handle on this madness, or I need to ask for help. I don't want to tell him any of this, but not for the obvious reason. Sure, he will probably think I'm losing it and he'll want me to call Dr. Lesser or worse—check myself into a facility for a while. And even though both options terrify me, I think I could handle it. It's the look I'll see on his face that I can't handle. It's one I know too well and one I hoped to never see again.

Everyone wears defeat a little differently. Some carry it on their shoulders. Others bear it in the curve of their spine. For Marcus, it settles in his eyes, and when he's really in it, they seem to sink back into his skull. I saw it that day he climbed in through my window, telling me horrible tales of his father drugging his mother and walking out on their family.

There's a light that lives deep in his irises, and it's one I have the power to extinguish with all my confessions. Sometimes these things aren't permanent. His light dimmed after his father left and nearly went out entirely when his mom died, but little by little, over time, it came back. You can recover from despair and the effects will mostly go away. Mostly, but never completely. And if I tell him these things. If I say that I'm seeing and hearing strange phenomena, the valley of creases on his forehead will deepen with worry, and many will never iron out. Marcus is resilient, but he isn't impervious to the scars that come from trauma. Even if this situation improves, the evidence of what I put him through will live on forever in those wrinkles, and I'll be reminded of it every time I look at him. He's been through so much—too much. There has to be a limit to how much a person can take. I don't want to be the one that finally breaks him.

"You're up." Marcus breezes into the room clutching a large rectangle in his hands.

"I am. Whatcha got there?" I ask, squinting up at him.

He turns the object around, revealing a dark wooden framed mirror. I catch a glimpse of myself and startle, quickly looking away. Marcus's eyes narrow. "Sorry," I say with a sheepish grin. "I haven't brushed through this mane yet." I run a hand through my stringy hair. His gaze softens, but there's still a trace of doubt in his expression. I have my work cut out for me.

"Your dad found this mirror in the attic, so I ran over and picked it up. Thought I'd swap it out for the broken one."

I nod, letting his words sink in. It's clear how my mom feels about my husband, but my dad is much more reasonable. He always calls himself "Switzerland," and it fits. He sees both sides of every coin. Normally, I wouldn't be alarmed to know that Marcus spoke to him, but after what happened last night, I have concerns. I find it hard to believe their conversation started and ended with the replacement mirror. A lump forms deep in my throat at the thought of the two most important men in my life talking about me. It would be one thing if their conversations were limited to bonding over shared irritation at my eccentricities. But after I put my hand through a mirror, I can't imagine they chose to talk about "silly April." No. If my name came up, I'm sure they discussed how worried they are about me. Great.

I look at Marcus, avoiding his eyes. "Well, I'll let you get to it. I'm gonna head into the kitchen and make some coffee."

"This shouldn't take long. I'll join you for breakfast then."

As I lumber into the hall, Marcus calls out, "I fed Clyde, so don't fall for any of his tricks." I snicker. That dog lives for two things: food and sleep. He's always trying to act as though he's starving, and it almost always works. I find him in the kitchen, sitting dutifully in front of his empty bowl. His somber eyes slide to mine and his tiny nub of a tail twitches.

"Sorry, buddy. Daddy got to me first," I say, patting his head. "But don't worry," I whisper. "You know I never finish my eggs."

He licks my hand and trots off toward the living room, no doubt in search of a bed. I shake my head, chuckling. Clyde is a constant source of amusement, and right now, I'll take anything I can get.

I move through the kitchen, brewing espresso and plucking eggs from the refrigerator. I've just popped bread into the toaster and am waiting for the butter to melt in the pan when strong arms wrap around my waist. Marcus rests his chin on my shoulder, tipping his head to smell my hair. My first instinct is to bat him away. I haven't showered yet. But I stop myself—Marcus has never cared about any of that. And at this moment, I don't really care, either. The nearness of him is enough. It's comforting, and that's a welcomed feeling compared to how weird things have been lately.

Life inside this house has been strained. For me, but

also for him. He doesn't like feeling helpless, but I haven't given him much choice.

I weave my arms around his and lean into his face. He places a kiss just below my ear, and I feel it everywhere. He takes my injured hand in his and turns it palm side up. "How's this feeling?"

"It's okay. A little sore, but no big deal."

"You were lucky, you know that?"

I nod. "I do."

He lets out a sigh and releases me, strolling across the room to retrieve two plates from the cabinet. While I make the eggs and butter the toast, he finishes brewing coffee. We move around the kitchen in a rehearsed kind of way. Like how it is when you do something so many times, it just becomes second nature. We carry the food and coffee over to the little table by the window. We rarely use the dining room, and after last night, I'm fine with avoiding that room altogether for a while.

I take a bite of my egg, turning my head to gaze out the window. A hummingbird is drinking nectar from the feeder we hung under the oak tree. "Marcus," I whisper as if the bird might hear me and fly away. "Look."

He follows my line of sight and leans in. "That's pretty cool." His voice betrays his words. He looks away and resumes eating—such a contrast to only a few minutes ago when he was hugging me at the stove. This hot and cold thing is enough to make me crazy, and I don't need any more help in that department.

"Is this how it's gonna be now?" I snip.

He leans back in his chair, folding his arms across his chest. "You tell me."

I throw my hands up in the air. "Oh, come on, Marcus. Why are you making such a thing out of this?"

His eyebrow shoots up. "Really? You put your hand through the fucking mirror last night."

"I already told you it was an accident!"

He looks away. His throat bobs with a swallow. "Yeah, I know that's what you said."

"I said it because it's the truth." And in a roundabout way, it is. I didn't mean to slam my palm into the mirror, but I didn't know how else to get the vision to stop.

He doesn't say anything. He doesn't look at me, either.

I stand and waltz over to him. Shoving his arm aside, I sit on his lap and take his face in my hands. "Listen to me. I am fine. My hand will be fine. Even the mirror is fine now, thanks to you." I smirk. The corner of his lip quirks, but he fights the smile. I cock my head. "Don't worry about me."

"Baby, I worry about you twenty-four seven. It's not something I can just turn off."

"I know that and I love you for it, but really, I'm good."

He leans forward, resting his forehead against mine. "Would you tell me if you weren't?"

"Maybe. Maybe not."

He sighs. "Yeah, that's what I thought."

"How about this, if things get out of hand and I can't pull myself out of it, I'll come to you."

He pulls back. "Out of hand like maybe you putting your fist through a mirror?" His eyes sparkle with a challenging gleam.

"Marcus," I warn.

His palms rub up and down my back. "Fine, but believe me when I tell you, I do not want to be lied to."

"Okay, I hear you." My teeth grind together, holding back my confession. I know all about lies of omission, but this is different. I need to figure out what's going on first before I can let anyone else in. "Speaking of lies …"

His brow raises as he pulls back to study my face. "Yeah?"

"We should probably talk about the pack of cigarettes stashed in your truck." I narrow my eyes at him.

"I was wondering when you were gonna bring that up." He chews on his lower lip.

"Well, now you can stop wondering and start explaining."

"I suck and I'm sorry." He laments. "But if it means anything, I've really stopped now."

I lower my chin. "And how do you expect me to believe that?"

He grips the sleeve of his shirt and raises it up to reveal a small square patch. "'Cause this time I called in the reinforcements."

I grin. "Good for you," I say, tapping him on the nose.

His hands glide lower on my body, settling at my waist. "Know what else is good for me?"

"Hmm?"

"If we made good use of this current situation." He lifts me up and guides my leg around so that I'm straddling him. "What'd ya say?"

My arms encircle his neck, pulling him closer. "I'd say you're an opportunist and I like the way you think." I press my lips to his and welcome the distraction.

A BOX CONTAINING my latest order from Ulta spills out onto the table in front of me. I rifle through it without ever really seeing anything. My mind is elsewhere—fixated on the vitamins I stopped taking.

I thought I had cracked the code, finally figuring out the root cause for all my hallucinations. It seemed simple. Stop taking the vitamins and stop seeing and hearing odd shit that isn't really there. And it worked. At least I thought it did. But last night changed all that. Now I'm back to square one, staring down the harsh possibility that it could be me that's the problem.

A familiar voice starts singing "Thank You for Being a Friend," and it snaps me out of my trance. Somewhere in this room, my phone is buried again. I jump up, following the sound to my recliner. Shoving my hands between the sides and the cushion, I find it wedged deep in the crevice.

I swipe my finger across the screen and press it to my ear. "Emma," I wheeze.

"Jesus, you're never calm when you answer the phone, you know that?"

"Sorry."

"Stop apologizing. Where was your phone hiding this time?"

I chuckle. "My recliner tried to eat it again."

"Ahh, that bitch is always hungry."

We both laugh.

"So what are you up to?"

I look around the room, surveying the mess of makeup on my table. "Well, I *should* be going through the stuff that just came from Ulta, but—"

"Let me guess, you're too distracted, right?"

My nose wrinkles. "Why would you say that?"

"Oh, April, April, April," she sings. "What am I gonna do with you?"

I gnaw at my lip, eyeing my open door. "Marcus called you, didn't he?"

She sighs. "He did, but don't get mad at him. The big dork is just worried about you. And now, so am I."

"I don't understand why." I huff. "Like I told him and my parents, it was an accident."

"Come on, you don't really expect us to believe that, do you?"

I pull my chin back and scrunch up my face. "The truth? Hell yeah, I do!"

"Listen, honey, suppose you did trip—"

"Suppose nothing. I did!" I stalk across the room and shut the door.

"Okay, hear me out for a second. This is *me* you're talking to. And bestie to bestie? It doesn't make sense. How would you get so tangled up in a throw rug that you accidentally put your hand through a mirror? And why would you yell, 'Stop'?"

My body starts to tingle, and my legs feel like they might give out. I hobble over to my recliner and sink into the cushion. I let my head fall between my knees and concentrate on breathing. Emma doesn't push any further.

She just waits in silence. As my inhales and exhales become more even, she says softly, "You okay?"

"Uh-huh." I feel almost as if I'm waking up in a hospital bed. Everything is happening to me, and I have zero control. Not only did Marcus tell Emma about the mirror, but he also told her what I said. It feels a little like a betrayal. And now I'm on the receiving end of an intervention.

"April, we all love you and we just don't like seeing you like this."

"Like what?"

"Like you're giving up. You stopped leaving the house, but you were seeing a therapist. I guess I figured the situation was only temporary. But now I hear you're not even meeting with Dr. Lesser anymore. It's like you're just resigned to living like this."

I let her words swirl inside my head. Am I? I know I haven't really been living, but I never thought of it like I'm surrendering. "I'm not giving up. When Marcus was telling you about my accident and Dr. Lesser, did he also tell you I went to the grocery store?"

"You did? Wow, that's great! I bet it was weird being inside a building that wasn't your house, huh?"

I rub at my nose and feel a flush on my cheeks. "Well, I didn't exactly go inside."

"April," she scolds.

"But I did let Marcus drive me there and I waited in the car for him." I spit the words out as fast as my mouth will allow. I need her to know I'm making progress. And maybe I need myself to know that, too.

"Okay, well, that's a start and a good one. I'm proud of you."

I smile. "Thank you."

"So, now that you're getting back out in the real world, think you may want to grab a taco with me sometime?"

"I don't know that I'm quite ready for that yet, but I'll get there."

"You will. And hey, I know it feels like we're all ganging up on you, but just try and remember we wouldn't push you if we didn't care."

"I know that. But I also need you all to trust me, okay? I've got this."

"Got what, exactly?"

I think on that for a moment, and then I'm nodding. "Life. I've got a handle on it." The power of positive affirmation, right? It's worth a shot.

"Word," she bellows, making me laugh. "Okay. Go organize some makeup. I'm all caught up on my videos and could use something new to watch."

I snicker. "You're my number one fan."

"Will you stop," she chides. "I am, in fact, your number one fan. And don't you forget it."

"Believe me. I never will."

"Good. Now get to work."

I END up filming my unboxing as a mini Ulta haul. As usual, it's nothing fancy, but that's the nature of my channel. It's also kept me busy for the last hour and a half.

Not long after I hung up with Emma, I heard Marcus's door open. I immediately launched into filming mode when I sensed him hovering by the door. I can't stand this push and pull with him, but I'm upset that he called my best friend and even more hurt that he told her about Dr. Lesser and what I said before the mirror broke.

I haven't let myself think about it much since it

happened, but screaming, "stop," affected me deeply. I wasn't just yelling at the girl in the mirror; I was pleading to anyone and anything that would listen to make all of this go away. I need it to end.

And I know that word is responsible for all the side-eyed glances and disbelieving tsks thrown my way. No one yells, "stop" when they're falling. They yell out nonsense or maybe "whoa" or even "no," but not "stop." Hearing Marcus question it—followed by Emma—has me feeling exposed. I'm running out of places to hide.

My stomach has been protesting for the last half hour. With a groan, I push up from my chair and head to the kitchen.

Marcus sits at the table; his hands wrap around a mug. He's studying the contents with unwavering precision. I clear my throat as I enter the room, jolting him out of his stupor.

A genuine smile fills his face. "Hey."

"Hey, yourself." My smile is tentative, reserved.

"Want some coffee? I could make you a cup."

I shake my head. "No, I'm good. I need to eat something, though."

"There are plenty of leftover meatballs from your mom."

I chuckle. "I believe it."

I tug open the refrigerator door and find the Tupperware of food. Marcus is up and at my side with two plates and a serving spoon. Wordlessly, we take turns filling our plates and heating up our food in the microwave. When we finally sit down across from each other, my irritation with him begins to slide away. He called Emma—so what? He knows how close she and I are; he probably thought she might have some insight. I can't hold that against him.

We continue eating, trading bits of filler conversation. He tells me about a new headset he's thinking of ordering, and I say I tried out a new eyeliner and ended up poking my eye no less than six times. He cringes. We laugh. It's nice. We've fallen back into a routine, and I feel immense gratitude for it. Just the little things like talking about our day had begun to fall by the wayside. Moments felt heavier and laced with dread on my part and concern on his.

We get all the way through dinner when he looks up at me. And I know before he says a thing that he's going to pop this beautiful little bubble we've been in. "So, uh, did Emma get a hold of you?"

I grit my teeth but then remind myself it's only because he cares. That's his motivation. I relax my jaw and nod. "Yeah, she called earlier."

"And what'd she have to say?"

I bite the inside of my lip. He never asks why Emma calls because he knows with us there doesn't have to be a reason. We can fill two hours' worth of conversation about nothing and everything in between. "Oh, you know, a little bit of this, a little bit of that." If he wants to beat around the bush, I'll grab a stick and join him.

"Hmm," he hums, nodding several times.

Yeah, I can't do this.

"Oh Jesus, Marcus." I snap. "You want to know if she talked to me about last night, right? Well, to answer the question you're refusing to ask, she did. And I told her the same thing I told you. It was an accident."

He opens his mouth then pinches it shut. The way he's sitting so still reminds me of something my dad always says, "Quit thinkin' so hard. I can hear your gears rattlin'." I almost say it to Marcus, but I stop myself. I'm frustrated that he isn't letting this go, but he's not wrong to worry about me. After all, I keep peddling a lie. Last night was no accident.

He's quiet for so long—long enough that the guilt

begins to churn deep in my gut. I'm desperate to make it stop, maybe more for me than him. So without thinking, I spit out the one thing I know will help ease his worries. "Emma asked if I wanted to grab a taco with her soon, and you know what? I think maybe I will."

That gets his attention. He sits up straight, pulling his shoulders back. His eyes gleam, and the grin on his face stretches from ear to ear. If relief were a living, breathing, palpable thing, it would be Marcus right now. "Wow, baby, you mean it?"

Do I? I have no clue, but I said it, so ... here we are. My head dips in a short nod. I pull at my lip and then rest my jittery hand in my lap. "Uh, yeah. I'm not sure when, but maybe next week."

His face pinches. "Why wait? What's wrong with this week?"

I scratch my neck. "Well, um, I guess maybe that could work."

"I think it would be good for you—both of you. Emma said she hasn't been doing much since you've stopped going out."

Huh. That's interesting. Just how long did my husband and best friend talk about me? I assumed it was a quick phone call. One where Marcus expressed his concern and Emma reciprocated. But now he's tossing out extra tidbits, and it doesn't sit right with me. The two of them have always had a relationship of mutual tolerance. When I first started dating Marcus, Emma was the first to say she thought I could do better. And Marcus didn't like how she was "always there." Their history is rocky at best, but they were civil for me. I should be happy that they've put aside their differences for a common cause, but not when that common cause is me.

I'm not sure how to respond to Marcus, so instead, I

stand, clearing my spot and loading my dish into the dish-washer—I'm not sure if my aloof behavior is obvious. He's moving around the kitchen as if everything is as it should be. And really, why wouldn't he? He may pay attention, but he's not inside my head. He can't see what I won't show him, and he can't hear what I don't say.

He joins me in the kitchen, rinsing his plate in the sink before depositing it in the dishwasher. "I'm gonna run to Target in a bit to pick up some things. Need anything while I'm out?"

"Actually, why don't I come with you?" The words come flying out of my mouth without much forethought, but maybe this is what I need. The more I leave the house, the easier it'll become.

His eyes widen. "Uh, actually, I need to stop by Zach's place on my way home, and you know how that can go. I'll probably be there awhile. You should stay here and enjoy the quiet." He smiles, but it doesn't reach his eyes.

My shoulders sag, but I just nod. I haven't been finding a ton of enjoyment from the quiet lately.

As I amble toward the hallway, he calls out, "Hey, baby?"

"Yeah," I say over my shoulder.

"Go get that taco with Emma. Don't overthink it, okay?"

I press my lips together and turn to face him. "Okay."

I SLUMP into my desk chair with a harrumph. Two days ago, I promised Marcus that I'd plan a lunch with Emma, but I have yet to call her. I should probably stop putting it off. I'm surprised Marcus hasn't checked in with me about it, but I'm sure it's coming.

Scanning my desktop, my eyes zero in on the left corner. I may have tossed all the vitamins, but I have yet to get rid of the bottle. It sits perched on my desk, mocking me for being so gullible. I snatch it, squeezing it in my fist. Time to get rid of this. The bottle hits the bottom of my empty trashcan with a *clank*. There. Now I can move past those repulsive gummies and what they represent. I'm still not convinced they weren't at least partially to blame for my behavior the other night. It's been over a week since I last took one, but maybe that whole bathroom mirror incident was because they still hadn't fully left my system. Maybe the argument with my mom triggered the last remaining fragments in my body. I know how unlikely that sounds, but right now, it's all I've got.

I flex my injured hand, examining the few cuts and scratches that have scabbed over. Marcus replaced the broken mirror, and once these marks are healed, there will be nothing left to remind me of what happened. Nothing except my memories, which I've been working really hard to suppress.

I wonder how Hemply Simple took the news about my refusing the sponsorship. I'm actually surprised they haven't tried to contact me on my backup email. Marcus said he would take care of ending things. Maybe I'll check the business email just to see what they said.

Aside from checking it a few times after the weird flower delivery, I haven't spent much time in this account in quite a while. Once I handed over the reins to Marcus, I never looked back. It's been so freeing to just create and edit without having to do all the marketing and behind-the-scenes stuff. And for the most part, we've made a good team. But this vitamin issue has made me realize we have different approaches when it comes to sponsored content. I know this is a job, but I also have my integrity. It's not always about the bottom line.

With the email account pulled up, I move the cursor over to select the sent mail, but before I can do that, an email near the top catches my attention. It's from Hemply Simple and the heading is *re: Vitamins*.

I click without hesitation, opening the email to find a lengthy back and forth between Marcus and someone named Troy Arello. From the signature at the bottom, it seems Troy is a public relations and marketing specialist for Hemply Simple. Scrolling down to the beginning, I find Marcus's original email where he tells them I'm not interested in the sponsorship. From the time stamp, it appears he sent it the day after I put my fist through the mirror. Huh. Why didn't he send it sooner? Maybe he didn't have time between my parents' impromptu visit and my bathroom incident.

My eyes scan the contents of the email, anxious to hear how Marcus told them I wouldn't be continuing to work with them. Except that's not exactly what he said. In his words, I am "not really sure how I feel about the taste." He goes on to say that I am not able to give them a positive review as it stands right now. My jaw is rigid and clenched tight. Why is he behaving like there's a possibility I could *ever* give them a positive review? It's not just a matter of taste. That's not even the real issue. At the bottom of his email, there's a brief mention about how I wasn't sure they were helping, but it's almost an afterthought.

I move on to Troy's response. He isn't very quick to withdraw the request. He starts offering other options—things he's "sure" I'll be more apt to like. As I read on, my chest starts to feel tight, and my teeth grind together. According to Troy, they've started developing a liquid vitamin and he's wondering if maybe I'd be willing to try that. Apparently, it's tasteless, and it "provides a more fulfilling energy experience." What is it with this company and vague descriptions?

It doesn't matter, though. After what I told him, I'm sure Marcus will say, "Thanks, but no thanks." But as I scroll up, I see the unthinkable. There in literal black and white, my husband has replied, *Yeah, actually. That could work. How about you send us some and we'll give it a try.* Troy said he would overnight it to the PO box. So they didn't want to send the gummy vitamins to the PO box, but for these new liquid vitamins, it's totally fine? I roll my eyes. Sure, that's not suspicious.

Troy sent that email a few days ago, and so far, Marcus has said nothing.

I lean back in my chair, tapping my finger to my lips. Thinking back on Marcus's behavior over the last couple of days, I can't say I've noticed him acting strange, other than his general obvious concern for me. He did run out to Target the other day, which just so happens to be in the same vicinity as the post office. He could've easily picked up the vitamins when he was out. And he conveniently talked me out of joining him. My face warms and my cheeks flush.

My eyes dash around the room as I try to piece things together. There are a few explanations for why Marcus would hold off telling me about this email, but there's one, in particular, I'm trying desperately not to entertain, even though my gaze is frozen on the glass of water he brought me an hour ago. A glass that's nearly empty.

I shake my head, trying to push the thought away before it takes root. No way would Marcus add something to my drink without telling me. That's the same as drugging me. He wouldn't do that. Not after what happened between his parents. That would make him no better than his father. It's his worst fear.

And yet …

He's made it known how worried he's been about me, and he claimed the original gummy vitamins were supposed to "help my mood." I told him they did the opposite, and then that night I put my fist through a mirror. I've noticed him watching me when he thinks I'm not looking. Not in a creepy way, more like he's keeping a close eye on me so that I don't hurt myself again.

Maybe he's feeling desperate. People have been known to act out of character when they're convinced there's no other choice. And in Marcus's case, his dad drugged his mom to make her more compliant. Then he left, and the drugging stopped, but his mom killed herself two weeks later. What if Marcus is afraid I'll meet the same fate and he's trying to intervene the only way he knows how?

I rub my hands fiercely over my arms, trying to smooth out the goose bumps that have erupted. A growing nausea starts to churn deep in my gut as saliva builds in my mouth.

I launch out of my chair and make a mad dash into the bathroom. I fling open the toilet seat just in time to expel all the contents of my stomach. Sinking to my knees, I scrub my face in my hands. Well, I guess if Marcus did put something in my water, that's one way to get rid of it. I grimace, rubbing my stomach.

I flop onto my bottom and slide against the wall. Resting my head back, I close my eyes and try to reason with myself. I've been going through a lot lately, and it's got my mind spinning in so many directions. Maybe I should just do what I should've done right from the start. Talk to Marcus.

I feel a little woozy when I stand. I flush the toilet and take small steps to the sink. Before I can turn on the water, the smell of something familiar catches my attention. After a few deep inhales, I can finally put my finger on it. Japanese Cherry Blossom. It was Emma's and my favorite scent from Bath and Body Works. I'm confused at first, until I notice the steam wafting from the diffuser. My smile is wide as my mind drifts back to simpler times. High school had its own set of issues, but I'd take them over this any day. Emma and I spent most of our time concerned with our appearance, and we always gave ourselves a once-over of body mist before we went anywhere. This sweet, fruity-floral scent is one I will forever equate with some of the happiest times in my life.

Feeling lighter, I turn on the water and begin washing my hands.

"There you are."

I scream, flinging water all over myself and the mirror. Marcus's presence in the doorway catches me off guard—more than it normally would. His eyes flash wide and he takes a step back. "Whoa, why are you so jumpy all the time? I thought you heard me."

"Apparently not," I say, drying my hands on the towel, grateful that he didn't come in a few minutes earlier.

He's quiet for a moment, and when he speaks again, his eyes don't quite reach mine. Like he's focusing on my forehead. I find myself standing on my tiptoes, trying to get my line of sight even with his, but it never lines up. "I was just gonna make some mac and cheese. Want any?"

Under normal circumstances, I wouldn't even blink at that question, but I'm pretty sure normal died. It's been replaced with this living nightmare of sorts where I feel like I'm not in control of anything; it's all just happening *to* me. I shake my head. "No, thanks. I'm not really hungry right now." I'm still reeling from clutching the porcelain throne.

He taps his hand along the molding and nods. "Okay, I'll be in the kitchen then, if you need me."

I smile, and it takes everything I have inside of me to make it look real. I'm not sure I pulled it off until he smiles back.

As he begins to turn away, I have an idea. "Hey, Marcus?"

"Yeah?" He spins back around.

"I was just curious. What ever happened with the vitamin people?"

Is it just my imagination or has the skin on his face turned sallow? He swallows a few times and then says, "Oh, they understood. They had a few ideas, but I told them we weren't interested."

Now I'm sure my own face is growing pale. He never said that. I can't find words, so I just nod and force the corner of my lip to raise slightly.

He heads to the kitchen, tossing over his shoulder, "Let me know if you change your mind about food."

I'm alone again with my dark thoughts. I didn't want to believe Marcus would secretly add something to my food or water, but then why didn't he just come right out and tell me about the liquid vitamins? None of this makes sense.

My stomach churns with unease. I turn the water back on, scooping it in my palms and splashing it onto my face. As I towel off, I notice the mirror speckled with water droplets. I grit my teeth—all warm and fuzzy nostalgic feelings long gone—and swipe the towel across the glass. It smears, blurring my reflection, but after a couple more wipes, it's crystal clear again. So clear, I can't turn away. I catch my eyes and nearly gasp at the sadness I see in them. A deep unrest dwells in the wetness that's beginning to pool. But then my reflection blinks and the well of tears in her eyes dry up. She cocks her head and her lips quirk. I step back, and she steps forward.

This isn't happening.

Tossing the towel into the sink, I rush out of the room. I swear I hear laughter echoing behind me.

I PICK up my phone for what feels like the seventieth time today. I have nowhere to go with these feelings, and if I don't let them out soon, they're going to force their way out —leaching from my pores and streaming from my eyes. I want to talk to Emma, but every time I think about calling her, I'm reminded of the last time we talked. When Marcus was an informant and she defended him. Suppose there is something going on with Marcus—I just don't know who to trust anymore.

These are crazy thoughts; I know that, and yet I'm not sure there's a rational methodology here. My husband is acting suspicious and clearly keeping things from me. It hurts to know I can't confide in him, not that I've even tried. But even knowing that, I've always had Emma. Do I still have her?

Maybe there's a way to find out. I grab my phone again and tap on Emma's face. When she answers, she sounds bright and cheery, and I hate myself for ever doubting her.

"What's up, bitch?"

"Nothing much, bitch." I chuckle.

"Ahh, so you just needed to hear the sound of my voice then, right?"

I close my eyes, fighting back tears. She has no idea how right she is. I clear my throat, composing myself. "Yep, you got it."

She laughs.

"Actually, I've been thinking a lot about what you said the other day about us grabbing tacos."

"Yeah?" Her voice lifts an octave. It makes me feel guilty for refusing her so many times. Marcus said she hasn't been out much. I shake my head, pushing thoughts of him away.

"What are you doing tomorrow for lunch?"

"Wait. Are you serious?"

"As serious as a—" I stop myself before I can say, "heart attack," but it's not soon enough. A flash of Walker Dolan pops into my head, but I blink it away. "Um, yeah, I'm totally serious."

"Oh, April, that's just … that's amazing. I'll pick you up at noon. Sound good?"

I grin, and it's the first time in a while that it's genuine. "Sounds perfect."

I'VE MANAGED to avoid Marcus for most of the night. When I finally feel hungry, I amble out to the kitchen and find he has scooped some leftover mac and cheese into a bowl. It's been covered and placed in the fridge with a sticky note on top—*For April.*

I scoff. There's no way I'm eating or drinking anything he's prepared for me. Not until I get to the bottom of things.

I end up having a bowl of cereal, which makes me roll my eyes, thinking of my mom. She's always convinced this is the sort of dinner Marcus would make for me, and now here I am proving her right—well, sort of. He actually left real food for me, but since I'm afraid it might be drugged, I've decided to eat Lucky Charms instead. I hang my head, cradling it in my hands. Do I really believe Marcus would do that to me after everything he's been through? I could confront him, but if I'm wrong—and I really hope I am—how would he react to being compared to his dad? Would we even survive that? I have to keep it to myself for now, but I'll be paying close attention to everything. If I learn he is drugging me, then I'll deal with it, and if he isn't, well, then he never needs to know it was ever a thought.

When I finish eating, I trudge down the hall, stopping in the doorway of my bedroom. Marcus isn't the only thing I've been avoiding all day. A bad taste forms in my mouth as I eye the bathroom.

I pull back my shoulders and set my mouth into a grim line. Here goes nothing.

I plow through my nighttime routine, never once looking up at the mirror. It works as well as could be expected. After all, you can't see something if you don't look.

When I finish getting ready for bed, I expect to see Marcus strolling into the room, but he still hasn't emerged from his game room. So I slide under the covers and start rifling through the sea of TikTok links Emma sent me over the course of the day. I'm laughing at one when I hear the squeak of Marcus's game room door.

Like a child afraid of getting caught staying up too late, I lay my phone on my nightstand and roll onto my side. My eyes squeeze shut so tight I have to remind myself to relax.

Marcus doesn't make a sound when he enters the room, but I still know when he does—the energy shifts the second he steps through the door. I'm not sure how long it takes him to get ready for bed. I may have dozed off for a bit. But I'm acutely aware of the moment he lifts the covers and positions himself underneath them. The mattress dips and shakes as he adjusts himself, and for a moment, I swear I can feel his eyes on the back of my head, but he never says a word.

I feel like I'm sleeping next to a stranger. How did we get here?

I LOOK up at the inky black storm clouds and roll my eyes. If anyone has ever wondered if it's possible to get annoyed by your dreams as they're happening—it is, and I am. I expect the funnel cloud any minute and barely bat an eye when I see it begin to form in the sky. I might feel less annoyed if I could understand the point of these.

Taking a look around, I realize I'm standing in front of the post office. I pause, listening. Despite the wind and chaos around me, I can still make out the faint hint of Nana's humming coming from inside. My body begins to move of its own accord, heading toward the sound. I give the front door a hard shove, and it pushes wide open. I breeze inside, surveying the vacant lobby. No one stands behind the counter, and there doesn't appear to be any activity in the back, either. The humming is louder in here. At first, it feels as though it's surrounding me, coming at me from all angles. But as I stand still in the deserted post office, Nana's song seems like it's beaconing me. The PO boxes are located around the corner down a darkened hallway, and as I tilt my head, the steady hum seems to be coming from that direction. My feet begin to move, and when I reach the hall, the humming stops. It's narrower than I remember and there's only one box on the wall. Number two fifty-eight. The door is open, and Marcus is rifling through the contents. He hasn't noticed me, and I watch with rapt attention as he plucks a small padded envelope from inside. He tears it open and pulls out a medicine bottle with a dropper lid screwed on top.

The wind outside is nearly deafening. It reminds me of the sound inside a plane after it takes off. It roars in a way that can't be ignored, no matter how many distractions you brought with you. And despite my husband standing in front of me, holding what looks to be the liquid vitamins he secretly agreed to receive, my gaze still snaps to the left. There's a window here now that wasn't there a second ago. The funnel cloud has touched down in the parking lot and is tossing cars aside like they're toys. It picks up a red sedan and sends it careening into the building. That gets Marcus's attention. His eyes fly to the window and then slide over to me.

We stare at each other, unmoving, as the tornado dices up the asphalt outside. The ceiling starts to pop and crack. And when I look outside, I see nothing but spinning darkness. The roof begins to lift off the building in bits and pieces. Marcus tips his head up and then back down at me.

"Baby," he says. "This isn't what it looks like."

My face pinches. "It looks like we're about to be sucked up inside a tornado, Marcus."

Neither one of us is yelling, despite the thunderous noise surrounding us. Yet, we can hear each other as clearly as if we were in a doctor's office waiting room.

He shakes his head, and his hair whips around. "That's not what I mean." I narrow my eyes at the bottle in his hand, and he holds it up. "Don't worry about these." Then he tosses the vitamins into the air, but instead of getting pulled into the funnel, they slam into what's left of the wall. Liquid flies from the bottle and lands on us both. It's so much fluid for such a small container. I rub my thumb and index finger together, feeling the slickness between them. It feels so real.

The spiral of dirt and debris begins to engulf Marcus. I can barely see him anymore. Just before he vanishes entirely, he gives me a sad smile.

My eyes spring open. Morning light cuts through the blinds. I knew it was a dream the whole time, and yet I'm still panting. My heart thumps like a low drum. I blink rapidly, trying to clear away the last thing I saw, but the haunting expression on Marcus's face is hard to ignore. It was unsettling; even more so than the other dreams I've had. Each one feels like I'm being given part of a story, but nothing is in order, and it's up to me to assemble it. Except I'm too afraid of how it ends.

There's an odd smell in the air. It's sweet and almost metallic. I sigh and begin to stretch out my limbs. I notice right away that Clyde isn't in the bed. He's probably in the living room. As I move the fingers on my right hand, something gives me pause. They glide together just like in my dream.

Raising my hand in front of my face, I find it covered in a curious red liquid. It's dark crimson and thick in places. I'm still hovering in the in-between stage of sleep and wake, and I can't quite make sense of what I'm seeing. My brain feels like it's misfiring. Did Marcus spill sauce in the bed?

I hold my fingers close to my nose and catch a whiff of that metallic smell again. I bolt upright, kicking the covers off. The entire right side of my body is speckled with blood. I gasp and whirl around to face Marcus's side of the bed.

I've never known true horror like I feel in this moment. My husband is lying prone beside me. Despite his large frame, he looks small. His arms are at his sides, and his legs are straight. His chest is bare and covered in blood. It pools in the center where there's an obvious gaping wound. My eyes zigzag across his body where I notice several gashes just like the one on his chest.

"Marcus?" My voice is weak and sounds more like a croak.

My gaze travels from his shoulder to his neck, finally

landing on his face. A fresh wave of terror washes over me. The skin on his face is unmarred, but no less terrifying. His lips are parted like his mouth froze when he was in the middle of speaking. His eyes are wide and fixed on the ceiling. Unblinking. Rigid. I used to get lost in the soulful depths of rich brown and flecks of gold. But now, I turn away, unable and unwilling to see them this way. Cold. Lifeless.

My hand clasps over my mouth, but it doesn't stop the sob that comes out. Or the others that follow. Shock and horror wind around my neck like a noose, and waves of nausea wreck my body.

I dive across the space to Marcus, gripping his face in my hands. "Marcus! Wake up! You can't leave me!" His skin is cold and firm, and yet, I continue shaking him and screaming his name. Loud wails bellow out of me until I'm gasping for breath.

I need to get help.

Pushing up to my knees, something hard presses into my side. The sheet is wrinkled, concealing whatever it is that jabbed me, but I can see a bit of black peeking out among the spotted white sheets. I yank the fabric back, and there on the bed, right between where Marcus and I sleep, is a knife covered in blood. I recognize it immediately. It's the same Santoku knife that lives at the top of the butcher block in our kitchen.

I scramble off the bed, my eyes shooting between Marcus and the knife. Back and forth and back and forth. Then I hold out my hands in front of me, examining them from all angles. There's blood speckling the tops of both — more on the right than the left. My right palm is also smeared with blood that seems concentrated along the outside edge of my hand up to my pinkie. I gasp and grip my hair in my hands. What the fuck is happening?

There's a thought hovering just out of reach, threatening to unravel my last bit of sanity. I can't let it form. I keep shaking my head. Because there's no way. It's not possible.

I didn't kill my husband.

I race around the room, looking for my phone. I need to call someone. 911. Emma. Zach. Anyone. My body uncontrollably shakes as I look under piles of clothes and inside drawers trying to find my phone. I keep looking back at Marcus and crying out every time I see his blank stare.

The bathroom. Maybe it's in there. I rush inside and look around, finding it resting on the side of the tub. Grabbing it, I unlock the screen, poking at it with blood-stained fingers. Who do I call? What do I do?

"Easy now, April. Take a deep breath."

I whip around, scanning the room. "Who's there?"

No answer. I recognize that voice.

With tentative steps, I inch toward the mirror. My erratic breathing is the only sound. When I reach the sink, I stare into it, trying to calm my racing heart. It's no use. I raise my head and stare into the eyes of my own reflection. I blink as if moving in slow motion, and so does she. I close one eye and then the other. My reflection dutifully obeys.

What am I doing?

I look down at the phone in my hand. It shakes and jostles as my body spasms. 911. I'll start there.

"Hold on a minute. You don't want to do that."

I jerk my head up and meet my own gaze. She winks. I close my eyes. This isn't happening. It's not real.

"Come on, April. You're wasting time. Let me help you."

"Who are you?" I ask, immediately shaking my head. "Nope. This is crazy. *I* am crazy."

"Don't talk about us like that."

My eyes widen. Am I dreaming? Yes. That has to be it. I drop my phone onto the little table next to the sink and squeeze the skin on my arm. I feel the sharp pinch and watch the skin pinken beneath my fingers. This is no dream. "No, no, no, no, no," I scream. "Marcus! Oh my God!"

"Shh," my reflection croons. "It's gonna be all right."

"How can you say that? My husband is dead and I've lost my fucking mind! Nothing will ever be okay again!" My face burns with fury.

"Listen," she leans forward, eyeing me carefully, "you just need some time. That's all."

"Time? Time won't change a thing. No. I need help!" I reach for my phone, but she makes a tsk sound.

"Stop, just for a moment. I only know as much as you do. We're the same, after all." She flaps her hand between us. "But I happen to be the part of you that reasons, and from where I'm standing, I don't think anything is as it seems."

My lip quivers as I take in a shaky breath. "What does that even mean?"

"It means, don't be hasty. It's too late for Marcus." I choke on a sob and she frowns. "I'm so sorry about that, but you don't even know what happened. Were you involved? Was someone else? Are they still in the house?"

I gasp and spin around to face the open bathroom door. *Is* someone here? I can hear my own heart beating as though it were outside of my body and my ragged breaths push through my open mouth in shaky puffs. I can't hear anything else, but that doesn't mean I'm alone.

"Okay, here's what you need to do," she says, commanding my attention back to her. "You need to get out of here."

I shake my head. "No, that's the wrong thing to do. I have to call an ambulance or the police. Someone."

"Maybe, and if that's the right move, you will. But trust

me on this." She sighs. "Go somewhere and clear your head. It will help."

"I-I don't think my head will ever be clear," I whisper.

"One thing at a time. Wash your hands," she directs.

I hold out my palms and watch as they bounce and jerk from shock and adrenaline. They're still splattered and smeared with Marcus's blood. My eyes fill, and when I blink, thick tears cascade down my cheeks. I can barely see as I turn on the faucet and use the back of my hand to press a pump of soap onto my open palm.

"That's it," she says. "Now dry them off."

I do as she says, my movements short and robotic.

Slowly, I lift my eyes to hers. "Now what?"

She smiles sadly. "Now you take care of you. Go for a drive and then come back and face whatever is waiting for you."

A drive? I haven't driven in nearly a year. "I'm in no shape to drive right now."

"You'll be fine." She nods.

"But what about Marcus?" I sob. "Oh my God, I can't believe he's dead," I cry.

"Hmm," she hums. "Is he, though?"

There's a dull ache above my left ear. I press a finger to it and massage in small circles. "What does that mean?"

She doesn't answer, and when I look up at the mirror, she's gone. I'm left alone, staring into my own dead eyes.

23

I SHOVE the front door closed and lean against it. My palms rest along the wood. They're free of blood, but it still polka dots my arms and my pajamas. None of this feels real. I try to take a deep breath, but it feels impossible. My throat constricts and my chest is tight.

How will I live without Marcus? I don't even know if it's possible. I couldn't even look at him before I left. I raced out of the bathroom, pausing only to grab my purse. As for Clyde, I never saw him. I feel a pang of guilt for not looking harder. I can only hope he's sleeping somewhere in the house.

I turn around and move zombie-like onto the stone walk that leads to the driveway. Other than my recent trip to the grocery store parking lot, I haven't left the house in months. It's been even longer since I've driven. My Subaru sits next to Marcus's truck. Aside from his gaming PC, it's his most prized possession. Was.

With shaky hands, I root through my bag in search of my keys. I can hear them jingle as I probe the black abyss, but each time I make contact with them, they slip out of my fumbling fingers. As I struggle, my hand slips and the entire contents of my purse dump out onto the driveway. I frantically grab at things, tossing them back inside. A tube of nude lipstick, a small wallet, a pack of tissues, my phone—so glad I remembered to grab it before I left the bathroom—and finally my keys.

I stumble toward the car, my shoulders tipping forward and my head hanging. This must be what shock feels like.

I drop into the seat, heaving my legs inside like they're cinder blocks. What am I doing?

I sink the keys into the ignition and give them a turn. The car rumbles to life and I have Marcus to thank for it. He made sure it was driven this past year. I close my eyes as fresh tears begin to fall.

Slowly, I back out of the driveway, keeping my eyes on the rearview mirror. As I near the road, I glance back at the house. The curtain in the living room is parted slightly as though someone is peeking out, watching me. I slam on the brakes and the car bucks as it jolts to a stop. I watch as the curtain is pulled shut. The fabric sways and then the movement stops altogether. I blink several times and rub my hands down my face. My eyes snap back to the window, but everything is still. It's as if it never happened. Did it? I don't know what to believe anymore.

My lower lip quivers as I exhale, continuing the drive. Once I'm on the winding road, I watch my home disappear in the rearview mirror. Only it doesn't feel like a home. Not anymore.

My hands grip the wheel tightly, and I lean forward, acutely aware of my driving. If I wasn't so upset by everything that's happened, I'd probably be celebrating this accomplishment. Instead, I feel like I'm on the run, driving my own get-away car. This isn't right. I should go back.

Thoughts buzz in and out of my head like a bevy of flies, each one more of a pest than the last. One, in particular, refuses to budge, forcing others to swarm around it. The knife. Why was it in the bed between us? And why was my hand all bloody—the way it might've been if I had held the knife as it pierced Marcus's skin, over and over?

"No!" I grab my head, trying to squish the thought out of existence. The car swerves, and I grab the wheel, righting it just in time before I drive off the road.

I struggle to catch my breath. My phone buzzes from inside my purse, startling me. I reach my hand in, fishing it out. The doorbell app is alerting me that someone is at my front door. I tap the notification and pull the car off the road as I wait for the app to load.

Emma. She's at the house, letting herself inside with her key. In all of the madness of the morning, I completely forgot about our lunch plans.

Dropping my phone onto the passenger seat, I grab the wheel and spin it hard as I push my foot against the gas.

She's going to find Marcus. There's no way I'll make it home in time. But I have to try.

TEN MINUTES LATER, the road to my house comes into view. My tires squeal as I whip around the turn. The bottom of my car scrapes against the driveway. There's always been a dip, but at this speed, it feels like a crater. Once I pull up in front of the house, I'm filled with confusion.

Emma's car is the only one in the driveway.

Marcus's truck is gone.

Wait a minute.

His truck is *gone*.

I barely have time to register that thought when I remember Emma is in the house. I have to get to her. I have to explain.

I grab my purse, but the straps tangle in the gearshift.

"Ugh!" A frenzied tugging and yanking ensues, but all of that frantic energy just makes it worse. I end up leaving my purse.

I fly up the stairs and into my unlocked house. "Em?" My voice doesn't even sound like mine. She doesn't answer. I race through the house and into the hallway.

My bedroom door is ajar, and I can hear water running from the bathroom.

"Emma! I know I should've called you, but please, let me explain," I cry.

"You better," she calls from inside. "I mean, from the state of this room, I don't know how you live with yourself."

She sounds so blasé. It stuns me. I lumber down the hall, closing the distance between us. As I enter the bedroom, I'm shocked and confused. There's no blood. No knife. No Marcus. The blankets are disheveled, looking slept in, but not the way they did this morning—like they'd witnessed a murder.

"You know," Emma's voice drifts out of the bathroom. "You could've at least made your bed." She struts into the room, but the smile she's wearing melts off her face as soon as she sees me. "You're not even dressed. I know it's only tacos, but you still can't go in your PJs."

I look down at myself. The blood that was marbling my clothes earlier is gone. My mouth hangs open. Frozen. Just like Marcus's was this morning. When he was dead. In our bed.

"Honey, what's wrong?" Emma takes small steps toward me, keeping her eyes trained on mine. "April, you're freaking me out. You look like you've seen a ghost." She takes my hand, tugging me out of the room.

Once we're in the kitchen, she pulls out a stool by the counter. "Sit." She grabs two glasses out of the cabinet and fills them with water. Placing one down in front of me, she nudges it with her finger. "Drink." I do as I'm told, grateful for some direction. I feel as though I'm trapped in a dense fog. She watches me closely. It's only when I put the glass back on the counter that she continues questioning me. "Okay, let's start from the beginning. You weren't here when I arrived and your car wasn't in the driveway, either. April, did you drive yourself?" Despite her growing concern by my mood and disheveled appearance, there's a glimmer of hope in her voice.

I open my mouth to speak but never have the chance. The front door opens, pulling our attention to the hallway. I rise out of my seat, stunned by what I see.

I HEAR the sound of clicking, and then Clyde appears, bounding in our direction as soon as he spots us.

"April? Are you here?" a familiar voice calls, sounding frantic.

My body begins convulsing and my legs feel as though they're about to give out. When Marcus steps into view, I gasp, covering my mouth with my hand. His face scrunches, and he cocks his head. "Everything all right?" I sprint toward him, throwing my arms around his neck. My heart pounds against his chest. I'm sure he can feel it.

"What's wrong with her?" He grips my arms in his hands and pushes back slightly, scanning my face.

Emma answers him from somewhere behind me, but it's like she's talking underwater. I can't understand a word she's saying.

Something's happening to me. It feels like I'm being sucked backward into a tunnel. Sound is muffled, and my vision is fading. The edges are getting fuzzy. I blink several times, but it only gets worse.

I feel his breath on my cheek as he leans in close.

I smile. "The gold flecks are back."

Marcus's face is the last thing I see before everything goes black.

A STEADY BUZZ ROUSES ME, and for a moment, I'm suspended in happier times. Tucked away in my bed, hovering in that blissful place between waking and dreaming. It's not until I begin to move that memories start to flood my consciousness, assaulting me in a barrage of fierce attacks. Marcus is dead. Emma is here. Marcus is alive.

I spring upright, startling Clyde. The buzzing stops, and I realize it was the sound of him snoring.

The last time I was in this bed, something awful happened. Now I'm terrified to turn my head in fear of what I might see. I start with a survey of my own body, shoving the covers back to reveal me still in my pajamas. There's no blood. And when I shift my position, there's no knife and no dead Marcus, either.

I hear voices coming from outside the room. One sounds angry—Emma's. She's firing off questions at Marcus, but I can't quite make out his answers. "How long has this been going on?"

There's another voice, too. "Relax. He has everything under control." Zach. What is *he* doing here?

I need answers, even if it means I'm going to have to give my own as well. Things I've kept hidden from the people I love most. Can they handle it? Can I?

People tend to say they want the truth when, in reality, they'd much prefer a watered-down version. That way, they can connect their own dots and draw their own conclusions. It's much easier to hide from awful things when you aren't forced to face them head-on. The truth doesn't offer excuses. It doesn't care about your feelings or your inability to handle hard things. It just is what it is, and sometimes, it's fucking hideous.

I can only make out parts of their conversation. Marcus

seems to be assuring Emma. "She's getting better. Trust me."

But Emma doesn't sound convinced. "How can you even say that after what just happened?"

What *did* happen? And what *didn't*? I have to get to the bottom of this, no matter how awful it may turn out to be.

Before I have a chance to get out of bed, the door swings open. "You're awake!" The relief in Marcus's voice is like a living, breathing thing. "She's awake," he calls behind him.

"Let me talk to her, please," Emma says as she pushes her way past him.

His chin lowers. "Okay, but just … we'll be right outside."

Emma doesn't acknowledge him. She hustles over and perches on the side of my bed. The door clicks, and she doesn't hesitate. "Honey, are you okay? I mean, really. And please don't sugarcoat it. I'm your best friend. I can handle it, you know?" She takes my hands in hers, imploring me with hopeful eyes.

I clear my throat. "I've had some dreams that have felt very real, and this morning, I had the most lucid one I've ever experienced. I thought Marcus had died." I hear her quick intake of breath, and her hands tighten around mine, but she stays silent. Listening. "I know he didn't, but it felt so real and when he walked through that door, it was like seeing a ghost."

"Wow, that must have been terrifying."

"It was." I nod. "It still is."

"But you know it didn't actually happen, right?" Her forehead wrinkles.

"I do, but that still doesn't change the fact that I saw him, Em. And I *felt* him. He was cold and so still." I shiver.

"Maybe you were just dreaming."

"Emma." I groan. "Have you been listening? I told you I physically touched him. I've had realistic dreams in the past, but this went beyond that."

She stands and begins pacing beside my bed. "It could've been like you were stuck in some sort of trance or dream-like state. You know, how people sleepwalk?"

I feel as though I'm watching her unravel, and I want to ease her worries, but how can I when I'm unraveling too? I know we have a lot to discuss, but right now, I need to see Marcus.

"I'm feeling a little tired." I yawn. "And I think I'd better talk to Marcus before I collapse from exhaustion."

She stops moving and leans down, taking my hands in hers. "Of course. You've had quite an exciting day." She chuckles, but it's laced with sadness. Letting go of my hands, she begins moving toward the door, but stops, calling over her shoulder, "Oh, and listen, I'm letting you off the hook on lunch today for obvious reasons, but you better call me soon to reschedule."

"I will," I say, giving her a smile even though it feels foreign on my face.

She opens the door and calls for Marcus. When he approaches, she's still blocking the doorway. "You better fix this," she warns. And then she's gone.

Marcus watches her leave, then turns to face me. His throat bobs with a hard swallow as he approaches the side of the bed. He looks exhausted with droopy eyes and a downturned mouth that he seems to be wrestling into a smile. Anguish is etched into the deep creases on his forehead and between his eyes. His skin is sallow, and I may be mistaken, but his clothing hangs off him oddly, like he's lost some weight. All this time, I've felt alone in my downward spiral, but it's clear Marcus has been along for the ride.

He ambles toward me, and even that seems off. Like his

gait has changed over time to that of a less self-assured person. Someone who second-guesses themselves and rates their self-worth below everyone else's. That's not Marcus. That's never been him. He's always cared for me while simultaneously caring for himself. We've been on equal rungs of the ladder, but from the look of things, as I've been stepping down, he has, too.

I reach for him, and he closes the gap, linking our hands. "Hey, you," he says, plopping onto the mattress beside me.

"Hey, yourself." I give him a smile, and I'll admit, my reason is a little selfish. I just want to see his eyes sparkle. That gleam they've always held is still there, but it's faded. My plan seems to have the desired outcome as his jaw works back and forth, unleashing a bright smile. One that reaches his eyes but doesn't stop there, continuing up where it softens and smooths the hills and valleys on his face. And there, even if for a few brief moments, is the man that I married.

Too bad it doesn't last long—and that's my fault, too. I shift my body to sit up a little straighter, and in doing so, I wince. I must've bent my arm funny when I fell. Just putting the slightest bit of pressure on it sends a shock of pain from my elbow to my shoulder. Marcus clocks all of it. Tormented eyes assess me, rapidly scaling my body in search of bruises. "Careful. I caught you when you fell, but with the direction you were heading, your arm got pinned behind you."

"Yeah," I say, rubbing my shoulder. "I can tell. It'll be okay, though."

"You will," he agrees, but his furrowed eyebrows are at war with his words. "So, what happened?"

"Marcus, I need help." The words I should've said weeks ago come tumbling out.

He shifts his body closer to mine and leans in, letting go of my hands while placing his on either side of my face. "Talk to me."

"Things have been happening, and I thought I could get it under control, but I'm not strong enough." I think of Nana. She said I had strength, but if that's true, it's been evading me.

"What do you mean 'things have been happening'?" His lips rub together.

"That's just it. I can't even describe it except to say that I'm pretty sure I'm hallucinating. Actually, I'm positive I am because the things I've seen can't be real. This morning, after another one of my tornado dreams, I woke up to find you dead, Marcus. You were lying right here." I pat the mattress beside me. "And there was a knife!" I rest a hand on his chest, pushing him back as I sit up. My hands are frantic as they scour the bed for the weapon that was there this morning.

"April, April, please try to calm down. Baby, there's no knife in the bed. I promise."

My heart pounds out of my chest and my breathing is labored. "What's happening to me, Marcus? Am I going crazy?"

"Shh," he whispers. It's meant to relax me, but it only stirs up memories of my reflection when she tried to shush me earlier. That's the problem. I've stayed quiet when I should've been loud.

"No!" I shout, startling him. He rears back as though he's been slapped. "I'm sorry, but I can't stay silent anymore. Not about this. I need help. I think you should take me to the hospital."

His body freezes, and he turns, looking away for a moment. When his gaze returns, I see something new in his eyes. There's a clarity that wasn't there before. He begins nodding and it continues as he speaks. "No, that's not what you need."

"But I—"

He presses a finger to my mouth. "Ah ah, let me finish. April, I know you feel out of control, but maybe you should embrace it. Maybe it's what you've needed all along. Think about it, you've stayed inside for so long, you're probably just going stir crazy." His eyes are alert and almost feral.

"This is more than just being stir crazy, Marcus," I say his name slowly, enunciating every letter. How could he think any of this is good for me?

"Maybe so, but baby, you've been doing things lately. You went for a drive with me and today you went for one by yourself. That's huge! I think you've been so focused on the things you can't explain you're missing all of these big milestones."

I lean back, letting my head fall against the pillow and feeling more confused than ever. Is he right? "I don't know what to think," I mumble.

He leans in close, his lips hovering inches from my temple. "You're not sick. You just need to get out more. That's all." He chews on his lip, looking pensive. "Tell you what, why don't you give it a few more days? If you still feel like you need outside help, then we'll go that route."

Could I do that? Is giving it more time the answer? I've had nothing but time and I'm not so sure it's been helpful. But I can tell from the set of his eyes and the way they implore me that he needs this from me. I'm sure he's remembering his mom's numerous hospital stays and how all they seemed to do was make things worse for her. For him. For his family. I give him a nod and a small smile.

He plants a kiss on my head and promptly stands. "Now, how about I make you something to eat. "

"Marcus, was I right?"

His face pinches. "Right about what?"

"Did you die? Am I talking to an impostor? Because you just offered to cook for me and other than box macaroni and cheese, cereal, and toast, I don't think you've ever made anything by yourself in the kitchen."

He smirks. "Okay, well, I didn't say *what* I would make you. But if you insist—Cap'n Crunch or Apple Jacks?"

I grin. "Apple Jacks."

"Coming right up." He strolls out of the room with more confidence than he had when he came in.

Closing my eyes, my thoughts drift back to the last tornado dream. Marcus was at the PO box.

I jolt upright. "Marcus?" He closed the door when he left, and I hear the faint sound of muffled voices and dishes clanking from the kitchen.

I slide my legs off the bed, testing my balance as I stand. Pins and needles shoot from the base of my feet to my ankles, but I ignore them as I trudge out of the room.

When I enter the kitchen, Marcus's back is to me. He's hovering over two bowls while Zach stands nearby—I forgot he was here. He's leaning against the counter watching Marcus but spots me as I walk further into the room. His eyes flare and he clears his throat.

"What's going on?" Marcus's body grows rigid at the sound of my voice, but when he turns around, there's a small vial in his hand.

"SO I WAS RIGHT—YOU *are* drugging me!"

"Baby, what are you doing out of bed?" Marcus walks toward me slowly, but I hold up my hand and he stops.

"April," Zach croons. "Good to see you up and about. How're you feeling?"

My eyes zing to his. "Are you really asking me that right now?"

He shrugs, shoving a hand into his pocket. "You gave us quite a scare, you know?"

"Right, and we can't have that now, can we?" I look back at Marcus, pointing a finger at him. "That's why you're drugging me, isn't it? To keep me compliant." My eyes swim with hurt as I scan his face. "How could you? After everything you went through, you really think this is the answer?"

"Whoa, hold up. Baby, I'm not drugging you. Jesus! Do you really think I could do that?" His head shakes, slow and disbelieving.

"I don't want to," I whisper. "But Marcus, I saw your emails with the vitamin people. I know all about the liquid vitamins and how they were going to overnight them to the PO box. And now I find you standing over my cereal holding that bottle …"

"Listen to me. This," he says, pointing to the vitamins, "isn't for you. Please. I just need you to let me explain. I promise it's not at all what it looks like."

The words zing through my veins. He said the exact same thing before, only it wasn't real then. I'm stunned, feeling like my conscious and unconscious worlds are colliding. How is any of this possible? My knees knock together, and if I'm not careful, I might faint again.

Stumbling toward the small table by the window, I sink into the chair. Marcus follows me, taking the chair across from mine. He set the bottle on the table. It feels like a chasm between us. His hands fidget in his lap and on the table and then back in his lap again. I can tell he'd like to hold mine, but he's not sure I'll allow it.

Zach clears his throat. "I'm gonna head out to the garage. I'll give you guys some privacy." He pats Marcus's shoulder as he passes.

We hear the front door softly close and Marcus turns to face me. "So, yeah, they did send these." He taps the bottle. "But they aren't for you. They're for me," he whispers.

"I don't understand. Why are *you* taking them?"

"Well, I was ready to give up the sponsorship, but then they mentioned these and, I don't know. You said they didn't help you, but I guess I thought they might be different for me. I hoped they would, anyway. And I know I should've told you, but you have enough on your plate. You don't need to be worrying about me, too." He sighs. "I haven't exactly had the best time of it lately, you know?"

I didn't know—not really, anyway. But there's no way I can deny it now. Not after really seeing him. "I'm sorry. And you're right, you should've told me, but it's not like I haven't been keeping secrets too. Looks like it's been a rough few months for us both."

"You can say that again."

I sit in stillness, thinking about all he's just confessed. Something doesn't add up. "Marcus?"

"Hmm?"

"You said those are for you." I point to the bottle. "But I read the back-and-forth emails, and you never told him you'd be taking them. In fact, Troy only mentioned me, and you didn't disagree."

"Yeah, so there's where the lie comes in." My expression hardens, but he holds up his hands. "Hear me out. If you go back to what I told him …" He whips out his phone, pulling up the email and sliding it across the table. "Look, I said, 'We'll give it a try.' We. As in me. But see, you're the influencer, and I'm just the guy who answers emails. I doubted they'd agree to send them if I told them straight out it would be me taking them instead of you."

"So what was your plan?"

"I didn't really have one exactly," he continues. "I never completely thought it through. I'm not even sure I'm gonna keep taking them. It feels kind of weird now. But if I did, I *could* just get on camera with you and talk about them."

"Really." I scoff. "You've never wanted to film with me before. And I've asked. Several times."

"I know. I know. But loads of other influencers have their significant others join them for videos. Maybe it's time I did it, too." A sheepish smile fills his face.

"You know, something else happened with that company," I say, scratching my chin.

"Like what?"

"So, a little while ago, I sent them an email. They're super vague with their list of ingredients and I wanted clarification. When they replied, they called me by my name only I used a fake email and never told them who I was." I grit my teeth at the memory.

Marcus tilts his head. "For real?"

"For real," I mime.

"Well, that's fucked up."

I nod, agreeing with his assessment.

I'm still reeling as I mull over everything involving Hemply Simple. It's a lot to process. I'm not sure about a lot of things lately, but I know one thing for sure. I believe Marcus. Doubting him never felt right. It's like a part of me always knew there was more to the story. And here's where someone could say, "I told you so." Because all I needed to do was talk to him, and all this suspicion never would've happened. That company, on the other hand, is about as untrustworthy as they come.

There's still so much Marcus doesn't know and I'm not convinced I shouldn't be locked in some hospital room right now. I shiver just picturing it. But he knows the worst of it —I thought he was dead this morning—and even with that knowledge, he said I should take some time. He wants me to lean in to the chaos and use it as fuel. So that's what I'm going to do. For now, I'm not going to tell him about my reflection coming to life or any of the other bizarre things that have happened. I'm not even going to go into detail about the tornado dreams I've been having. What I'm going to do, instead, is continue to push myself to do more things outside these walls. Marcus is right. It's vital for my sanity that I get out of the house more regularly.

And who knows, maybe it's working. I drove my car today. I still can't quite wrap my head around that. And maybe that's because I was fueled by my own adrenaline. I was caught up in so many things at the time, but it was nice to be in control, for once.

I try not to think about what led me there, but it's impossible. Memories filter in and out of my head like a slideshow, pausing on an image of my car parked in the driveway right before I got inside. Marcus's truck was next to it, meaning he was still inside the house when I left. My arms tingle and twitch, and my nostrils flare. At the time, I knew he was inside, but I thought he was dead. I saw the curtains move when I backed out of the driveway. Was he the one watching from the front window?

"Marcus?" My voice wavers slightly.

"Hmm," he answers, his gaze locked on the pine tree gently swaying outside.

"You were home this morning when I woke up." It isn't a question, and although I try to sound casual, it comes out like an accusation.

His attention is pulled from the window as his eyes snap to mine. "Yeah, I was."

"Okay …" I draw out the word, taking my time on each letter. "Well, if that's true, where were you? And did you know I left? Were you watching me drive away? And where'd you go after I left?" I rapid-fire the questions at him, carefully aiming to hit my intended mark each time. It works. He shifts uncomfortably in his chair, uncrossing his legs and leaning in on his elbows.

"I woke up early and you were still sleeping. You looked so comfortable. I left you alone. Clyde was pacing, so I took him for a walk on the path behind the house. Zach was in the backyard laying down mulch and I talked to him for a bit before coming back in. We were gone for maybe an hour or so, and when we came back, your car was gone. I couldn't find you inside and I don't know, man, I fucking lost it. I grabbed my keys and yelled for Zach. He took off in his car and Clyde and I drove off in my truck to look for you." He runs a hand through his hair, making it stand on end.

"Wait, Zach was here?" I think back on the short time I spent outside and I don't remember seeing his car.

"Yeah, why?" His brow furrows.

"Do you know if he came inside the house?"

He shrugs. "I only saw him when I was finished walking Clyde. I guess he could've come in to use the bathroom or something."

I nod absentmindedly as I try to connect the dots. It feels like a few are missing. "When you saw I was gone, why didn't you try calling me or checking the tracker app?"

"Yeah, that would've been smart, huh? But I was too wound up. It didn't even occur to me, at first. I got maybe fifteen or twenty minutes down the road before it dawned on me to use the locator app. So, I pulled over and when it loaded, it showed you were home. I fired off a text to Zach, then turned around and found your car and Emma's parked outside. And, well, you know the rest."

It all sounds plausible, but I still have an unanswered question. I stand, and Marcus watches me carefully as I move toward the front window. I tug the curtain back the same way I saw it move this morning and then I let it fall. I'm about to walk away when I notice a smudge on the sheer fabric. It's dark and about the size of a fingerprint.

"Hey, Marcus? Think you could grab Zach for me?"

"Yeah, sure, one sec," he says as he stands and walks toward the door.

A few minutes later, he's back, with Zach following closely behind. I've known Zach for years, and yet right now, I feel as though I'm looking at him through a different lens. Am I imagining things or is that a smirk on his face? Do his eyes look shifty or am I just projecting? "April, looks like you're feeling better." He smiles. Is it just me or does it seem a little insincere?

"I'm getting there." I cock my head, studying him for a beat. "So tell me, Zach, were you watching from this window when I left the house this morning?" I lift a hand, letting my fingers brush along the curtain.

He remains silent for a moment, but he doesn't look away. Marcus's head whips back and forth between us. "Wait, Zach, is that true? Did you see April leave?"

Zach turns toward Marcus and gives a half shrug. "Yeah. I came in for a glass of water and I heard a car. Thought it was weird 'cause I knew you were out back with Clyde—I saw you off in the distance when I was working. Anyway, so I peeked out through the curtain. April's car was halfway down the driveway." His tone is relaxed, and his posture is casual, as though he doesn't see anything bizarre about what he's just confessed.

"For real, bro?" Marcus's eyes practically bulge out of his head. "Why the hell didn't you say something when I stopped and talked to you after walking Clyde?"

Zach runs a hand through his dirty blond hair. "I don't know, man. I didn't really think anything of it. I mean, April's been getting out more so I figured it wasn't a big deal." He shoves his hands into his pockets and casts his gaze to the floor. "Then when you saw she was gone, and you freaked out, I didn't know how to tell you. I feel like shit for not yelling for you sooner. I'm sorry." He lifts his head, looking at Marcus, and then he turns and locks eyes with me. He rests his hand against his breastbone. "April, I'm so sorry. If I had said something, maybe Marcus could've caught up to you and it would've saved you both some heartache."

Maybe it would have lessened things a bit, but it wouldn't have stopped all of the emotional turmoil I experienced before I left. Zach isn't to blame for any of that. I cross the floor until I'm standing right in front of him. Cupping his shoulder in my hand, I give it a squeeze. "It's okay. I know you didn't mean any harm. And no one in this room is in any position to judge another for withholding information." I glance at Marcus and he nods.

Zach gives me a sad smile and mouths, "Thank you." He looks over at Marcus, "Hey, man, I think I'm gonna take off. We good?"

Marcus shoots him a wry grin. "Yeah, man, we're good."

"Cool." Zach smiles wide, giving me a wink before strutting toward the door.

"Whew." I widen my eyes, trying to fight my growing exhaustion.

Marcus sidles up next to me and tugs on my sleeve. "Come on, you. Let's get you into bed. You've had a day. Time to relax."

"I like the sound of that." I sigh, leaning against him.

As he guides me into the hallway, he stops short before we reach the bedroom. "So, tell me something. When you drove off this morning, did you think I was dead in there?" He tips his head toward the room.

I did, but I'm acutely aware of how that makes me sound. Leaving my dead husband in the house while I flee the scene is extremely suspicious. "No. I mean, I thought you were dead, but I knew it wasn't real," I lie. "That's why I left. I just needed to clear my head."

His shoulders relax, and he chuckles. "Okay, 'cause I was gonna say, shit, if you just took off and left me bleeding, man. That's harsh." He laughs.

"Yeah." I choke, feigning humor. "Way harsh."

He wraps a strong arm around my shoulders and pulls me close. I lean in and inhale his rich, musky scent. My eyes fill with tears, thinking about how I was sure I'd never smell that again. I nestle into the crook of his neck, and he kisses the top of my head.

When we reach the bed, he helps lower me onto the mattress. I don't need the guidance, but it feels nice to be cared for. He pulls the covers up around me, patting my arms beneath the blankets. "You get some rest. I'm just gonna go play a round with the guys to unwind."

I smile. "Okay."

He leans down and kisses me. As he strides out the door, I call to him, "Hey, Marcus?"

"Yeah?" He pops his head back into the room.

"What are you gonna do about the vitamins?"

His eyebrows shoot up. "Do you even have to ask? I'm throwing that shit out."

"Good." I smile, feeling relieved.

He taps the doorframe. "Get some rest. I've got plans for you later." He winks.

"I'm counting on it." I wink back.

His soft laugh trails behind him as he leaves the room.

WITHIN THESE LAST SIX DAYS, I've gone to lunch with Emma, drove Marcus to the grocery store where I actually got out of the car and went into the building, took myself on a short outing to Target, and today, I'm getting ready to head over to my parents' house for dinner. I'm pushing myself, trying to make a real effort. I promised Marcus that I would give it time and I'm not gonna lie—I'm kind of shocked that it seems to be working.

The vitamins are long gone. Marcus tossed the liquid ones like he said he would and then he fired off a strongly worded email to Hemply Simple. I was right about them tracing my IP address. They claimed it was standard practice at their company in order to "gather data about potential clients," but that's insane. I'm so relieved we won't be working with them anymore.

I've also enjoyed a reprieve from hallucinations and terrifyingly real nightmares. I'm not deluding myself into thinking they're a thing of the past, but the break has given me some perspective. I think it's more a case of mind over matter. Maybe keeping busy is helping. And if anything happens again, I'm ready.

Honestly, I'm not exactly thrilled with going to my mom and dad's house, but I can't put it off any longer. She called me last night. Her shrill voice shocking my eardrum —"April, you've been gallivanting all over town. When are you going to come and see your poor old parents, huh?"

She's a master, I swear. She knows I have a hard time saying no to her when she reminds me that she and my dad are getting older. I don't consider myself cured—not by a long shot. I still worry and fret over death every single day. And the idea of losing my parents is crippling. So, naturally, when she asked, I couldn't argue.

"April? Have you seen my belt?" Marcus pokes his head into the bedroom, gripping his pants at the waist.

"Hmm," I mutter as I take in his disheveled appearance. His shirt is untucked and unbuttoned, revealing toned pecks and rows of sculpted muscle. I can tell he's been trying to tame his hair, but his efforts have been futile. His dark waves have gone rogue, swirling off his face in delicious rebellion.

"Ahem." My eyes instantly flash to his lips. They curve into a smug smirk, and when my gaze roams up his face, I find him regarding me behind dark eyes and thick lashes. "You're staring." He crosses his arms over his taut chest.

"Maybe I am." I shrug, returning a smirk.

"You know," he says, dropping his arms to his sides and stalking toward me. "We could just skip this." His hand rests along my cheek and then glides up to tuck a lock of hair behind my ear. He leans in close, whispering, "It's been months since you've been to your parents' house. What's one more day?" His warm breath sends shivers down my arms.

Of all the experiences I've had recently, my reconnection with Marcus has been my favorite. We are closer now than ever. We talk about everything and nothing at all. And the sex? It's on a whole other level.

I tilt my head, looking up at him. "Listen, I would if I could, but …"

"I know. I know." He backs away. "Raincheck?"

I bite my lower lip. "You know it."

He grins. "I'm gonna hold you to that. And, baby?"

"Yeah?"

"I really do need my belt. Any idea where it is?"

"Oh!" I giggle. "Um, have you checked the floor next to your side of the bed?"

He hobbles over and retrieves it. Holding it up with a smirk, he asks, "Now remind me, how did it get over here?"

My body floods with warmth from the memory. Pressing a finger to my lips, I smile.

With the belt secured in place, Marcus buttons up his shirt while I fight the urge to shove his hands away. I can't remember the last time I felt this insatiable. I'm not sure I ever have.

"You finish getting ready. I'm gonna go feed Clyde."

"Sounds good." I nod, refocusing on the disaster of a drawer in front of me.

Before he leaves, Marcus leans over my shoulder. "You know it doesn't matter what you wear, right? Your parents just want to see you. And besides, you're always beautiful." He plants a kiss on my cheek and strolls out of the room.

I sigh. He's right. I know they're just excited to see me, and yet … if I choose wrong, there's always that chance my mom will make a comment.

I root through my clothes, stirring up a bevy of smells. There's a pouch of lavender in here, but that's not what gets my attention. I select an off-the-shoulder top with delicate pastel flowers on it. The last time I wore this, Marcus and I celebrated our anniversary with dinner at Olivio's. The memory is almost as strong as the scent on the fabric. Pressing it to my nose, I catch a whiff of the perfume I wore that night. Kate Spade's Walk on Air. It's a fragrance that lingers, but I'm still shocked it's managed to last this long, even after being washed. The more I inhale, the stronger it gets.

I slide the shirt on, deciding to pair it with jeans, and make sure nothing is too tight to stave off potential comments about my slender body. My appetite has started to increase little by little, but I still have a ways to go before I put on enough healthy weight. I'm a work in progress, but my mom won't see it that way. She's more of an instant gratification kind of lady. She'd have me eating a sleeve of Oreos every night before bed just to "add some more meat on my bones." I roll my eyes. Marcus and I haven't really talked about starting our own family. It's a long-term plan. We're not in any rush. But if and when I'm a mom someday, I vow to hold my tongue with my kids and remind myself that words are like tiny swords, except the wounds never fully heal.

The bathroom window is open, and a gentle breeze slips in through the screen, making the curtains dance. I've been avoiding this room like the plague, only using it out of necessity. And I never look at the mirror. If I need one, I use the desk mirror in my office. But right now, I need my tweezers, and even though I'm kind of a beauty influencer, I only have one pair—and they're in the medicine cabinet right below the mirror. Standing in the doorway, I suck in a breath. *I can do this.*

I'm sure I must look ridiculous. I'm moving at warp speed, tugging at the door while keeping my head down and my eyes on the task at hand. I want zero chance of seeing my reflection. With the cabinet door open, I let my eyes roam the shelves. They're filled with neat rows of antibiotic ointments and creams, a few boxes of Band-Aids, spare bottles of Tylenol and ibuprofen, and there on the bottom shelf sits my nail scissors and tweezers. I snatch them and push the door shut, immediately leaning in close to the mirror as if I'm on autopilot.

I'm examining my right eyebrow when I notice it raising and lowering in the reflection while the one on my face stays still. Shit. This is exactly what I wanted to avoid.

I pull back from the mirror and catch my reflection winking at me. I squeeze my eyes shut so tightly, water springs from my tear ducts. The tweezers fall from my hand, landing in the sink with a *clank*. My fingers plug my ears just in case she decides to talk to me again. Shaking my head, I repeat the words "this isn't real" over and over in my head while slowly backing out of the room. I don't stop until my calves hit the bed.

Not bad. I mean, it isn't great that it happened, but I handled it okay. Unfortunately, I left my tweezers in the sink, and since I'm not about to go back in there, I guess I'll just have to deal with a few rogue brow hairs.

MY MOTHER HASN'T STOPPED TALKING about my weight since we got here. She's relentless, constantly shoving food in my face and pleading with me to eat. Marcus and my dad have both tried to speak up on my behalf, but Mom is having none of it.

"I can practically see every bone in your body, April. Here, eat another slice of pie, why don't you?"

She keeps giving Marcus these looks, too. Like they share a secret, but it's one she doesn't like. It's odd.

"Mom, I'm eating. I promise. I mean, look," I say, holding up my empty plate. "I cleared my plate, see?"

Her hands perch on her hips. "What, you want a medal for that? You barely had anything on it in the first place." I catch her looking at Marcus again. Her eyes widen and her jaw clenches. Marcus turns away quickly, but not before I notice him mirror the same expression.

"What's going on with you two?" I flick my finger back and forth between them.

"Huh?" Marcus asks at the same time my mom says, "Don't worry about it."

He glares at her, and she clams up.

"Someone better spill." I narrow my eyes at both of them.

Marcus sighs but doesn't say a word. My mom looks at him, a helpless expression on her face. "Oh, fine," she says, smacking her hands against her thighs. "I know all about you fainting, so don't even try to deny it."

"I'm not gonna deny it, but"—I face Marcus, shooting daggers at him with my eyes—"I thought we weren't going to worry my mom. What happened to that plan?"

He scratches at his forehead and then smooths it. "Listen, baby, I didn't want to get your mom upset, but—"

"I'm your mother. I have a right to know when something happens to you," my mom interjects.

I groan. "Yeah, but now you're hovering even worse than normal. I'm not so sure it was a good idea to share any of this with you." I scowl at Marcus, but he only shrugs.

My dad speaks up, surprising us all. "Kiddo, we're your parents. It's our job to worry about you. We'll never stop. And telling us when something bad happens doesn't make the worrying worse. In some ways, it makes it better because if we know what's going on, we can help. It's when we're out of the loop that it feels unbearable."

I can't remember the last time my father spoke so much. He's usually the king of one-liners, sprinkling them in like confetti when a conversation needs a pick-me-up. He isn't known for his profound soliloquies, and the rest of us are stunned into silence. I ponder his words, turning them around in my head. He makes a lot of sense. Maybe I should tell them more, let them be the judge of what they can and can't handle.

My mom leans on my dad's shoulder, and he pats her hand. It's a small gesture, but one that speaks volumes. "Fine," I concede. "I'll try not to keep so much hidden from you if you promise not to nag so much. Deal?" I look between them.

My dad nods instantly, but my mom hesitates until he nudges her. "All right, all right. But just promise me you'll take care of yourself. And you"—she narrows her eyes at Marcus—"see to it that she does."

He nods stoically, and she crosses the room, placing a hand on both of our cheeks. With a quick pat, she's off, pulling more food out of the fridge and setting it on the already overflowing counter. Marcus catches my eye, giving me a *you good?* kind of look. An easy smile fills my face because, yeah, I think I finally am.

27

"AHH." I sigh, raising my arms above my head.

Another dreamless night of sleep and another blissful morning. I've enjoyed this reprieve from nightmares. I hope it continues.

Of course, I'm sure my late-night activities with Marcus aren't hurting, either. I was tired when we left my parents' house last night, but got a second wind when Marcus grabbed his shirt behind his neck and pulled it off. It gets me every time. My lips curve in a wry grin. I roll my head to look at my husband, but he's not there. The floorboards in his game room creak from the rocking motion of his chair. He can never sit still when he plays, always bouncing in place.

Lifting my phone, I'm shocked I slept so late. It's nearly ten thirty. I have a sponsored video to film today. Swinging my legs over the side of the bed, I wiggle my toes into the plush carpet. I rise and stroll over to the window. The sun is fighting to peek out from behind the clouds. They've overwhelmed it at the moment, but as I stand watching, they begin to part. Sunrays cascade through the narrow opening and spill out onto a patch of wildflowers in my yard. I smile, celebrating the triumph. The sun wins this round.

I can't remember the last time I started my morning off

with my song and dance routine. I've been out of sorts for so long, but I'm finally starting to feel like myself again. A *better* version of me. My smile is wide as I call out, "Alexa, play—" Hold on, what's that smell? I breathe in deep. Oranges. It's strong and familiar. I'm sure I smelled something similar not long ago, though the memory is just out of reach.

It feels like it's wafting in from somewhere. My eyes cut to the open bathroom. I think it's coming from there. As I tiptoe toward the smell, I hear the faint sound of my Echo apologizing for not knowing what song I was asking for.

The scent grows vastly stronger the nearer I am to the bathroom. It's not an artificial smell. It's as if someone cut open fresh oranges and laid them out all over the floor. My eyes cascade around the small space and land on the diffuser. A telltale mist snakes out of the top and has me shaking my head, feeling foolish. I always forget about that thing.

As I turn to leave, a voice calls out. "Wait."

I lift my gaze to the ceiling, groaning aloud. And my morning was going so well. On instinct, I want to run. But it's time my reflection and I have a little chat. And not like the time, where I was caught off guard and hysterical, thinking my husband had died. I'm in a much different head space now.

I stride into the room with my shoulders back and my head held high. "You know I don't believe any of this is real, right? You're not even you. You're me. And this"—I flick a finger at the mirror—"is all in my head."

She nods, but in a way that you might if you're worried about someone's mental state. It's patronizing, and it's bullshit.

I shake my head, marching toward her. "Don't do that.

Don't act like I'm some poor broken soul who needs saving. I'm not, and I don't."

"I know that," she whispers.

"Do you, though?" I narrow my eyes at her. At me.

Hers widen. "Of course. We're the same person, remember?"

That word. *Remember.* It causes me to think back to that morning not so long ago. I was terrified—not only that Marcus was dead, but that I might have been the one to kill him. I held a conversation with the April in the mirror. She told me to clear my head. As I replay the moment, I feel it start to dissipate. Slowly, at first. It's fuzzy and then becomes hazy, like I'm seeing it through a blanket of fog. And then it's gone.

I blink furiously, trying to get it back. But …

Get what back? There was something. A memory was just there, but it's lost now.

I flick my eyes up and meet my own. There's something off with my reflection, but what is it? I feel like I knew what it was. I held it in my hand only moments ago, but now I can't remember what it was or why I'm standing here. It's as though my memories are leaching out of my head.

Oranges. Fresh and strong, the citrus smell permeates the air. It's so potent I feel as if I can taste it.

Stumbling out of the bathroom, my eyes zero in on the unmade bed. Marcus was dead, slashed open, and bleeding all over those sheets only days ago. I rush toward it, rubbing my hands along the fabric. It was here. Wasn't it? His chest was splayed open, and his mouth was parted. Yes. I see it now. I remember.

A dense fog rolls in and coats the memory of my dead husband, covering him in a thick cloud, and when it's gone, so is he. I'm left staring at my empty bed.

Did something happen here? There's a nagging feeling in the back of my mind, but I can't quite grasp it. What's happening to me?

I feel queasy and wrap my arms around my middle. The scent of citrus is overwhelming. I stagger into the hall and out into the kitchen. There are no oranges on the counter. The aroma is so strong out here, I was sure I'd find some sliced and arranged on a plate.

The pantry door is ajar. Something happened in there. My eyes close as I sift through my mind in search of the memory. Yes, I can see it now. Nana was in there, only it wasn't her. It may have been a mouse, but I thought I heard her humming "Will You Still Love Me Tomorrow." I sing the lyrics. The melody swirls inside my head, slowly at first, in time with the rhythm. But as it starts to pick up, the notes begin to scramble, and the words are lost. And then there's nothing left.

The light in the pantry is on, so I turn it off and close the door. I have a strange déjà vu feeling, but I can't figure out why.

Sumo oranges are my favorite, and right now, they're all I smell — but it's not their season. Still, I feel like I may find some if I keep wandering around the house. The hallway is empty. On my way to my office, I pause, eyeing the door to the basement. Was I locked down there? A memory flits in and out of my head like a bird. Something about laundry and Nana's recipes. But when I reach out to grab on to the moment, it disappears. Goose bumps erupt on my arms.

With a shake of my head, I push open the door to my office. Nothing is out of place, but it feels off in here. Maybe it's me.

The citrus smell is intense and inescapable. Nausea flows through me in waves. Standing in the center of the room, an onslaught of memories barrages me. Marcus turned into Walker Dolan. There was a knock at the door, but no one was there. I heard laughter when I was alone. And the nightmares. Tornado dreams so real I swear I felt the surge of wind.

The images flash in rapid succession, bringing me to my knees. Yet as I try desperately to cling to them, they're plucked out of my head. It's as if there's a vacuum sucking memories out of my brain like they never happened at all. One by one, the recollections disappear, leaving me with only a feeling of profound loss. I press my hands on either side of my head and cry.

"Stop! Stop," I scream, but no one is listening. I think I said that before. Yes, I remember. I yelled at my reflection and then I smashed a mirror with my hand. I glance down, but it's all healed now. I turn my hand back and forth as yet another memory is erased.

I rock back and forth as quiet sobs wrack my body.

Nana hums from somewhere in the room. I whip my head up, twisting my neck in every direction in search of her.

"Remember, they said this part would be hard," she says. I follow her voice to the open doorway and find her standing there. She's wearing her blue dress with the little white flowers. I blink a few times, expecting her to vanish like everything else, but it doesn't happen. She's still there, watching me with sad eyes.

"Nana?" My throat aches and my voice is raspy. "What's happening?"

"Sweet pea, take a minute. Catch your breath. You're so close."

I shake my head violently, but the movement only serves to strengthen the pounding behind my eyes. "There's something wrong with my head. All my thoughts are scrambling, and I'm losing memories. I can feel them being tugged from my mind."

"Yes." She nods. "I suppose that's to be expected."

"What are you talking about? Expected? Expected from what, exactly?"

"You'll have the answers soon, I promise."

I crane my neck, scanning my surroundings. There's steam coming from the diffuser in the corner. That must be where the smell is coming from. But I already knew that, didn't I? Yes, there's one in the bathroom. And there are two more—one in the bedroom and another in the kitchen. They're all emitting the same fragrance. That's why it's so strong.

"How do I turn these things off? I can't think straight with that smell. It's making me sick."

"No, honey, it's making you well." She bobs her head up and down while pressing a hand to her heart.

"Huh?"

"It's okay. Give it time. New memories will come."

I slide back onto my bottom, letting my legs splay out in front of me. I have no idea what she's talking about. I'm losing memories; not gaining them.

She says the diffuser is helping me. It perplexes me, and yet there's something there. I feel it beginning to come back to me.

"This orange smell. It's happened before. And I knew it would happen again. It's like a reset button." I glance back at the copper cone. "They're not just ordinary diffusers, are they?"

Her smile is wide as she nods.

The memory comes back in tiny pieces, slow and pixelated. Marcus and I talked about this before he accepted the sponsorship. He was curious, but cautious. It was me who decided it was worth a shot.

I crawl across the floor toward the diffuser. My body is weak, and my arms tremble beneath my weight. The device is beautiful. The copper shines, and when I lean in, I see my eyes looking back at me, full of wonder and something else. Recognition. Each diffuser rests on a square patina base, and there, in raised letters, is the name *Diffuse-ology: a new kind of therapy*. It's been there the whole time, but I've never bothered to look.

"It's amazing, isn't it? It's like a miracle."

I whip around, squinting at her. "Miracle?" The word tastes sour on my tongue. While some elements of this story have become clear, others are still unknown. I agreed to these devices, knowing they would have an effect on me. But what kind of effect? I close my eyes.

Marcus pushed his way into my office, talking a mile a minute. "Baby, I think this might help. I mean, I don't know. Maybe it will. It's worth a shot, I think. But I'm not sure."

"Hey, hey, deep breaths," I said, holding up a hand. He complied, inhaling and exhaling. Then he slammed his laptop on my desk, making us both jump.

"Sorry," he said through gritted teeth. "Just read this, okay?"

I did as he asked, skimming over a vague sponsor email from some company calling themselves Diffuse-ology. I wrinkled my nose. "That's a strange name."

Marcus nodded. "I know, I thought so, too, but click on the attachment."

I navigated down to the paperclip icon and selected a file simply called "More info." A document loaded on the screen, explaining in much more detail what these devices are used for. I read aloud, "At Diffuse-ology, we believe immersive therapy is the key to overcoming large obstacles that can debilitate our lives or the lives of those we love. That's why we created a unique blend of olfactory therapy designed to immerse the user in a sensory environment where they will come face-to-face with their worst fears. They will be forced to deal with each obstacle as it appears, ultimately leading to their success." The document went on to explain that the program begins and ends by using a special potent concoction to erase your memory. That part seemed a little frightening, but in order for it to work, you needed to forget what it does so it could just exist in the background and do its job. And once the cycle was complete, it came in again, erasing all of the experiences you had. Leaving you well and whole again.

"It's weird, right? But you haven't been able to leave the house. This could help with that." He gnawed at his lip. "You know what, forget about it. I don't like the idea of you being a part of some fucked-up mind experiment."

I leaned back in my chair, keeping my eyes trained on the screen in front of me. He had a point—it did sound experimental. But maybe that's what I needed. I'd been trapped in the house for months. Trapped by my own fears. I had Dr. Lesser, but she could only help me as much as I was willing to allow. And now another option was dropped in my lap and I didn't even have to leave my home. It sounded too good to be true, but maybe it wasn't.

"What are you thinking?"

I regarded him for a moment. He wore his emotions like an old suit. I could see fear etched in his frown lines and worry on his forehead. But it was his eyes that convinced me. Deep within the flecks of gold was a glimmer of hope.

"I think it couldn't hurt."

I was so wrong. "Nana, what did I agree to? These diffusers are torture devices. I thought I was losing my mind." All those smells—Nana's apple crisp, my lip cream, Marcus's cologne, even his blood—were all manufactured from these devices. Weaved so seamlessly into my everyday life, I never suspected a thing. I was never supposed to.

Her brow furrows. "Oh, sweet pea, I know you were scared, but you told them everything you were afraid of."

She's right. I answered a detailed questionnaire,

providing them with all the ammunition they needed. I handed them all my triggers. It was tailor-made for me. That's why no one else ever smelled anything. It wasn't meant for them. And Marcus never brought it up. I think he may have wanted to. That day after I fainted, he looked like he had something to say after I asked him to take me to the hospital. But he didn't because that's not how the program works. Now the scent of citrus is cleansing my mind of all that's happened, and soon, it will take these memories away, too.

I look up at Nana. "Who else knows about this?" I watch her eyes, but they give nothing away. I keep talking, processing my thoughts out loud. "I think Emma does and Zach, too. Emma didn't know at first, but she does now. Marcus had to tell her because I was acting so erratic. That's what they were arguing about the day I passed out. I don't think she's happy about any of it, but she kept the secret. And Zach probably knew right from the start. Marcus never keeps anything from him." I pause. "Do my parents know?" Nana cocks her head and I shake mine. "No. My mom would never go for it. I think it was supposed to stay between Marcus and me, but he would've told Zach just so he'd have someone to talk to and then Emma found out, too. How do I know all of this?" It's like I have an awareness I didn't have before.

She presses her hands together and leans forward. "Do you remember what I told you when I came to visit you in your dream?"

I stare off across the room, trying to filter through my dissipating memories. "You're strong." We say the words in unison.

"But Nana, I haven't even been in control of myself. How can I possibly be strong?"

She smiles. "April, it's like I said. You've always been

strong; you just forgot, that's all. And now that you're coming out on the other side of things, it's time for me to go."

I'm an exposed nerve, feeling each new bit of information as though it's a jolt of electricity. "Wait, you're leaving? But I need you."

She shakes her head. "You don't need me, honey. In fact, I'm not even here. This is all you. You're remembering the way you need to remember. It's the way the program works. And the fact that you're here means you made it through. You're gonna be okay. I promised you that, didn't I?"

"Yes, but I can't do this alone."

"You're not alone. Just listen," she whispers.

My body stills until the only sound is the pounding of my own heart. And then I hear it.

"Damn, bruh! You snuck up from behind! How'd I not see you?"

Marcus. He's in his game room yelling at his friends, completely oblivious to my mental disintegration. And he knew about this from the very beginning. What does he think about it now? Am I *cured*?

From a purely factual vantage point, I have made significant progress. I hadn't left my house in six months, and now I leave it all the time. I drive myself, go into stores, dine in restaurants, and even visit my parents. I faced my fears with more bravery than I've felt in years, maybe ever. But at what cost?

No, I haven't been cured. I've been tricked. And it's my own fault. I did this to myself. I was duped into believing I was strong enough to overcome all this on my own. But I wasn't. I was only reacting to my delusions. Delusions brought on by these fucking things. I stand, fury coursing through my body like a pulse. I was terrorized, thinking I was losing my mind. Living in fear of my own home—the one place where I'm supposed to feel safe. It used everything against me. And now what? I'm supposed to go on camera and tell my subscribers about these *amazing* devices? No way. I shake my head. I can't do that.

My feet pound on the floor as I march toward the door. I have to stop this while I still have the chance. The outcome of this diffuser "therapy" isn't worth the horror that I went through.

When I reach my nana, I lift my arms to hug her, but my hands plunge right through her. She dissipates like a puff of smoke. I'm stunned, but I feel the edges of my memory begin to fray. I'm losing my focus. All of the horrible memories related to the diffusers are going to leave me, and all I'll remember is that it helped. I have to talk to Marcus before it all goes away. I prod on, shoving the game room door open with such force, it bounces off the wall.

"Marcus, I—"

My husband spins around with wide eyes. He whips his headphones off his ears and grips the armrests on the chair. "April? What is it? Are you okay?"

Am I okay? Am I …

Huh. I don't know what I'm doing in here. Oh, well, maybe it'll come to me later.

"Sorry." I chuckle. "I completely forgot what I was gonna to say."

THE LIGHTS ARE bright and warm. I give myself one last look in the mirror, fluffing my hair and dabbing at the corners of my lips. Then I look up into the eye of the camera and smile.

"Hi, guys! Welcome back to my channel. And if you're new here, hi, my name is April and I'm so glad you're watching. If you like what you see, please give this video a thumbs-up and subscribe if you want to see more content from me. I upload every Monday, Wednesday, and Friday at twelve p.m. eastern time."

"Today is a special day because this video is kindly sponsored by an amazing company. And you guys, believe me when I say, this product completely changed my life. I would not be where I am today without them."

Reaching off camera, I slide the elegant copper cone into view. Keeping a hand rested on it, I beam at the camera. "Let me tell you a little bit about Diffuse-ology."

ACKNOWLEDGMENTS

To all of my readers, thank you so much for taking a chance on me. You could've chosen ANY book and I'm deeply honored that you chose mine.

To my amazing beta readers, Angela and Marissa. I am so grateful for your honesty and your willingness to wade through my messy first drafts. You have both helped me tremendously, especially with this book.

To Liz, I dedicated this book to you because you were in my head the entire time I was writing. I will forever be humbled that you always drop everything and read my books the second I send them to you.

To Traci, you have an incredible ability to help me uncover the pieces of my story that I missed the first time. With your help, my good books become great ones. I don't know how you do what you do, but I'm so glad I have you in my corner.

To Murphy, we are most definitely connected by some unseen force. You give my books life with your gorgeous covers.

To Marla, your eagle eye is always appreciated. You

help clean up my pesky comma problems and let me know when words appear way too often.

To my friends, family, and neighbors, you are my number one fans . You're always cheering me on and sharing my books with others.

To my fellow authors who are far too numerous to mention, you are the ultimate hype team. I am so appreciative of your constant, unwavering support.

And to my husband, Adam, and our two kiddos, Stella and Jasper, thank you for putting up with my ramblings and making it possible for me to do what I love.

ABOUT THE AUTHOR

Layne Deemer aims to push boundaries with her writing. Her stories deconstruct the ordinary until it becomes something else entirely.

She has a degree in Communications with a minor in English and has worked in the fields of public relations, marketing, and advertising, but writing has always been her true passion. When she isn't writing, she's reading. Her wish list of books will take her a lifetime to get through.

She resides in Pennsylvania with her husband, Adam, their two kids, Stella and Jasper, and their bulldog, Archie.